# Lone Wolf

OTHER SAGEBRUSH LARGE PRINT WESTERNS BY
## BENNETT FOSTER

Dust of the Trail

Rawhide Road

# Lone Wolf

## BENNETT FOSTER

**Sagebrush**
**Large Print Westerns**

## Library of Congress Cataloging in Publication Data

Foster, Bennett.
  [Turn loose your wolf]
  Lone Wolf / Bennett Foster.
    p.  cm.
  ISBN 1-57490-199-0 (alk. paper)
  1. Large type books. I. Title.
[PS3511.06812T87  1999]
813'.54—dc21                                99-30784
                                                           CIP

Ca         T   102333           ı is available from
the British Library and the National Library of Australia.

Originally published under the title *Turn Loose Your Wolf*. An earlier version of this story was serialized as "Cut Loose Your Wolf" in *Argosy* (8/6/38-9/10/38).

**Sagebrush Large Print Westerns** are published in the United States and Canada by Thomas T. Beeler, Publisher, Box 659, Hampton Falls, New Hampshire 03844-0659. ISBN 1-57490-199-0

Published in the United Kingdom, Eire, and the Republic of South Africa by Isis Publishing Ltd, 7 Centremead, Osney Mead, Oxford OX2 0ES England. ISBN 0-7531-6015-3

Published in Australia and New Zealand by Australian Large Print Audio & Video Pty Ltd, 17 Mohr Street, Tullamarine, Victoria, 3043, Australia. ISBN 1-86442-248-3

Manufactured in the United States of America by Sheridan Books in Chelsea, Michigan

# Lone Wolf

# CHAPTER 1

## FRANKLIN

THE TWO MEN WERE OF ABOUT THE SAME AGE AND both were white men. There the resemblance ended. Father Paul's years had been kind to him, while at fifty Judge John Lester's hair was snowy and his face seamed with lines. The two sat now in the patio of Lester's home in Franklin while the sun slid down its invisible chute behind El Oro, and to the south and west the two passes in the saw-toothed range of Los Cantandos mountains grew blue with evening. Lester tapped the heavy hand-hewn arm of his chair with long ascetic fingers and stared across the patio to where a door was half open behind a thicket of hollyhocks; while Father Paul sipped the good Celeste wine, product of his own vineyard at Tumac Mission, and watched his host.

"The boy made it purely an affair of business," said Father Paul, continuing a discussion. "He came to me this morning, bringing his brother. I was to take the younger boy, Don, in charge. The older boy, Larry, had it all planned."

Lester nodded, continuing his tapping on the chair arm.

Father Paul laughed ruefully. "Larry must be all of twelve years old," he said. "Don is ten and has a pathetic faith in Larry's abilities."

From the door behind the hollyhocks came a rasping, hacking cough that was instantly stifled. John Lester started and the lines in his face deepened. Father Paul's

1

benign countenance showed sudden sympathy.

"You were saying . . . ?" Lester reminded, breaking the priest's long silence.

"Oh yes. Larry told me that he would get work—'a job,' as he phrased it—and send me money for Don's education. He seems determined that Don shall be a lawyer."

The priest stopped again, interrupted once more by that hacking cough.

"And you want . . . ?" suggested Lester.

"I want both the boys." Father Paul leaned forward in his chair, the Celeste in his glass, forgotten in his earnestness, tipping until it crossed the brim and trickled down the side. "Don is a good boy, and young; Larry is a better boy and worth saving. I want them both."

Judge John Lester ceased his restless tapping and touched the tips of his fingers together. "You understand, Father, that this is a matter that must go through the court," he said gravely. "Legally I can do nothing for you now. I will tell you this: If you petition for guardianship I will look favorably upon it. More than that I cannot say."

Father Paul leaned back. He was satisfied. So much was indeed a great deal from John Lester, the Hanging Judge of the Tenth Judicial Circuit. A very great concession indeed. John Lester seemed to feel it so, and another feeling as well. He spoke again.

"You understand, Father, that I could do nothing else but sentence Tom Blue as I did." Judge Lester's voice was calm and unhurried. "The evidence against him was final; the jury found him guilty, and I sentenced him to hang. I could do nothing else."

Father Paul placed his unfinished Celeste upon the table beside him. "I know that the law cannot take

2

account of small boys," he said slowly. "I sometimes wonder that the law takes account of humanity at all. You are a harsh man, John Lester, a harsh man."

"I am a just man!" Lester's jaw set firmly.

"And one that believes in his justice." Father Paul arose from the chair. "Perhaps some day . . ."

Another burst of coughing came from behind the hollyhocks. The priest paused. "She . . . she will not be with you long, my son?" There was compassion in the deep voice.

"She will be with me always!" John Lester flung the words at the priest. "She . . ."

Father Paul raised a hand and, head turned toward the hollyhocks, made a little gesture. John Lester bowed his head. Father Paul had made the Sign of the Cross.

There was silence in the patio ind the dusk, deep now, crept closer. The priest moved. "Then I will take the boys with me," he said. "Don is already at the Mission. Larry I can find. He will take handling, that young gentleman, I can tell you." The priest's laugh was deep. "I owe you thanks for a problem, Judge Lester."

John Lester, coming from his chair, nodded. "You will petition the court," he said formally. "I am sure that the petition will be granted. Good night, Father."

"Good night, my son, and thank you." The priest moved away through the gloom. From the shadowy hollyhocks came a faint voice calling:

"John . . . John . . ."

Father Paul let himself out of the patio through the great wooden gate. Outside he paused once more and turning looked back at the iron barred door. "I would not," said Father Paul, "I would not be you, John Lester..." Then, as though ashamed, he turned again and hurried to where his patient mules stood waiting before his buckboard. Down in Franklin, where the street lights blossomed one by one as the lamplighter made his rounds, there was the sound of a shot and then, swiftly, another. Father Paul climbed to the buckboard seat and lifting the lines spoke to the mules:

"Angelica! Francesca!"

The mules lifted long-eared heads and walked forward sedately. Father Paul drove down the hill.

Franklin was waking up. In the afternoon Franklin, borrowing from its southern neighbor, took a siesta, the better to prepare for a hectic night.

The passes—one to the south, the other to the west—made Franklin possible. Through the southern pass there came goods from Mexico, some to be declared at the customs port, some to enter illicitly across the invisible line that separated the countries. Los Cantandos had many a hidden cove, many a snug retreat for men who cared not to pay duty.

To the west the pass opened the way for the stages and for the wagon trains that moved snail-like across the mesquite-dotted sand through the heat haze. A good town, Franklin, a good tough town; hard as granite and tough as a sow's snout; proud of its wickedness and, oddly, proud too of its Hanging Judge. Geronimo had raided within five miles of Franklin. A month did not pass but that the stage came into town carrying flint in the shape of arrow heads, or lead in the form of bullets. Franklin lived and throve on blood and wickedness, and on the traffic through its dusty streets.

At the outskirts of Franklin, as the dusk fell, three children sat and wriggled their bare toes in the sand of an arroyo. One of these, a girl, held her shoes and stockings in her lap and sat as close to the fair-haired,

4

blue-eyed boy as possible. Another, lounging with native ease on the arroyo bank, toyed with the tongue of a home-made wagon. The girl, dark eyes intent on the blue-eyed boy's face, stirred slightly and a vagrant breeze ruffled her fair hair. The blue-eyed boy was talking.

"If we'd of had money for a smart lawyer," he stated, his voice matter of fact, "my father wouldn't of been hung. Don's goin' to be a lawyer. I fixed it up with the priest at the Mission."

"And what are you going to do, Larry?" asked the girl.

"Make money." Larry Blue's answer was positive. "Make a lot of money and send Don to school. I'm goin' to get a job."

"I've got five dollars," the girl spoke tentatively. "You can have that, Larry."

"Five dollars!" Larry Blue scoffed at the amount. "I need lots of money. I need a hundred dollars anyhow."

The girl drooped her fair head and instantly Larry reached out one scratched and grimy hand toward her. "Don't you cry, Annette," he comforted. "I . . . well, I can't take money from a woman, can I, Tomaso?"

Tomaso Patron, thus appealed to, lifted his head and smiled, his teeth white in his dark face. *Por que no?"* questioned Tomaso. "Me, I will take money from anybody. When I grow big I shall be a bandit. Then, Larry, if you need money I will give it to you."

Larry Blue had no thanks for this magnanimous offer. He was looking at the girl. Annette Bondreaux, eight years old, a fairy-like wisp of a child, snuggled closer to him. Larry Blue was her hero, her god, her one object of worship. "Do you need some money now, Larry?" she asked.

5

"I need a lot," Larry answered gravely.

"My papa would give you some," tentatively.

Larry shook his head. He knew Jules Bondreaux and he knew just how fond of Larry was that volatile little Frenchman. "No," he said. "I've got to get some more bottles, I guess. We got two dozen today. If I could get about that many more I'd have four bits. I could give that to Father Paul. . . ."

"There are cases and cases of empty bottles behind papa's saloon," proffered Annette. "You could have them, Larry."

Again Larry Blue shook his head. "They belong to your dad," he said sternly.

"But I can give them to you." Eve, the temptress, held out an apple. Empty beer bottles were coin of the realm to the junior desperadoes of Franklin. They were worth a cent each, cleaned and washed. "You wouldn't be stealing them if I gave them to you, Larry."

Larry Blue pondered the ethics of the problem. Twelve years is no great age even when for six of those years their owner has been fending for himself. Necessity and temptation worked vigorously.

"I'll go with you and help you get them," Annette urged.

"Well . . ." said Larry Blue finally, ". . . all right."

Tomaso Patron, future bandit, got up from his place. "I am going home," he announced. "It is supper time."

"You are afraid!" The girl flung the words at Tomaso.

Tomaso grinned. "I am hungry," he said, "and my papa has a strap. Adios, amigos." Tomaso departed.

"You're not afraid, are you, Larry?" Annette voiced her worship.

Larry Blue, sturdily upon his feet, shook his head. "I ain't afraid," he answered.

The two, boy and girl, stayed beside the arroyo while Annette donned shoes and stockings; then, with Larry pulling the wagon, the empty bottles in its bed clinking together, they walked toward the town. The street lamps, an innovation in Franklin, glinted as they were lit and the girl, sighing a little, put her hand in the boy's fist.

"You won't ever go away and leave me, will you, Larry?" she asked.

Larry, looking straight ahead, shook his head a little. "I'll have to get a job," he answered.

"But if you do go away, you won't forget me?" Annette sought for some word of assurance.

"I won't forget you, Annette."

Shoeless feet and shod feet crunched into the sand. The girl's hand tightened. "Here's the alley," she announced needlessly.

Side by side they entered that dark passage. The uneven tin wheels of the wagon made a little rattling noise, and on either hand board fences loomed, cutting out the remainder of the night. Larry stopped beside a gate.

"You better wait here, Annette," he directed. "You keep the wagon."

The girl nodded. Larry, reaching out, noiselessly opened a gate. The dark spaces of a yard showed beyond the gate, and at the end of the yard a square adobe building. Larry released the girl's hand and slipped through the gate.

As he reached the back porch of the "EXCHANGE SALOON, JULES BONDREAUX, PROP." Larry paused. There were voices inside the building and a light shone from a side window; but where Larry stood the building was dark and quiet. The porch ran its length. At one end

7

a stack of cases filled with empty beer bottles showed Larry his goal. At the other end two heavy timbers, forming skids, ran down to the ground; and just above the skids were three empty kegs, one piled on top of the other two, and held in place by a wooden chock. Larry, finishing his inspection, slipped stealthily up on the porch.

He was not entirely satisfied with what he was about to do. There was a certain obliquity in stealing beer bottles, a sort of hair-thin line between right and wrong. And, too, there was always the chance of being caught. Larry, reaching up to the top case, paused a moment and then went on. After all, Annette had given him these bottles and they belonged to Annette's father. In a measure that made them Annette's. A resolve formed in Larry's mind. He would not sell the bottles to Jules Bondreaux. That would make it all right. Bottles clinked as he relieved a case of part of its contents.

He was reaching for more when the knob of the back door rattled faintly. Larry froze, motionless, beside the boxes. The knob rattled again, then the door opened swiftly and a man came through. In the momentary light Larry caught a glimpse of the man's familiar face. Then the door was closed and the light blotted out. Larry could hear his heart beating. That man who had come through the door was Abe Seemans, and Abe Seemans was the city marshal of Franklin, a man feared in only one less degree than Judge Lester.

Seemans paused a moment on the porch. Larry gathered himself to run. In another instant Seemans would turn and then . . . Seemans stepped from the porch, moving toward the corner of the building that stood on the bisecting alley. Larry Blue swallowed his heart again and was motionless.

At the corner of the building Seemans paused. Larry could see him there, a dim shape, dark against the dark wall of the saloon. The marshal crouched, and, listening, Larry could hear voices in the alley, voices lifted in altercation. Noiselessly the boy moved toward the end of the porch. He stopped beside the empty kegs. Seemans had moved a little. Was he turning to look? Larry placed his hand on the top keg, ready to jump. The marshal was still. Soundlessly Larry moved forward a foot. Then, suddenly, there was noise and movement. In moving Larry had rubbed his foot against the loose chock that held the kegs. Freed of that restraint, and with the boy's hand pushing against the top one, the kegs rolled. With a rumble from their empty bellies and a clatter of their heavy staves, the kegs rolled down the skids, rolled straight toward Abe Seemans.

Larry yelled once, his voice a hoarse squawk, and jumped. He lit, running, in the yard, making straight for the gate where Annette waited, a white ghost in the gloom. Behind Larry a man swore and a pistol exploded once and then again. Those shots lent the boy wings. He was through the gate and had seized Annette's hand before the reverberations died.

"Run," gasped Larry. "Run!"

Annette needed no urging. Her flying feet kept pace with Larry's. They did not hear the hoarse voices behind them, did not see the lights that bloomed suddenly behind the Exchange and in the alley that flanked it. Their hearts were in their mouths and their eyes were devoted to but one task: picking a way through the gloom.

At the end of the alley they turned. Neither needed to ask of the other their destination. They kept on running. Breathless, at last they paused beside a house. Larry

9

released the girl's hand.

"You better go in," he panted. "You tell your mother . . ."

"Where are you going, Larry?"

"That was Abe Seemans," Larry answered, all his fear in his voice. "Maybe he seen me. I'm goin' to hide. I'm goin' to get away."

"Maman will hide you. You . . ." Annette was talking to the empty night. Larry Blue had brought her home. So far chivalry had carried him, but no further. Now he was looking out for himself.

"Larry . . . Larry . . . !" the girl called.

The door of the house opened. A woman's voice, sweet even in exasperation, spoke. "Annette come in here. Where have you been?"

There were two big tears in Annette's dark eyes as she turned to answer that voice.

Larry Blue, freed of all incumbrances, circled back the way he had come. A block behind the Exchange Saloon there was a livery and a wagon yard. Larry lived in that wagon yard, unknown, so he thought, to its owner. Now like a frightened alley cat seeks its empty box, Larry made for this retreat.

Gaining it, he slipped over the fence and into the dark interior. He moved cautiously there and made toward his dwelling place—a wheelless old stagecoach body propped up on saw-horses. He was half way there when a light appeared, coming from the livery, and Larry heard voices. One he recognized.

"The kid's been hangin' out in that old stage," said the livery man. "You'll probably find him there."

Larry waited for no more. He dived over the tailgate of an adjacent wagon and finding a tarpaulin and a pile of sacks occupying the bed, pulled the tarp over him and

10

waited. The tarp muffled all sound. Larry did not hear Father Paul's voice calling his name, nor did he hear the livery man comment on his absence. Larry Blue cowered against the grain sacks and huddled beneath the tarp.

The livery man was frankly exasperated. That blame' boy had been hanging around and he could not account for his absence. Father Paul listened to the livery man and thought swiftly. He could, Father Paul knew, stay the night with the parish priest in Franklin. Morning would be time enough to find Larry Blue. Thanking the barn man Father Paul asked him to watch for Larry and if possible keep him at the stable in the morning. Assured that his wishes would be carried out the good Father withdrew, unaware that the frightened object of his search was a scant thirty feet away. The barn man escorted the priest to the gate, lighted his way through it, and went back to the barn. But not for long. Two men, one supporting the other, made their appearance at the livery door.

"Sam," greeted the supporting member of the pair, "get the team hitched, will you?"

Sam, the barn man, swore feelingly. "Yo're a damn' nuisance, Duck," he said. "I thought you was goin' to stay the night."

"So did I," answered the man called Duck. "But I'm responsible to Clark an' I got to get his precious brother-in-law home before he leaks out of his skin. He's drunk as a lord, an' lookin' for trouble. Come on, Esk."

With that statement, Duck moved forward, his waddle showing the manner in which he had acquired his name. Larry Blue heard the double trees of the wagon rattle, he felt the canvas of the tarpaulin move, felt a heavy body

11

that fell partially upon him and lay still.

"Come on with that team, Sam," commanded a rasping voice.

A fainter voice answered it. Larry lay still, not daring to move, scarcely daring to breathe. So it was that Larry heard the clink of tug chains being hooked, felt the wagon stir as a man mounted to the seat, and heard a profane, "Giddap!"

Beneath Larry Blue wheels revolved. The body that lay across him stirred and shifted a little. Larry held his breath. He was leaving Franklin; for where he did not know, but he was leaving.

# CHAPTER 2

### THE WOLF CUB

LARRY STAYED IN THE WAGON BED, HUDDLED UNDER the tarp, for what seemed an endless drive. Now and again the body that had been pitched in on top of him stirred, and occasionally a boot thumped against him. Then the wagon stopped, moved, stopped again, and moved once more. Larry knew that they had gone through a gate. Lifting himself cautiously he peered out from under the canvas. A black silhouette of humped shoulders and big hat showed against the sky, and that was all. Larry moved until he almost reached the seat of the wagon, settled himself stealthily, and pulled up the tarp once more.

The next time the wagon stopped the boy knew that they had reached their destination. There was a clatter of metal as the driver climbed down and departed, and after a time a light shone, edging in under the tarp. The driver was having trouble moving the other man. Larry could hear him grunt. Then a deep voice said: "Home so soon, Duck? Who you got there?"

Duck grunted profanely. "It's yore precious brother-in-law," he answered. "Drunk as a hoot owl. Lend me a hand, will you, Mr. Andrews? We got to put him to bed."

The deep voice said, "Sure," and the limp body in the wagon bed went up as though lifted by a chain hoist. Duck was feeling around in the wagon. Suddenly Larry felt a groping hand fasten upon his leg.

"What in the hell?" complained Duck.

The lantern, lifted high, disclosed a pale-faced, tousle headed boy, his leg in Duck's grasp. "Who are you?" demanded Duck. "How'd you get in here?"

Duck stopped. Larry's eyes, blue and direct, were fixed on his face, unafraid and calm.

"I'm Larry Blue," answered Larry. "I got into the wagon back in town."

"No time for that now, Duck," Clark Andrews' voice interrupted. "Let's get Archer into the bunkhouse. I don't want Mrs. Andrews to see him."

"You come on, kid," admonished Duck. "Come on now, an' don't try to run away."

Larry climbed out over the sideboards of the wagon. When he got to the ground Duck needlessly clapped a hand on the boy's shoulder. There was no place to run and anyhow Larry did not intend to run. He went with Duck, following the giant figure of Clark Andrews who strode along, carrying the limp body of the man he called Archer.

Inside the bunkhouse Andrews dumped his burden on a bunk. The room was deserted, empty and lonesome in the lantern light. Duck had released his hold on Larry's

13

shoulder and stood looking at the boy. Andrews turned, finishing a long scrutiny of the man on the bed. "Well?" said Andrews. "What happened?"

"Usual payday night," Duck answered. "The boys are sheddin' their money in Franklin. They'll be back tomorrow."

"What happened to Archer?"

"To Esk? He just got lit a little quicker than the rest, that's all."

"So you brought him home?"

"So I brung him home before he got into some real trouble. He was ridin' Abe Seamans in town, an' that ain't supposed to be healthy."

"Hmm," Andrews seemed to be considering the statement. He turned suddenly and looked at Larry Blue. "What did you say your name is?" the big man demanded.

"Larry Blue," steadily.

"Old Tom Blue's kid." Duck put in information. "Tom was . . ."

"What were you doing in the wagon?" Andrews took up the questioning as Duck checked his sentence.

"Gettin' out of Franklin," answered Larry. "I was out back of a saloon an' somethin' happened . . ."

Duck started violently. Andrews turned from Larry to the bow-legged man. "What is it, Duck?"

"Nothin'," answered Duck. "Nothin'. Go on kid."

"I run and hid in that wagon an' came on out with it," Larry completed. "I want to get a job, Mr. Andrews."

The boy knew now where he was. This was the Cross C, the big ranch northeast of Franklin. Clark Andrews owned the Cross C and Larry remembered things he had heard in town. He looked steadily at the big man.

"A job? What kind of a job do you want?"

14

Larry took a deep breath. "Most any kind of work," he stated. "Will you give me a job, Mr. Andrews?"

Andrews looked at the boy. He glanced at Duck. "Put him to bed," the ranchman said. "We'll talk about a job in the morning." Turning abruptly, he stalked out of the bunkhouse. When Andrews was gone Duck turned to Larry.

"Did you roll them barrels?" he snapped.

"Yes, sir," answered Larry honestly. "I didn't mean to, but I must of knocked out the block that held 'em."

Duck's little mouth set firmly in his broad face. "You done a damn' good job, kid," he commented. "Yes, sir! You take that bunk over there. Bill Williams won't be back tonight. Turn in now."

Obediently Larry turned toward the designated bunk.

When morning broke, a battered alarm clock rattled in the Cross C bunkhouse. Larry, almost thrown from bed by the clamor, was on his feet instantly, rubbing sleep from his eyes. It had not taken him long to go to sleep, once he had huddled down in Bill Williams' blankets. Across the long room he saw Duck sitting up and sleepily rubbing his eyes. Duck yawned, stretched, yawned again and then stood up, an oddly humorous figure in his underwear. On the bunk next to Duck's, the body of the man Archer Bolton—he whom Duck called "Esk"—still lay outstretched. Duck looked at that bed.

"Still dead to the world," he commented. "He drunk a gallon yesterday. Come on, kid. We'll start a fire an' cook some breakfast. Not many to cook for today. Just you an' me. He," with a jerk of the thumb toward the bed, "won't want to eat."

Larry was already dressed. All he had to don was shirt and trousers over his skin. Duck took more time, stamping his feet into boots and getting into a three button shirt. Clothed, the two left the bunkhouse and made toward the cookshack close by. There Larry carried in wood and removed ashes while Duck kindled a fire. With that done they washed at a bench outside the cookshack door, combed their hair with a broken comb, and re-entered the kitchen.

"So you want a job, do you?" asked Duck, dumping coffee into a pot.

"Yes, sir," answered Larry sturdily.

"Hope you get it," commented Duck. "Know who that was we brung in last night?"

"No, sir." Larry rearranged the wood in the box.

"That," said Duck with evident relish, "was His Nibs. That's Mrs. Andrews' brother: Archer Bolton, Esquire. Gets his mail addressed that way. We call him Esk."

"Oh," said Larry.

"An' he's a damn' fool," announced Duck. "How'd you like yore eggs?"

"Just any way," Larry answered.

Duck broke eggs into a sizzling frying-pan.

Larry drank coffee, ate salt pork and eggs and biscuits for breakfast. It was the best meal that he had ever eaten. The boy stuffed himself and Duck watched him, grinning at the amount of food that Larry put away. They had finished the meal and were washing dishes when Clark Andrews came into the cookshack. Andrews stood beside the door watching Larry. Suddenly he spoke.

"You're Tom Blue's boy?"

"My father's dead," Larry answered steadily. "I got a brother, Don."

"But Tom Blue was your father?"

"Yes, sir."

Looking at the big man, Larry could feel there was some essential quality lacking in Andrews. Andrews was big, physically a giant. He was handsome, with a bold nose and dark eyes. Still there was something indeterminate about his face, something in the set of his lips, perhaps, that gave the lie to his boldness.

"You can help Duck," Andrews said suddenly. "I'll give you a job."

Larry tried to speak his thanks but Andrews turned sharply on his heel and stalked out of the cookshack. Larry looked at Duck.

"I got a job," he said. "He . . ."

Duck grunted. "You got Clark Andrews' word for it," he said dryly. "Mrs. Andrews does the hirin' an' firin' around here, kid. It'll be her say-so if you stay. By golly, if I was Clark I'd . . . I'd run this place! My name ain't Duck Bunn if I wouldn't!"

When the dishes were washed Larry watched while Duck searched in a cupboard. Duck brought out a whisky bottle. "Goin' to fix up a hair of the dog that bit him," explained Duck. "You get out to the woodpile, kid, and wrangle some wood. That'll keep you busy."

Obedient to orders Larry got the ax and fell to work at the woodpile. He saw Duck Bunn cross from the cookshack to the bunkhouse carrying a glass. Duck grinned at him. Larry grinned back. He liked Duck Bunn. The cook was friendly and pretended to be nothing but what he was. Larry hacked at the wood, swinging the heavy ax. Little by little the pile of chopped wood grew.

Still engaged with that task but with the ax grown heavy, Larry, mauling a particularly tough chunk of mesquite, paused for breath. He straightened, leaning on the ax, and hearing a movement behind him turned to

17

find its cause. There was a young fellow, a boy of not more than twenty, standing there.

The newcomer had approached so silently that Larry, busy with the ax, had not heard him. Now he stood looking at the boy. Larry returning that look, saw a narrow, sallow-skinned face with prominent blue eyes and long yellowish teeth that protruded slightly. There was no expression in the eyes or on the face, no expression and no color. The youth's hat was pushed back, and his hair, a mouse brown, was slick with water. There was a gun on the man's hip, a heavy gun in a low-cut holster and he toyed with the butt of the weapon as he looked at Larry.

"Who are you, kid?" demanded the youth.

"Larry Blue," answered Larry stoutly.

"Blue?" the word was a drawl.

"Yes, sir."

The youth turned and sauntered toward the house. Larry watched him go and then lifted the ax once more. He had struck but a few blows before Duck Bunn came out to the woodpile.

"What did George want of you?" demanded Bunn.

"George?" Larry leaned on the ax and looked at the cook.

"George Whiteman. That was him."

George Whiteman! Larry knew that name. George Whiteman had killed a man in Franklin. Rumor had it that he had killed other men in other places. Larry's blue eyes widened. George Whiteman!

"Gosh!" exclaimed Larry Blue, "was that him?"

"That was George. What did he want of you?"

"He asked my name."

"You tell him?"

"Sure," Larry answered.

Duck shook his head. "Never tell a man like Whiteman nothin'," he advised. "You cut a little more wood an' knock off. You got 'most enough."

Duck went back to the cookshack and Larry returned to his work.

He had finished the tough mesquite root and was attacking another, sure that when he finished it he would have enough wood, when the back door of the ranch house opened and two children, a boy and a girl, emerged. The boy, black-haired and handsome, was bigger than Larry and walked with a swagger, the girl, also dark-haired, skipping along beside him. It was plain that they were brother and sister—their resemblance was striking—but the girl was two or three years younger than the boy and pretty as a French doll. Larry paid no heed to these details. Boy-like, he was interested largely in the physical potentialities of the boy.

Beside the woodpile the two paused and the boy thrust his hands in his pockets. Larry, chopping at the mesquite, did not deign to look up.

"Hello." The girl spoke in a friendly voice.

"Hello." Larry was gruff.

"Who are you?" Still the girl talking.

"I'm Larry Blue."

"Do you work here?"

Larry swung his ax. "Looks like it, don't it?" he answered. The girl danced around until she was in front of Larry. Larry ceased chopping. The girl was smiling. "You've cut an awful lot of wood," she said. "You're strong."

Larry felt his muscles swell. She was a mighty pretty little girl.

"He ain't as strong as I am, Connie," the boy spoke.

19

"I'll bet I'm stronger."

"You said 'ain't.' " There was malice in Connie's voice, malice and achievement. "I heard you. I'm going to tell Aunt Luella on you, DeWitt."

"And I'll tell on you," the boy threw the words back at her. "Talking to a servant. Go on and cut wood, boy."

Larry leaned on the ax, his square, face belligerent. "Who's a servant?" he snapped.

"You are! Go on an' cut wood."

"Who was your nigger last year?" Larry knew how to deal with this situation. He had had plenty of experience.

"You were. Yah! Cut your wood!"

The girl was watching, her dark eyes bright. Larry looked first at the girl, then at the boy. Here was a fresh kid that needed taking down a peg. From the cookshack came Duck Bunn's voice.

"Larry, got that wood cut yet?"

Recalled to the job, Larry scowled. He had to have this job, had to keep it. There was Don back at the Tumac Mission, and Larry's promise to Father Paul. Reluctantly he lifted the ax and swung it down viciously.

Under the impact the mesquite gave suddenly, weakened by many former blows. A piece flew up, describing a swift parabola, and came down to strike against the black-haired boy's leg. The boy yelped as though he were hurt, caught at his shin with his hands and danced momentarily upon one foot. Larry let go the ax handle.

"You meant to do that!" accusation was flung at Larry. "You threw that wood at me. You meant to!"

"I never neither." Larry's voice was more sturdy than his feelings.

20

"You did. You did . . . !" Assured by his size and by the fact that he had never had a battle, DeWitt charged in. Larry saw him coming.

Larry Blue had won his place among the youngsters of Franklin, won it honestly with hard fists. The black-haired DeWitt got in one blow, one swinging hand struck Larry's face. Then DeWitt backed away before a torrent of clenched hands. Larry went at the business wholeheartedly. The way to win a fight, Larry knew from grim experience, was to hit hard and hit a lot. He put his hard-won knowledge into practice. DeWitt, before that avalanche of fists, recoiled, retreated, and went down. Larry pounced upon him.

"Holler, 'Calf rope!' " commanded Larry, pummeling. "Holler, 'Calf rope!' "

He was jerked from his triumphant squat by firm hands seizing his arms and pulling him erect. A hard hand slapped his head, making his ears ring. "You little ruffian!" shrilled an angry voice. "You ragamuffin. I'll . . . !"

Twisting and squirming, Larry freed himself. Almost he renewed his attack upon this fresh adversary, but not quite. It was a woman who had pulled him from the squalling DeWitt, a woman with a thin face that in repose might have been handsome, but was now a scowling mask. She pursued him as Larry went around the woodpile at a run. He gained the further side of the woodpile and was prepared to dodge when another voice stopped him short.

"My dear sister," drawled this fresh voice, "is that quite necessary?"

Larry turned. There was a man standing behind him, a man who was thin and dark-haired. His face was puffed with liquor and his eyes were red-rimmed. Still there was that in his voice, in the indolent gesture he made, his very poise, that caused Larry to halt his flight, and stopped the woman as she advanced around the woodpile.

"He attacked DeWitt," snapped the woman. "He was pummeling him. He . . ."

"But Luella, I saw it all," the man with the puffed face drawled. "You must be mistaken. It was DeWitt who attacked, and the child defended himself. Surely you would allow anyone to do that?"

"You are drunk, Archer." Luella Andrews threw the words at the man. "You . . ."

"Surely, my dear, but drunk or sober I know right and wrong. Grant me that." Archer Bolton turned, staggered a little, and made his dignified way back toward the bunkhouse. The woman glared at his receding back, encompassed Larry in that glare, and then turned to the sniffling DeWitt and to the girl, Connie, who giggled.

"Come, children," she commanded, and without looking back, walked toward the house. Connie followed her, but DeWitt, emboldened by her presence, shook his fist at Larry. Larry did not return that threat. Duck had come out from the cookshack and was standing beside him, and Duck looked very grave.

"You go on into the kitchen, kid," commanded Duck. "Go on in out of sight."

Like a puppy slapped for jumping on its master, Larry obeyed the command.

Duck had little to say when he joined Larry in the kitchen. Duck came waddling in, carrying an armload of wood, and dumped it in the box. He busied himself around the stove and with sundry pots and pans, but he did not comment.. Larry, moping on a chair, made the first break.

"I reckon I sunk myself," he said woefully and yet hoping for some reassurance from the cook.

"I reckon you did," agreed Duck Bunn.

Larry Blue was still sitting on the chair, staring at the floor when Clark Andrews came in. Andrews, somehow, did not look as big as he had in the morning. His lips pouted and his eyes were uncertain. He spoke to Duck and then, turning, looked at Larry.

"You'll have to go back to town," he said shortly, averting his eyes from the boy. "Can't have you around here making trouble with my niece and nephew."

Larry said no word.

"Well?" Andrews almost snarled the word, as though he hoped that Larry would make some defense, as though he wished that a weaker, younger being would try to override him.

"Yes, sir," agreed Larry dolefully.

"That DeWitt kid took a swing at Larry," offered Duck. "I seen him do it, Mr. Andrews."

Andrews growled at Duck, turned, took a step toward the door and stopped. "You'll have to go," he said again, the while he fumbled in a pocket. "Can't have you around here making trouble. Here . . ."

The hand came from the pocket holding a bill. Without looking at Larry, Andrews held it out. Larry made no move to take the proffered money.

"Don't you want it?"

"I didn't earn it." Larry's voice choked a little. That was five dollars that Andrews had in his hand.

The ranchman turned his head, looked oddly at the boy for an instant and then returning the bill to his pocket, stalked on out.

"You're a fool, kid," announced Duck.

"Yes, sir," Larry agreed.

23

Duck said nothing for some time. Then, opening the oven, he slid in a pan. "Damn me if I wouldn't wear the pants around my own place!" the cook exploded.

Larry made no answer and after a time Duck walked out. He was gone for quite a while. When he returned he was carrying a bundle which he thrust toward Larry. "You take this when you go," said the cook. "It's some clothes for you. Goin' to be cold around here pretty soon."

Larry accepted the bundle. "Thanks," he said.

Duck looked at the boy, grunted and scratched his head. "Why would you take that from me an' not take Clark's money?" he demanded.

"I don't know." Larry shook his head.

There was the sound of uncertain steps outside the kitchen door. Boy and man looked up. Archer Bolton came through the door, stopped, and smiled at Duck. The smile illuminated his dark face, lifting the somberness from it.

"Have you another drink, Duck?" asked Bolton.

Duck Bunn shook his head. "I got one but you don't get it," he answered.

"And probably for the best," agreed Bolton. "I suppose by now that the wrath of the gods has descended on our young friend?" He looked at Larry.

"He's fired, if that's what you mean," answered Duck. "He'll be goin' in to Franklin the first way there is."

Bolton's face sobered. "My dear sister," he murmured, "I think . . . my brother's children are brats.'"

"If you mean that snotty nosed DeWitt, I'm with you," agreed Duck.

Archer Bolton leaned back against the door jamb and

his dark eyes narrowed. Presently he smiled and nodded. "I think I will," he said slowly. "I believe I will, if only on Luella's account. Do you want work, my young friend? 'A job' in the vernacular?"

"I've got to work." Larry looked straight at Bolton.

Bolton nodded again. "And I need a boy," he said pleasantly. "I am going to my ranch, or at least it is called that. I need a boy to chop wood and draw water, a general factotum. Can you chop wood and draw water?"

"Yes, sir!" Larry's voice was eager.

"And cook?"

Larry's face lost its eagerness. "No, sir."

"Ah well, one can't have everything. The wood and water will suffice. I'll take you with me."

Larry started up from his chair, took a step toward Bolton and then stopped. "How much will you pay me?" he asked.

Bolton looked at the boy and the dark eyes were no longer amused, but searching. "Does that matter?" he asked.

"Yes, sir," slowly. "I've got a brother. . . . I told Father Paul I'd send him some money."

Bolton's dark eyes sparkled once more. "And you shall," he announced. "Up, Horatio, and away! Make ready!" Straightening from the door jamb he smiled at Larry and Duck Bunn, turned on a booted heel and strode through the door.

Larry looked at the cook. "Does that mean . . . ?" he began.

"It means that he's goin' to take you up to his place,"

Duck answered soberly. "He's goin' to take you up there just to spite his sister. Kid, you'd better go back to Franklin."

Stubbornly Larry shook his head. "I'm goin' with

25

him," the boy answered. "It's a job an' I've got to have money. I . . . well, thanks, Duck."

Duck Bunn sniffed the air. "My bread's burnin'," he exclaimed, moving swiftly toward the stove. "I . . . well, kid, good luck. Damn it, I burnt myself!"

# CHAPTER 3

## THE HORRORS

LARRY BLUE RODE A BUCKBOARD WITH ARCHER Bolton back toward the west from the Cross C. At the end of the journey he was nearer Franklin than when he began, for Bolton drove toward the Rio Grande. In the river valley the dark faced man turned southward and followed along the stream, stopping eventually at a place where raw hills lined the valley and where the tornillo grew thickly about a small rock house. The team stopped beside the house and for the first time on that trip Archer Bolton turned and looked at his passenger.

"We are here," he said, and then more slowly, "God help us!"

Larry Blue climbed down from the seat of the buckboard and fell to the task of unhooking the team. Bolton watched him for an instant and then he also went to work. They stripped the harness from the horses, hung it in a shed, and, directed by Bolton, Larry led the horses to a gate and put them through it. At the house Bolton produced a key from under a flat rock, unlocked the door and pushed it open.

"Go in," he said, his voice strange. "Go in, Larry."

Larry went inside. The house was a hogpen, a muddle of bed clothing, wearing apparel, cooked and half-eaten food, dirty dishes and unidentifiable litter. But beginning at the door and marching grandly about the room were book-filled shelves. Larry looked at the litter, at the books, and at the man. Bolton was smiling bitterly.

"A mess," he said. "Well, Larry, it is no more messy than my life." Leaving the boy at the door he crossed the room, stepping casually upon a hand-carved saddle, a Navajo blanket and a pillow, and from beneath the table brought forth a jug. Looking at Larry he bowed politely.

"Will you join me?" Bolton invited. Larry made no answer and the man waited for none. Tipping up the jug, he drank. Larry, where he stood, could smell the whisky.

Fascinated, the boy watched the man. Bolton took another drink, put the jug aside and returned Larry's steady scrutiny. "You don't approve?" he asked mockingly. 'You are not alone, my friend. My sister does not approve, nor does my good brother-in-law and my brother. . . ." Bolton grimaced.

Larry made no movement or answer and Bolton, placing his hand on the jug again, scowled suddenly. "Get out!" he commanded, his voice rising. "Get out of here. Who asked your approval? This place is mine! Mine, do you understand? I bought it. It's mine. Get out, you little Buddha devil!"

Larry understood that command and he knew what caused it. Larry had seen just this sort of thing before. A kid who has had to fend for himself in such a town as Franklin knows the horrors when he sees them. Larry Blue, twelve years old, Larry Blue, whose father had been hanged for a murder, advanced steadily toward the trembling man beside the table.

27

"You better give me that jug," said Larry calmly. "You better go to bed, Mr. Bolton."

Bolton's hand relaxed as Larry took the jug. He reeled a little, clutching at the table. Larry, putting the jug on the floor, came close to the man, offering a shoulder for support. "I'll help you," he offered. "You'd better go to bed."

Bolton's black eyes were dazed. How he had kept control of his whisky-soaked brain for so long a time must rest among minor miracles. He placed his hand on Larry's proffered shoulder and stumblingly allowed the boy to lead him across the room to the littered bed. There he fell, rather than lay down, upon the tumbled bedding. Larry watched the man relax and then, bending, lifted the booted feet and placed them on the bunk. Bolton lay quietly and Larry stood watching him for a time, waiting for the next movement.

None came immediately and Larry, wise beyond his years, left the bed and took the whisky jug outside. He secreted it in a tornillo thicket and returning to the house made further search. That search revealed another half-filled jug and a full one. Larry took them out and hid them with the first. Going back to the house once more he saw that Bolton was still motionless. Methodically Larry set to work. He carried out the ax, a butcher knife that he found, and a long tined fork. A pair of shears, a big sacking needle, a shotgun and a rifle: each, as it was found, was taken out and cached with the liquor. Then, reasonably sure that there remained nothing within the house that Bolton could use to harm himself, the boy went back. Bolton was sitting up on the bed and his black eyes were cunning, narrow slits. Larry was too young to heed the warning in those black eyes.

"I better get us some supper," he said, looking at the

man on the bed. "What can I get you to eat, Mr. Bolton?"

Bolton waved a hand vaguely. "Whatever you can find," he answered, his voice strange. "I'll take whisky."

Larry paid no attention to that last remark but crossed the littered room to the table. There was part of a ham on the table and remnants of an ovenful of bread. To carve the ham Larry would need the butcher knife. Momentarily he debated bringing it in. As he stood beside the table, his back turned to the bed and the door, he heard the door close and turned hastily. Bolton stood before the door, his face a mask of triumphant hatred. Bolton's lips were drawn back in a snarl and his hands were thin, curved claws.

"My precious brother," murmured Bolton, "you're here with me now. Let's see you wriggle out of this!"

As he spoke, Bolton began a careful, cat-like advance, more awful because of its slowness. The curved hands were extended now, the fingers talons. Larry Blue's eyes sought wildly for an avenue of escape. There was none. The boy backed away before that terrible advance, and high and full and shrill screamed his fright.

As though in direct answer to that scream the door behind Bolton was thrown open and a giant of a man, white hair flying, flung himself into the room. Two strides he took and then leather-encased arms swept Bolton from his feet and held him struggling but helpless.

"Git somethin' to tie him, kid," boomed a deep voice. "Move now. I've got him!"

Larry Blue was so paralyzed with fright he could not obey the command and the white-bearded giant seemed to realize that. With a grunt he deposited the squirming, screeching Bolton upon the floor, held him there with one mighty knee and looked around. The carved saddle caught the giant's eye. Reaching out a big hand he pulled the saddle to him and produced a shining knife from a belt sheath. With the blade he severed saddle strings and then returning the knife to its sheath, methodically captured flying arms and brought them behind Bolton's back. The saddle strings lashed the arms in place, another string fastened the threshing feet and with a heave and a grunt the giant lifted the bound man, carried him across the little room and dumped him down on the bed.

"There," grunted the giant. "That'll hold you. He hurt you, kid?"

Larry Blue, recovering from his fright, had found his voice. The kindly gray eyes beneath jutting white brows reassured him. "No, sir," said Larry. "He was goin' to choke me, I reckon. He's got the tremens."

"The horrors," said the giant grimly. "He gets 'em. Mistook me for his brother one night an' I had hell with him. How come yo're here, kid? Who are you?"

Larry spoke his name and, briefly, the tale of his arrival at the rock house. The old man listened.

"Yo're Tom Blue's kid," he commented when Larry had finished his recital. "I know Tom. How is he?"

"He was hung for killin' a man named Haslip," answered Larry, and his chin quivered.

"Sho, kid," the big man, moving swiftly on moccasined feet, was beside Larry and one buckskin-clad arm went around the boy's shoulders. "Sho no. Don't you."

Larry got himself in hand. That big muscled arm, so mighty and yet so gentle, resting on his shoulders, reassured him. He looked up at the owner of the arm.

"It's just . . ." said Larry, ". . . if we'd of had a good lawyer they wouldn't of hung Dad. He. . ."

"Yo're all unstrung," the giant diagnosed Larry's trouble. "Havin' a man with the tremens goin' to kill you ain't been exactly a help. Never you mind, kid, Ol' Jim will look after you. You just stick to Ol' Jim Cardwine."

It seemed as though Cardwine knew exactly what to do with a badly frightened, badly shaken boy. He released Larry and put him to work, talking the while in a monotonous and strangely soothing drawl. From those drawling words Larry got information.

"Allus goes on a toot when I'm gone," complained Cardwine of the now subdued Bolton. "Minute I pull out he takes to his books an' liquor an' don't think of nothin' else. Place is a hawgpen. Tell you what, Larry. You pick up an' I'll fix him some."

Occupation was exactly what Larry needed. He began to pick up the litter in the room and Jim Cardwine, hauling out a half barrel, took a pail in either hand and went to the door. "Cold water's what he needs," said Cardwine grimly. "An' I aim to give it to him."

With that the old man departed and Larry watched the door for his return. When Cardwine came back with the pails full Larry offered to carry water. The giant nodded agreement and crossing the room looked down at the man on the bunk. "I don't know what I fool with you for," he said. "I don't, for a fact."

Larry carried water and filled the tub. Cardwine stripped the squirming Bolton, handling the man as though he were a child, lifted him up and put him in the tub. Bolton screamed and fought but Cardwine held him there.

Gradually the struggling ceased. Lifting the shivering

man from the water, Cardwine carried him back to the bed, dumped him down and pulled up the covers over his wet body.

"There," he commented, "that'll hold you for a while. Now we'll go look after my horses an' then fix up some grub. Come on, kid."

Larry was more than willing. He did not want to be alone in the house with that wretched man on the bed. He accompanied Cardwine when he went out, staying close to the old giant while a pack saddle was pulled from one horse and a stock saddle from the other. Cardwine put the horses in the pasture and went back to the house, Larry at his heels. Bolton lay moaning on the bed.

"You see what you can do about finishin' yore job," directed the old man, "an' I'll get a little supper."

The two ate by lamp light. The disarray of the room was straightened, for Larry had worked diligently, putting things in place and sweeping. When the meal was finished Cardwine took Larry out to the shed.

"I reckon," he boomed, "that you won't mind sleepin' on my camp bed out here tonight. I'm goin' to have to set up with that loco in there."

Larry was more than willing and when Cardwine had made down a thin bed Larry crawled gratefully between the blankets.

Twice during the night he was awakened by Bolton's screams as the man fought delirium. Both times Cardwine seemed able to quiet Bolton and both times Larry drifted back to sleep. In the morning, just as the sun peered over the bare hills and down into the river valley, Larry awakened to see Cardwine looming over him. Weariness was written on the old man's face, still he smiled down at the boy.

"He's sleepin' now," said Cardwine. "I reckon I'll turn in a while. Look after things, will you, kid, an' call me if he wakes up."

"Yes, sir," answered Larry, his voice expressing a sturdiness he did not feel.

"Good kid," Cardwine approved. "He'll be all right." And with that he lay down upon the blankets that Larry had vacated and instantly, it seemed, was asleep.

Larry moped about the house and the shed. Looking in through the door he could see Bolton, motionless on the bed. There was food on the table but Larry did not enter the room to take any. He did not want to go inside that house.

Cardwine awoke at mid-morning and immediately went to look after his charge. Satisfied that Bolton was still asleep the old man ate some of the cold food and Larry, safe in the giant's company, sat at the table with the old man. They went outside when they had finished and sat down beside the door. Cardwine produced cornhusks and tobacco and twisted a thin cigarette. Lighting it he smoked reflectively for a while and then, putting out the stub as it threatened his white beard, looked over at Larry.

"Well, kid," he said, "what are you goin' to do?"

"I don't know," Larry answered.

Cardwine was silent for a moment, then his deep voice boomed. "I trap around here," he said. "I kind of work out of this place. Archer Bolton needs lookin' after some an' I come in every now an' then an' do it. Want to go with me, kid, an' learn the trappin' business?"

Larry thought that over. "How much money can I make?" he asked finally.

Cardwine shrugged. "All depends," he answered.

"Sometimes you make some, sometimes you don't. What you want money for?"

"For Don," Larry answered. With that as a beginning he told Cardwine what he intended to do. It was an ambitious plan for a twelve-year-old. Cardwine heard the boy through and made no comment. To Jim Cardwine who had made his own way all his life it did not sound so difficult.

"You got to make a lot of money," he said when Larry finished. "You got quite a chore cut out for yoreself."

"Yes, sir." Larry agreed.

"An' you ain't goin' to take up trappin'?"

Again Larry thought. "Look," he said, "I've got to send so much money to Father Paul every month for Don. I guess I'd better stay here."

Cardwine got up. "Even if he gets the D. T.'s again?" he asked, nodding toward the door.

There was fright in Larry's eyes but his voice was steady enough when he answered. "I got to have it for Don," said Larry stubbornly.

Cardwine made no answer but walked out toward the shed, leaving Larry sitting there beside the door.

That night Larry again slept in the shed, an uninterrupted slumber this time. In the morning he went into the house at Cardwine's call. The trapper was kindling a fire in the stove when Larry entered and Bolton was lying on the bed, his eyes wide open.

"Come here, kid," ordered Cardwine when Larry entered the room. "You might as well learn somethin' about cookin' if yo're goin' to stay here. No need of yore starvin' to death."

Larry cooked breakfast under the trapper's tutelage that morning. He cleaned and straightened the cabin.

Cardwine watched the boy work, grunting now and then, though whether in approbation or disapproval Larry could not tell. When the chores were done the big man strode to the door, turned and looked at Larry.

"I'm goin' out to look after the horses," he said brusquely. "You stay here."

Larry looked uneasily at the man on the bed. Cardwine searched Larry's face but offered no encouragement. It was up to the boy. Finally Larry looked back at the white-haired man. "All right," he said, "I'll stay."

With no comment Cardwine went on out, leaving Larry Blue alone with the man who short hours before had tried to kill him.

For some time after the trapper left Larry stood stock still. Then, as Bolton made no movement, the boy walked around the room. He touched the books on the shelves, timidly, using the tips of his fingers. He stopped beside the table and rearranged a pile of papers. He did numerous small things and then, turning suddenly, he found that Bolton's eyes were fixed upon him. Larry did not move. The man's black eyes were red-rimmed and expressionless. Bolton's voice was a hoarse whisper when he spoke.

"Larry?"

"Yes, sir," answered Larry.

"Will you bring me a drink of water, please?"

How much sheer nerve it took neither Larry Blue nor Archer Bolton ever knew or could ever guess. For a long minute after that request Larry made no motion. Then, very slowly, he went to the water bucket, lifted a dipper full of water, carried it to the bed and extended it. Bolton took the dipper, drank thirstily and returned the enameled iron cup.

35

"Thank you," he whispered, "thank you, Larry."

Larry put the dipper back in the bucket. When Jim Cardwine came back into the room the boy was beside the table and Archer Bolton was lying peacefully on the bed.

Cardwine stayed at the rock house for a week. During that week he watched the man and the boy. Bolton, recovering, was up and dressed the second day of Cardwine's stay. On the third day, Duck Bunn, driving a wagon, came over from the Cross C with supplies and mail. Larry gathered that Duck regularly made two trips a month to the rock house in the river bed. The Cross C cook had a great bundle of papers which he gave to Bolton and from then on the dark-eyed man was immersed in the *Boston Transcript*. Bunn unloaded his supplies and, as he brought them in from the wagon, talked to Jim Cardwine and to Larry Blue. The cook had a budget of news.

Mrs. Andrews, so the cook said, had departed for the East, taking Constance Bolton and her brother DeWitt with her. There was excitement in Franklin. A saloonkeeper had been found with a knife stuck in his brisket. Jules Bondreaux it was, Duck said. No one knew why he had been killed and there was no trace of the killer. And, here the cook looked at Larry, while in Franklin he, Duck Bunn, had been asked by the city marshal if he knew the whereabouts of Larry Blue.

"Did you tell him?" gasped Larry.

Duck shook his head. "It ain't none of his business," answered Duck. "Anyhow . . . you was out back of the Exchange that night, wasn't you, kid?"

Larry nodded, his face anxious.

"I ain't goin' to tell Seamans nothin'," announced Duck. "I don't like him anyhow. I'll say this, though: it

36

was sure lucky for Archer Bolton that you was out there."

The cook's departure left Larry uneasy. He was frightened by the report that Bunn had made. If Seemans was asking about Larry, he had knowledge of the boy. It would have taken very little to put Larry to flight, but he had nowhere to go and there was the ever-present need for him to carry out his plan. That plan was an obsession with Larry Blue, forever uppermost in his mind.

At the end of the week Cardwine departed. He did not announce his going, he was simply at supper one evening and when morning broke he was gone. Larry had come to rely so much on the old man that his leave-taking threw the boy clear offstride. So excited was he that he came into the house and told Archer Bolton.

Bolton looked up from the paper he was reading. His voice, cultured and even, was kind. "Jim comes and goes," he said reassuringly. "He will be back, Larry."

"When?" Larry demanded.

Bolton shook his head. "I can't tell you that," he said whimsically. "Jim has never taken me into his confidence. Sometimes he stays away a month or more; again he may come back tomorrow or the next day."

That was no assurance to Larry Blue. The boy turned to leave the room but Bolton called him back.

"Are you afraid of me, Larry?" he asked gently when the boy returned to stand beside the table.

Larry thought before he spoke. Then: "Yes, sir," he answered honestly.

A glint of pain shone in Bolton's dark eyes.

"You need not be," he promised. "I . . . I heard you talking to Jim, boy, that day when I . . ."

Larry waited. Bolton did not proceed for some time.

37

Then, quietly, he continued. "You want money to send your brother to school, you said. What are you going to do yourself?"

"Make money," Larry answered. "I'm goin' to put Don through an' make a lawyer out of him."

"I understand that, but what do you want to be?"

"Just anything." Larry looked at the man.

"As long as you make money. I see." Bolton stirred in his chair. Larry waited. "I'll pay you to stay with me," Bolton went on, after a moment's pause. "I promised you a job. Will fifteen dollars a month be enough, Larry?"

"Yes, sir, for right now," Larry answered. "I reckon I ain't worth more than that now."

"But if you thought you were worth more you would go where you could earn it? Is that right?"

"Yes, sir."

Bolton smiled and picked up his paper. "Get a book and sit down," he said. "There isn't anything to do now, is there?"

Larry shifted uneasily. "No, sir," he answered, "but I . . ."

"Well?"

"I can't read."

Again Bolton laid aside his paper. "You can't read? he questioned.

"No, sir."

"Or write either," Bolton mused. "Have you ever been to school, Larry?"

"No, sir!"

"Would you like to read and write?"

Eagerness covered the boy's face. "I sure would," he answered. "I . . ."

Bolton smiled. Here was something that he could do

38

for this fearless, honest youngster. "Then you shall," he announced. "I'll teach you."

Larry thought that over. A doubtful expression supplanted the eagerness on his face. "I can't pay you for it," he announced. "I got to send all the money I make to Father Paul."

Bolton kept his face sober. "I didn't expect you to pay," he said gravely. "I'm not a very good teacher. In fact I ought to pay you. Suppose we say that I'll give you fifteen dollars a month for taking care of the cabin and doing the cooking. Jim has taught you to be a pretty good cook. Then I'll add some clothes to your wages, because you are letting me experiment on you. Will that be all right?"

Larry thought it over. He digested the whole sum and substance of Bolton's offer. Then, without a word in answer, he went to the book shelves, selected the biggest volume that he could find and carried it back to the table.

"I'm ready at any time," said Larry Blue.

Bolton's lips twitched. "That's fine," he said. "But I don't think we'll begin with Schopenhauer, Larry. We'll try something a little more simple."

# CHAPTER 4

## THE THREE R'S

JIM CARDWINE DID NOT RETURN TO THE ROCK HOUSE for six weeks. When he did come it was in the morning and the house was quiet, not a sign of life visible save for a trickle of smoke from the chimney. Riding in, the trapper noted that the yard had been cleaned and there

39

was a pile of wood cut and stacked near the door. There were other evidences of industry, The horse-pasture fence, once a thing of sagging wire, was now tight and well strung. There was a fresh rope over the well pulley and a new bucket on the well curb. Someone had been busy.

Letting his horses stand, Cardwine walked to the door. Stopping there, he heard Bolton's voice, even and cultured, reading a sentence. Larry's voice followed Bolton's its boyish treble a pathetic imitation of Bolton's diction. Jim Cardwine stepped around the door and walked in.

Bolton and Larry were beside the table. The room was almost painfully neat, cleaned and swept within an inch of perfection. The old man's moccasins made no sound and he stood inside the doorway waiting for the two to discover him.

"You see, Larry," said Bolton, patiently, "you must learn to read without spelling out the word. You must recognize it at once and know its meaning. I know that is hard, but it is the right way to do."

"Yes, sir," Larry's voice was eager. "I know that's the way to do, but it ain't easy."

"Isn't easy, Larry."

" 'Isn't easy.' "

Cardwine stirred and made a small noise. At the table, man and boy looked up. "Hello, Jim," greeted Bolton.

"Hello, Mr. Cardwine," said Larry.

"Hello," Jim Cardwine returned. "I butted into somethin'?"

"Larry's reading lesson," Bolton answered. "You go ahead, Larry. Try the next sentence or two. I'll be right with you."

Larry's eyes sought the book page. "'He . . . valued...

40

the . . . sun . . . beam,'"Larry read.

It was not until night, when Larry was sleeping soundly on a cot in the room, that Jim Cardwine found out the exact status of affairs at the rock house. With Bolton the old man sat outside the door, sucking a cornhusk cigarette and peering off into the darkness. The fall air was cold and Bolton had armed himself against it with a Navajo blanket wrapped about his shoulders; but Cardwine, with only the buckskin of his shirt for warmth, apparently did not feel the nip of the wind.

"He wasn't afraid of me even after what I tried to do to him," said Bolton. "That first day he brought me a drink when I asked for it, knowing all the time that I might snatch at him and catch him. Then he told me about the plans he has for his brother. He wants his brother to be a lawyer. Imagine that! Plans to send money to put his brother through school. I've already written one letter for him. . . . Jim, what kind of man is this Father Paul at the Tumac Mission?"

"The kind you hold to," said Jim Cardwine shortly. "Nursed me through a arrer wound one time. The kid told me about his brother."

"He wants to learn to read and write. I'm teaching him," Bolton went on, apparently paying no heed to Cardwine's answer. "The boy fairly soaks it up. I've written words and sentences for him to copy and he will sit for hours making his letters and words look just like those I have written."

In the darkness Jim Cardwine's cigarette described a little glowing arc. "He's just a wolf cub," drawled Cardwine. "His daddy was hung for murderin' a man. You know that?"

"Certainly I know it!" Bolton's voice almost seemed

41

to bristle. "If you think that I . . ."

"Now wait," Cardwine's drawl was placating. "I know you think you owe the kid somethin' for skeerin' hell out of him that time, but have you ever thought . . . ?"

"I've thought all I need to think!" Bolton snapped the words. "That boy is going to stay with me. I'm going to teach him all that I can. I'm going to look after him. If I thought he would stand for it I'd get his brother and bring him out here too."

"How do you mean, 'stand for it'?"

Bolton hesitated a moment before answering. "It is a little hard to tell you, Jim," he said finally. "Larry's whole idea in life is to see his brother through school. To make a lawyer out of Don, as he calls him. If I brought Don out here I'm afraid that Larry would let down. I'm afraid that with Don taken care of he would lose incentive. Do you see what I mean?"

"You mean that he wouldn't have somethin' behind pushin' him," grunted Cardwine. "Maybe yo're right. You got any drinkin' liquor, Arch?"

Bolton got up. "Why . . . yes," he said, surprise in his voice. "I have some around here somewhere. I'm not sure just where. I asked Larry to put it away. I was wanting a drink and . . ."

"Never mind. Set down. You don't know where the liquor is. I see you got the yard cleaned up an the fence fixed. Duck been over?"

"No. Larry and I cleaned the yard and we repaired the fence yesterday. You see he thinks that he has to earn his money and he won't study until all the work is done. It keeps me busy thinking up things for him to do. You saw how clean the house was?"

"I seen it. So yo're teachin' Larry, are you?"

"Why . . . yes . . . I'm trying to teach him. I . . ."

"See you bought him a few clothes an' a bed, too."

"He needed those. He . . ."

Jim Cardwine laughed. "This is the first time I ever come in here when the place didn't look like the wrath of God," he said. "You been here three years an' you never bought anythin' for nobody, lessen mebbe it was a drink. I never come back here before but that you wasn't drunk, an' now you don't even know where the whisky is. *Ho! Ho! Ho!*" The big man's booming laugh was soft in the night. "Yo're teachin' the kid, Arch. Yo' surely are!"

Cardwine laughed again and after a moment Bolton joined him. "I know it's funny," said Bolton, when the laughter ceased. "I suppose I am a reformed character. I hadn't thought of it that way, Jim."

"You think about it that-a-way then," directed Cardwine, rising. "Why, hell! The kid's even turnin' you into a pretty fair cook. That was a right good supper you got tonight. Come on an' let's turn in, school ma'am!"

Cardwine was chuckling as he walked away through the darkness toward the shed and his bed. Bolton, standing on the doorstep, watched him go and then turned and went into the house. The lamp was burning there, a tin screen deflecting its light from Larry's face, Bolton stopped beside the boy's cot and stood looking down.

Larry. like any other healthy youngster lay sprawled. His face was dirty, not unclean, but simply dirty as a boy's face will be. There were freckles sprinkled across his nose and his yellow hair was tousled. Bolton stooped and drew the covers up under the boy's firm chin and then straightening spoke half aloud.

"I suppose Jim is right," he said musingly. "I suppose you have pulled me up, Larry. I'll do what I can for you too, but, God forgive me, I'd throw you and all the rest over for just one word from . . ." Turning abruptly Archer Bolton walked across the room to his own bed.

On his visit to the rock house Jim Cardwine stayed a week. During that week a tacit understanding grew between the old man and the boy. Larry, when he was free from his studies and the other duties he had set for himself, hung around the old trapper.

What boy would not? Jim Cardwine had a gun he fondly called "Ol Sal," an old Buffalo Sharps that, worn as it was, still was a miracle of accuracy. He let Larry shoot the gun a time or two, carefully instructing him how to hold and how to touch off the light set-trigger. Cardwine noted with approval that the boy did not flinch from the heavy recoil. And too, Jim Cardwine wore buckskin and moccasins and a wide felt hat. Jim Cardwine had a beaded bag that he said was his "medicine" and Jim Cardwine's softly booming voice could recount miraculous experiences: tales of hunting buffalo in Kansas, tales of indomitable white men who went into Indian territory after beaver; stories of Geronimo and of Cochise, and the Comanche and Sioux. Jim Cardwine! He had seen it all, done it all. Larry Blue listened with wide blue eyes and open mouth. Certainly there was an understanding between the boy and the old man. And then Jim Cardwine got ready to go.

"Want to go with me, kid?" asked Old Jim, eyes narrow, as he stood beside the shed looking down at Larry. "Like to be a trapper an' learn how to handle Ol' Sal, an' ride a horse? I know where there's a mighty pretty pinto I could get."

Larry Blue took a deep breath and there was a light in his eyes, a light that faded away. "I'd like to," Larry answered honestly, "but you see I'm learnin' how to read an' write an' figure some. Mr. Bolton's teachin' me. He ain't . . . I mean; he isn't done yet and besides there's Don. I got to send money to Don every month. I got Don to look after. But gee! I'd like to!"

Old Jim Cardwine's eyes resumed their normal width and he nodded. "So long, Larry," said Jim Cardwine. "I'll be back an' mebbe we can do all them things yet. I'm goin' to see Bolton a minute."

He padded away on noiseless moccasins and Larry took the lead rope of the pack horse and stood twisting it wistfully. At the rock house Cardwine spoke to Archer Bolton.

"That kid. . ." said Jim Cardwine.

"Well?" questioned Bolton.

"He'll do to take along, Arch."

Bolton stared at the old man. "Why do you say that?" he demanded.

Cardwine grunted. "I just tried to toll him away," he answered casually. "Helt up a right perty pinto an some other things for bait. He wouldn't go."

Bolton, coming swiftly across the room, took Cardwine's shoulder. "Look here," he said fiercely, "you let the boy alone! I have plans for that boy. I'm going to take him . . ."

Jim Cardwine shrugged off Bolton's hands. "You got plans, yes," he said. "An' yo're goin' to take him . . . if somethin' don't happen. If you don't get sidetracked. So long, Arch. I'll see you some time."

He turned then and walked out of the rock house and Archer Bolton, going back to the table, sat down in a chair and moodily studied the clean swept floor.

45

If something did not happen. If he did not get sidetracked. . . .

"Damn it," swore Bolton, "nothing's going to happen!"

For three months after Jim Cardwine had gone nothing happened. Things went along at the rock house in even routine. Every two weeks Duck Bunn brought supplies and the mail, books and papers and, rarely, letters. Also he brought a budget of news: Mrs. Andrews had returned from her Eastern trip; Apaches had raided a freighter's train in the west pass of the Cantandos; the stage line had put on extra coaches and was running two a day each way. To the man and the boy in the rock house these were but distant rumors. They were busy. October, November, December, wore along and were gone. Larry could write more than a little, his script a weirdly true imitation of Bolton's fine hand. He could read, read enough so that at night Archer Bolton had to tell him to put the book away and go to bed. Sometime in those three months Larry passed his thirteenth birthday. At the end of each one of those months Duck Bunn took a letter, a letter that held money, back to the Cross C with him, promising to mail it in Franklin.

At the end of those months disaster fell upon Larry Blue.

Duck Bunn, making his regular trip, drove into the neat yard of the rock house in the middle of the afternoon. Larry, coming from the door, greeted the friendly cook and Archer Bolton called a hello from inside. Duck answered that hail and pulled a bundle of papers from the wagon box.

"Here's yore readin' matter," called Duck, "an' Missus Andrews sent over a letter, an' I got another one

46

for you. Come out from town today."

Duck fished under the folded blanket on the wagon-seat and brought out two envelopes. Larry had taken the papers into the house and Bolton came out and reached up for the letters. He glanced at the note from his sister, thrust it idly into his hip pocket and looked at the other letter. Duck, having jumped down from the wagon, was waddling toward the house carrying a side of yearling beef and so did not notice the expression that came over Bolton's face as he ripped open the envelope.

Larry came out, got a load of supplies and took them in. Duck emerged from the house. As he reached the wagon Bolton caught his shoulder.

"We've got to go!" Bolton's voice was hoarse. "I've got to get to the ranch. I've got to get . . ."

"Bad news?" questioned Duck anxiously. "I thought that everything was all right. Missus Andrews . . ."

"Get on that seat and start!" ordered Bolton. "Get on that seat. My brother is dead!"

"That's too damn' bad," began Duck, moving to climb the wheel. "I . . ."

"My God, man," Archer Bolton almost screamed, "don't you understand? My brother is dead. I'm the only Bolton left. I can go to her now. I can . . ." Bolton had scrambled to the seat as he spoke. Now he snatched up the lines and pulled the astonished team around. Lashing their rumps with the ends of the lines he sent them lumbering out of the yard, leaving the surprised Duck still reaching for the seat. Larry Blue, coming from the cabin, saw the wagon rattling out of the yard, Bolton, a coatless madman, standing up in the wagon box and flaying the horses. There where the wagon had been, was Duck Bunn, his hat pushed forward over his eyes, and scratching his head with aimless fingers.

47

"I'll be damned," vowed Duck. "I sure will be damned!"

"What happened?" demanded Larry.

"He tol' me his brother was dead," announced Duck, "an' I was just fixin' to say how sorry I was, when he yelled that he could go to her, that he was the only Bolton left, an' made a runnin' jump for the wagon. Now by golly, I've got to git a horse an' ride clear back to the ranch. Dawggone it!"

The wagon had disappeared, only the rattling of its wheels coming back to the two in the yard. Duck Bunn looked at Larry Blue. "I declare," said Duck, "it looks like he'd plumb forgot you, kid."

"Yes, sir," said Larry.

"Kid," Duck looked speculatively at the boy, "you reckon you could go out an' bring in one of Esk's horses? I ain't exactly built for walkin' an' we got to wrangle afoot."

"Yes, sir," agreed Larry. "I can bring them in."

"Then you do that," ordered Duck. "I'm goin' after him. I got to go to the ranch anyhow. Likely he'll send for you when he gets there. He was some excited just now."

"I'll get a horse," said Larry.

He left Duck still standing in the yard and went through the gate into the little horse pasture. Bolton had kept two horses there, gentle enough animals. They were used to Larry; he looked after them. When he returned, driving the horses before him, Duck had brought Bolton's saddle from the shed. It was an English saddle, flat and with thin iron stirrups.

"An' I got to ride this postage stamp back to the ranch," Larry heard Duck mourn.

There were halters on the fence. Larry took them

48

both. Neither of the horses made a fuss about being caught. Larry led them out and through the gate to the waiting Duck.

"That's the idea," commended Duck. "You go with me, kid. He was sure in a hurry, wasn't he?" speaking of the absent Bolton.

"Yes, sir," agreed Larry.

Duck put a pad in place and lifted the light saddle. "Don't weigh ten pounds," he said. "You goin' to ride bareback, Larry?"

Larry nodded. He was tying the loose end of the halter rope to the headstall, making reins. Duck was fastening his cinch.

"Say," he announced, "it's a good thing yo're goin' in too. Save me a trip. I'd like to forgot it, what with Esk runnin' off that way, but I was told to bring you in."

Larry stopped his work with the halter. "Why?" he asked. "Who told you?"

"Andrews." Duck finished his saddling and looked apprehensively at the flat leather. "Seems like he was in Franklin an' they want you in there for somethin'."

"Who wants me?" There was fright in Larry's voice.

"Seemans, I reckon. Leastwise I seen him talkin' to Andrews yesterday."

"I ain't goin'." All Larry's careful training was forgotten in his fright. "I ain't goin' in, Duck."

Duck Bunn looked at the trembling boy. "You scared, kid?" he asked kindly.

There was no need for Larry to speak. His face was answer enough.

Duck scratched his head again. "I don't blame you," he said suddenly. "Look here, Larry. You stick here 'til Esk ketches up with himself. He'll be back for you. In the shuffle at the ranch they won't be askin' why I

49

didn't bring you in an' I won't say nothin' about it. I'll ask around a little an' when I find out why Seemans wants you we'll know what to do. How's that?"

Larry nodded, words refusing to come.

Duck Bunn grinned, gingerly mounted the horse and settled himself in the English saddle. "Ain't a damn' thing under me," he complained. "You stay right here 'til I get back, Larry, or 'til you hear from Esk. So long, kid!"

Duck Bunn rode off on that unfamiliar saddle and Larry Blue stood watching him go. When Duck was out of sight Larry turned and entered the house. There, carefully choosing those things which were his own, he made a small bundle, a thick bundle of foolscap. This was the copy book that Archer Bolton had made for him. Clothing, books, paper, made but a light load. When he had tied his bundle Larry Blue left the rock house. The second horse stood patiently waiting, the makeshift reins that Larry had fashioned trailing on the ground. Larry stripped the headstall from the horse, knowing that the animal would drift and find his way to other Cross C horses. Then, closing the door, Larry locked it and hid the key under the flat stone that served for its receptacle. He was leaving the rock house in the tornillo, leaving it for good. He was no more coming back than Archer Bolton was returning.

Larry swallowed something in his throat. There had been finality about Bolton's departure. There was finality in his own. Abe Seemans had talked to Clark Andrews about him. That was enough for Larry Blue. To the west was the river, and north along that river, somewhere, was a place where a boy could get a job. Bundle slung on his arm, Larry Blue took a twisting, winding cowpath through the tornillo.

# CHAPTER 5

## PARDNER

FRANKLIN WAS NOT COLD IN JANUARY AND THE WINDS had not yet begun to blow. The winds came in March and April, hurtling out of the west and sweeping sand and dust through the town. But now Franklin was peaceful, almost as peaceful, it seemed to Father Paul, as his own mission of Tumac. The good priest drove his mules, Angelica and Francesca, along Franklin's dusty street, now nodding to some native woman whose black rebosa shielded her face, now smiling at a sturdy teamster or native, or bowing to a merchant standing at the door of his store. A strange town, Franklin, thought Father Paul, a wicked town albeit a town that contributed liberally to the church. At the main intersection of the town the good priest stopped his mules. There was a rider, handsome as a picture, coming toward the buckboard, his blood bay horse curvetting. As the horse reached the buckboard, it shied and was restrained by a firm hand. The rider, black hat in hand, wide black tie blowing with the breeze, bright black eyes and full lips smiling, greeted Father Paul.

"Good evening, Father."

"Good afternoon, my son," replied the priest. Father Paul knew the man, knew him for what he was. Indeed any man of the period might have picked the profession of Royal Truman from his long smooth hands, his pale face, and his dress. Royal Truman was a gambler.

"And good-by, Father," continued Truman "I am leaving your fair city."

Father Paul, noting a slim roll behind Truman's

51

cantle, nodded slightly. "Leaving?"

"By request." Truman's smile was sardonic but not bitter. "It seems that those of my fraternity are not wanted in Franklin. We have been asked to go, by no less than one hundred citizens." From the pocket of his immaculate coat Truman produced a hand bill and held it out for the priest's inspection. The words, "Outlaws, Gamblers, and Road Agents," were flaunted across the top. Truman returned the bill to his pocket.

"I am sorry," said Father Paul, and meant it. Truman was a gambler, true, a man who lived by chance and the turn of a card, and yet there were many worse men than Royal Truman, and Father Paul knew it. He had seen some of the things that Royal Truman had done, knew of hidden charities that, spoken of, would have set the gambler's face into a hard carved mask and his eyes gleaming a warning.

"Thank you," Truman received the priest's tribute. "It was time for me to go. The railroad is pushing down through Kansas and into Colorado. I belong there."

Thoughtfully the priest nodded. "I suppose so," he said slowly.

"I know so." Truman was cheerful. "Still, I am glad that I got to tell you good-by, Father. I am glad that I got to do that." The blood bay was stirring restlessly, taking little mincing steps in the dust. Truman loosened his reins, swept his hat in a gesture, and horse and rider pounded up the street. Father Paul spoke to his team.

Atop the hill overlooking Franklin he found John Lester's house without a sign of life. Stopping the mules, Father Paul got down from the seat and knocked at the wooden gates that closed the entrance of the patio. No answer coming, he knocked again and waited.

Presently the gates opened a crack, a brown face

looked out and seeing the visitor, the gates were swung open.

"*Padre!*" exclaimed the native. "*Padre, la Señora Lester esta muerta. El Señor . . .*"

Father Paul waited for no more. Robe flapping about his ankles, he strode through the gates and into the patio. Straight to where the withered hollyhocks stood, brown and sere, he made his way, and then stopped, for John Lester, face lined with pain, was coming through the door behind the hollyhock stalks.

"My son . . ." said Father Paul, and all the age-old pity of his Master was in his voice. "My son . . ."

John Lester made a little, futile gesture. "I said," Lester's voice was low, "that I would keep her with me always. I said . . . She is gone, Father."

Father Paul's firm hand rested on the Judge's shoulder. "You will keep her!" said Father Paul valiantly. "You will keep her always in your heart. Come with me. Come!"

Obediently as a child John Lester allowed the priest to lead him away.

They were long together, those two. Gray-haired man of law and ruddy-faced priest, they sat together and from Father Paul, John Lester drew comfort of a sort. The priest's mules were put in the Judge's stable, and his buckboard was wheeled under a shed. Dark-faced men and women who knew the sorrow of their master waited upon the two, and late that night when the candles had guttered close to their sockets, John Lester spoke of something other than his grief, spoke with a strong resolve in his voice.

"I have done what I thought was right," said John Lester. "I believed, and I still believe, that law must come to this country, some law other than that of the wolf. But now I see a new course.

"I have sentenced men to hang. I believed that they deserved hanging. I have been stern, as a judge. They call me 'the Hanging Judge,' Father. But no more. I will resign from the bench."

Father Paul leaned forward, watching the strong face before him.

"She . . ." Lester's voice broke, "she was not stern and she did not believe that the law should always exact its tribute. I will follow her belief. I will uphold the law but I will try to temper it. The law was not tempered for her, it was not kind to her, and yet . . ."

"And yet she had your love, my son," said Father Paul, softly.

John Lester was silent then and Father Paul respected that silence. But the priest knew it is not good for a man to be too long with his thoughts. Gently he broke the silence. "I came today to ask you about my boy," said Father Paul.

"Your boy?"

"My boy Larry Blue. In town I asked the marshal, Seemans, if he had found him for me. He told me that the boy was living with Archer Bolton, Clark Andrews' brother-in-law. Seemans had sent for him, he said. I wanted to ask if you had any word."

Judge Lester shook his head. "Nothing," he answered. "I have given the boy's name to the United States Marshal and his deputies, but they have not found him."

Father Paul nodded. He smiled slowly. "The boy is somewhere close," he commented. "I'm inclined to believe that Seemans is right and that Bolton has him. I have received three letters, each containing fifteen dollars, and each well written by a man. The money was for Don Blue. I have put it away."

54

"Odd that someone hasn't found the lad," said Lester, aroused briefly from his sorrow.

Father Paul made a wide gesture. "It is a big country," he said.

Judge Lester rose from his chair, paced across the room and back. He stood looking down at the priest. "Father," he said slowly, "will you let me help you? Will you let me help you with Don Blue and his brother? I have influence. I can . . ."

"Surely you can help me," agreed the priest. "And now, my son . . ."

The candles guttered low and the two men knelt together. Across the patio the wind rustled in the dead hollyhocks.

North along the river Larry Blue curled down in the sand and shivered, for the night was cold.

The boy could not stay long in his sandy bed. The cold drove him out and set him in motion. He collected wood, dry poles of the tornillo, scratching his hands woefully in the process. He broke the poles carefully and then with a match from the block of sulphur matches he had brought from Bolton's, he kindled his fire. It burned, feebly at first and then more strongly. Larry Blue warmed himself beside the blaze, turning now this side, now that one toward the flame. Alternately toasting and freezing he was gaining some measure of warmth, when a voice spoke out of the black thicket to the north.

"Kind of takin' a chance with that fire, ain't you, Larry?" came the even drawl. "If a 'Pache saw that he wouldn't ask nothin' better."

Startled, Larry jumped back from the blaze. Jim Cardwine, Sharps aslant over his arm, stepped into the firelight.

"Jim!" Larry exclaimed.

"I seen the blaze an' taken a little walk to look it over," drawled Cardwine. "Yo're a long ways from home, Larry."

Larry said nothing.

Cardwine kicked sand toward the fire with his moccasined foot, partly extinguishing the flame. "Arch get drunk again?" he asked evenly.

Larry shook his head.

"Somethin' happen?"

"He got a letter." The boy's voice choked a little. "He read it an' left in the wagon. He never even looked back."

"Hmm," Cardwine cleared his throat softly.

"An' Duck told me that Seemans knew where I was an' wanted me," the boy finished with a burst of words. I pulled out."

"What for are you so skairt of Seemans?" asked Cardwine. By now the fire was a bare flicker.

"He . . . I . . . he seen me," answered Larry. It came out then, the tale of Annette and the beer bottles and the man who had crouched, gun in hand, behind the Exchange Saloon.

"He seen me an' he knows I pushed down the kegs," Larry finished. "He's after me."

"An' you don't aim to let him ketch you," added Cardwine, kicking sand over the last of the flame. "All right. You string with me, kid. I'm camped at a spring above here. I was goin' into Franklin but I reckon that can wait. Come on."

A big hand reached out and engulfed Larry's scratched paw. Larry, feeling the warmth and security in that hand, was glad to follow. Cardwine stalked off in

56

the gloom.

Moving through the night as surely as though it had been broad daylight, Cardwine reached his camping spot which was a scant quarter mile up the river. A horse stamped softly; Larry stumbled over a bed, and they were there!

The big man released his hold on the boy's hand. "Here we are," he said, low-voiced. "That's the bed yore standin' on. Kick off yore boots an' turn in, Larry."

Placing his bundle beside the bed Larry moved to obey Cardwine's command. "Just slip into the blankets," ordered Cardwine.

"Where will you sleep?" asked Larry.

"Right beside you," answered the trapper. "We'll talk in the mornin', kid. One thing you want to remember though: Don't go buildin' a fire in this country. Not if you want to live to keep warm."

Cardwine lay down. Larry, huddling into the blankets, heard movement and saw that Cardwine was wrapping himself in some sort of cover. The boy pulled the blankets up about his shoulder, reveling in their warmth. Cardwine grunted, turned, settling himself, and then his breath came, deep and regular in sleep.

Morning broke cold and gray. As Larry sat up and rubbed the sleep from his eyes he saw Cardwine hovering over a tiny fire. A black bucket steamed on the blaze and a savory odor, a mingling of coffee and something else, assailed the boy's nostrils.

"Mornin', kid," said Cardwine cheerfully. "Let's eat. Then we'll wash an' break camp. I aim to be a long ways up the river by night. Want to make Palo Verde. There's a Mexican up there that's got that pinto horse."

As he spoke the old man poured coffee from the bucket into a tin cup and held it out invitingly. Larry, rising from the blankets, took the cup and burned his lips on the scalding contents.

The two ate breakfast in silence. When the meal was finished Cardwine cleaned his few dishes, put them in a gunnysack and made his way to a spring, a pale green bowl, close to the camp. There he washed, Larry following his example. When the trapper walked on from the spring out to where his horses were staked, Larry went with him. Cardwine took one horse, Larry the other. Old Jim Cardwine, watching the boy's every move, almost voiced his approval at the way the boy followed the example set him. Almost, but not quite. Back at the camp-site Cardwine began to lay out his scanty outfit. Beside the gunnysack which held a coffee pot, a frying pan, and a tin plate and cup, there was another sack with a meager supply of food, the thin bedroll, a pack of pelts and an ax. These Cardwine distributed between the two horses, placing the bedding and the pelts across his pack saddle.

"You ride the pack," he commanded briefly when the loading was done.

Larry climbed up the side of the sedate pack horse and bestrode the load. Cardwine mounted his own saddle, nodded to Larry, and set out toward the north.

For a time Larry followed the lead horse. Then, when the trail widened Cardwine dropped back and rode beside the boy. "What you plan to do now?" he asked, watching Larry from the corner of his eyes.

Larry frowned seriously. "I got to get a job," he said. "I've got that money to send Don an' . . . Well, I got to get a job."

"Doin' what?" Cardwine's voice showed very little interest. It was as if the old man simply wanted to make conversation.

58

"I don't know," Larry answered. "If I could get to a town mebbe I could find some kind of work."

"Might stay out in the country a while." Cardwine looked ahead at the trail. "Might try trappin'. Coyotes are prime an' there's some beaver in the hills if you will go far enough north. Then there's always the chance of washin' a little gold, an' I know a swamp where there's plenty of mushrats."

"I don't know anything about trappin," objected Larry.

"I do." Cardwine pushed his horse ahead, for the trail was narrowing. "Learn, can't you?"

"Yes." Larry stared at the broad, buckskin-covered back.

"I've lernt lots of fellows to trap," said Cardwine over his shoulder. "I reckon you'd pay me back when you got to makin' money, wouldn't you?"

"Yes, sir," eagerly. "I sure would. I'd . . ."

"It's a deal, I reckon," interrupted Cardwine, his voice carefully calm. "I'll teach you to trap an' stake you to enough money to send yore brother, an' you'll pay me back. That correct?"

"Yes, sir," agreed Larry, and then, after some little time, "Thanks."

Cardwine grunted.

They had made an early start. Cardwine, careful not to overtax his companion, kept nursing Larry along. By noon they had covered what ordinarily the man would have considered a two hours' journey. When evening came they were almost at the tiny native settlement of Palo Verde. Cardwine pulled off the trail, seeking those three things that all travelers must of necessity seek: wood, water and grass. Cardwine found them— instinctively, it seemed—dismounted, and waited for

Larry to come up. The boy slid down from the pack horse and stood with wide-spread legs. His face showed the pinch of weariness and his shoulders drooped. Cardwine spoke slowly, disregarding the boy's exhaustion. Jim Cardwine knew that men must keep going even when they are ready to drop, and it was no part of his plan to let Larry down easily.

"You buscar some wood," he drawled. "Take the ax an' don't chop dirt or rocks. It's all the ax we got. I'll make camp."

Larry took the ax from the pack, squared his sagging shoulders and walked toward a cottonwood log. Jim Cardwine, unpacking the horses, listened to the ringing of the ax against the cottonwood, a ringing that never faltered, and smiled to himself. The kid would do. The kid would do to take along!

"I reckon that's enough wood, pardner," called Cardwine.

Later on, when frying-pan bread, coffee, and jerky gravy had relieved Larry's weariness, and when a long chunk of cottonwood was smoldering in the sand, Jim Cardwine leaned back against his saddle and looked across the fire.

"So Bolton pulled out, did he?" asked the old man, puffing reflectively on his tiny corn husk roll. "I figured that he would, someday."

"He got a letter," said Larry. "His brother had died an' he was upset."

Cardwine took two deep inhalations before he spoke. "Arch Bolton hated his brother," said Cardwine. "One night he was drunk an' he had to talk. He tol' me. His brother beat him out of a girl an' Arch went to drinkin'. Then his half-sister married Clark Andrews an' Arch come out here an' bought some land along the river. It

60

was old Mexican grant land an' he got a title to it. Clark run his cows on the land an' kept Arch in grub an' sort of looked after him. Arch Bolton was a weak sister, son."

"How did it come that you knew him?" asked Larry, comfortably sprawled beside the smoking cottonwood.

"I drifted in there one night when he had the horrors," answered Cardwine reflectively. "He was sure fightin' his head. I stayed with him an' somehow I got to likin' him. He'd read me stories out of them books an' . . . Did you bring any books with you, Larry?"

"Two. An' all that writing he made for me," answered Larry.

"Good. You keep up with yore readin' and yore writin'. Somebody in this concern has got to read an' write, an' I can't."

"You can't?" Surprised, Larry came up to a sitting position.

"No," Cardwine's voice was reflective. "I run away from a cowhide strap back in Missouri when I was younger than you. I never learnt to read or write or cipher. But you will. You'll practice every day."

Larry lay back again and Cardwine, throwing away his cigarette, began to fashion another. "Kid," he drawled, "would you mind talkin' some about yore daddy? I been pickin' up a little here an' a little there, about him. Yore daddy an' me packed for Crook when he went after Cochise. I was right fond of him."

Larry rolled over and pillowed his head on his arm. His voice was muffled when he answered. "No. I'll talk about him."

"Yore daddy," stated Jim Cardwine in the matter of fact voice a man uses when he relates history, "was hung for killin' a man named Haslip. Him an' Haslip

61

got into a argument over a card game an' that night Haslip got himself shot. Nobody seen who done it but yore daddy was clost by an' Seemans arrested him. Then at the trial it come out that Tom Blue had threatened Haslip. His gun had been shot an' the money that Haslip had won was in Tom's pocket. It was open an' shut, an' Judge Lester sentenced Tom to hang when the jury found him guilty. That right?"

"Yes, sir," the muffled voice was but a murmur.

"Tom was drunk when they picked him up?"

"Yes, sir." Larry rolled again until he was on his back, and then he sat upright. "Dad was drunk an awful lot, Jim. It seemed like he was always drinkin'. But he was awful good to Don an' me. He gave us money when he had it and he cooked for us an' he bought us clothes. That is, when he had the money."

Across the fire Jim Cardwine nodded. "I knowed Tom," he reminded. "He was good to you kids, all right. Losin' yore mother shook him up a lot. I knew her too." There came a long silence. Larry stared into the glowing cottonwood coals. Jim Cardwine smoked.

"This Haslip," said Cardwine suddenly. "You know anythin' about him, kid?"

"Not much. He lived north of Franklin. Out by the Deaf Smith tanks. He had a shack out there an' some cattle. That's all I know."

"The Deaf Smith tanks," mused Cardwine. "That's the only water in that country. It's right against Andrews' Cross C. I reckon Andrews didn't take kindly to Haslip havin' the water?"

"I don't know," said Larry dully. "I never heard."

Jim Cardwine said: "Hmm," deep in his throat. Then, rising, he addressed the boy again.

"You haul that burnin' log away an' throw some sand

over it," the trapper directed. "Put some sand on them coals an' ashes. Cover 'em fairly deep an' make down yore bed right there. You'll sleep warm an' I'll settle down beside you. I'm goin' out to look at the horses. Make sure all the fire is out, son."

# CHAPTER 6

## A WOLF CUB'S FANGS

AT SIXTEEN LARRY BLUE'S SHOULDERS ALMOST, BUT not quite, filled one of Jim Cardwine's shirts. The boy would never be so tall as his mentor, but chest and shoulders were deep and broad, and already there was the beginning of a golden beard sprouting on his cheeks, a fine fuzz that Larry felt surreptitiously and proudly now and then. In three years Larry Blue had shot up from boyhood almost to manhood, and in those three years he had learned.

Jim Cardwine's teachings had not been as those of Archer Bolton. Jim had taught by precept and example. The old man did things seemingly by instinct, and in doing the same things Larry developed the same instinct. It was, for example, instinctive in the boy to ride anywhere and anyhow upon his pinto horse. Jim Cardwine had learned from the Comanches, than whom no better horsemen ever breathed. Larry Blue learned from Jim Cardwine. Larry could shoot his light Sharps, a gun that weighed barely ten pounds, from any position, with speed and with deadly accuracy. Jim Cardwine shot that way. Larry could whip a knife—from his belt—a knife carefully made from an old file and tempered by a native smith—and throw it twenty or thirty feet as a man whips a baseball. That was the way Cardwine threw a knife. Larry could circle the fifty-foot rawhide rope he carried on his broad-horned saddle and snare neck, front feet, or hind feet of a running horse. Why not? Jim Cardwine could do it. An ax was a tool to do Larry's bidding in his hands or in the air. Traps that Larry set caught even the cunning coyote. Larry's blue eyes, earnest and alert, could read the sign along a trail plainly as a printed page. The boy had not learned these things; he had assimilated them. There was not much of sixteen-year-old Larry Blue that resembled the frightened, freckled kid who had hidden under Duck Bunn's wagon tarp or who had set out upon a lonely trail from Archer Bolton's rock house in the tornillo.

One thing remained of that boy. With all the rest, Jim Cardwine had insisted that Larry continue with his reading and with his writing. The dog-eared books that Larry once carried from the rock house had been supplanted by others, but the foolscap copy book that Archer Bolton had made still rode in Larry's pack. The boy practiced writing just as he practiced throwing the knife or his lariat, and while in those two arts he imitated Jim Cardwine, in the writing he imitated meticulously the loops and whorls set down upon paper by Archer Bolton.

On a March day Larry Blue stood in front of the half shelter that he and Cardwine had thrown together near a swamp on the Rio Grande, and looked Jim Cardwine in the eyes.

"It's time," said Cardwine, "that we went to Franklin, Larry. I reckon now's as good a time as any. The rats ain't prime no more."

Larry Blue thought through the statement, revolving

it and its implications in his mind. "Maybe we had better go back," he said slowly. "I've been sending Father Paul money for Don. I ought to go see Don."

"An' there's another reason," said Cardwine, watching the boy. "We got these furs an' we got 'em to sell. Old Bill Doliver at Pajaritos is dead, an we can't trade with him no more. An' then . . ."

"Yes?" Larry urged his companion on when Cardwine hesitated.

"This is my last year trappin'," announced Cardwine. "I'm slowin' down. I'm right at seventy-five, Larry."

"You want to stop in Franklin?" Larry's question was blunt.

Cardwine nodded. "For a while," he agreed. "I got somethin' I want to do there."

"How about Don?" Larry, as always, brought his brother's name forward. For three years he had sent money to Father Paul for his brother. Sometimes not money but other valuables. Once it had been a pack of beaver skins and once a pouch of gold dust, washed laboriously from a little creek high in the Cimarrons. "I got to have a job, Jim."

Cardwine nodded absently. "You can hire on with a freight outfit," he said. "Or else you could go north an' take a meat contract with some gradin' camp."

Larry considered both suggestions. He nodded agreement. "I could," he said. "What you got to do in Franklin, Jim?"

Between these two there were no secrets. What was Larry Blue's was Jim Cardwine's, and what belonged to Cardwine belonged to Larry, even to thoughts. For the first time in three years Jim Cardwine averted his eyes from the boy's.

"A little unfinished business," evaded Jim Cardwine.

"We'll go in the mornin', Larry. I reckon Bolton's old house will make us a good enough camp if there ain't somebody livin' in it."

"Uhhuh," agreed Larry.

In the morning, pack horses loaded, they left the swamp and the lean-to. As always Cardwine took the lead, and as always Larry followed. There were two hundred miles of twisting river basin between the lean-to and Franklin, a mere jaunt for Larry Blue and his partner. Riding along after the pack horses Larry watched the man ahead. Seventy-five, Jim had said. His shoulders, once so straight and broad, were humped a little, and his head was bowed forward. Three years had aged Jim Cardwine. He had gone down the hill as Larry climbed it.

Six days saw them pulling in through the tornillo thickets to the rock house. The house still stood but any eye could have seen that it was deserted. Standing at the door Larry noted that the shelves still marched around the room, but that was all. The roof sagged and the house was empty. Animals had made a playground of the floor that Larry had swept. Cobwebs hung in the corners, and rain had beaten in through the stovepipe hole and the cracked shakes of the roof.

"I reckon we'll make camp outside," said Jim Cardwine. And: "Yeah," agreed Larry Blue.

There was no need of speech as they made their camp and cooked and ate a meal. When the fire died they buried it and went to their blankets. Nothing disturbed their sleep, not the sound of a night bird flitting in the thickets, or the bright-eyed pack-rat that came from the deserted house and surveyed their camp.

In the morning as day broke, the two awoke soundlessly and set about their tasks. Jim Cardwine,

66

eating frying-pan bread and drinking coffee, gestured with his cup toward the house.

"He ain't never been back," said Cardwine.

"No," agreed Larry, "he ain't."

"A queer man," mused Cardwine. "Queer sort of duck."

"I wonder what's become of Duck Bunn," said Larry Blue.

"No tellin'. I'm goin' into town this mornin'," Cardwine announced after a pause. "Want to see what's goin' on. Larry . . ."

"Yes?"

"Why don't you ride from here over to Tumac Mission? It's shorter than goin' to town. You want to see yore brother, I reckon."

Larry's eyes lighted. "I'll go soon as I've cleaned up," he agreed.

"You go 'long now," urged Cardwine. "I'll do the chores."

Larry got up from beside the fire and wordlessly went out to where the horses were staked. He led the pinto in.

"I'll be back by sundown," said Larry.

"An' so'll I," Cardwine assured. "Good luck, kid."

"So long, Jim." Larry had the saddle in place. Stepping up into it he waved his hand and set out through the tornillo, taking the trail toward the river, and beyond the river, Tumac Mission. Left alone at the camp Jim Cardwine scraped the frying pan.

"Good kid," said Jim Cardwine to himself. "I hope he finds things the way he wants 'em." He paused then, the frying pan held reflectively in his hand.

"An' I wonder how I'll find things," said Jim Cardwine, aloud. "That Mexican said that it was George Whiteman that killed Haslip. I wonder . . ." Cardwine

67

put the frying pan on the ground.

Larry rode on west from the camp, finding his way through the thick tornillo, following along cow trails, and presently he struck the river. It lay broad and glassy before him. There was quicksand in the river, treacherous, sucking stuff. Some instinct, an instinct that he had not possessed three years before, told Larry where to find sound bottom. The pinto splashed across, emerging on the western shore, and struck again into the tornillo. Within an hour the square white tower of Tumac Mission shone at his right hand, and in another thirty minutes Larry was stopping the pinto before the gate.

At the priest's house beside the Mission, Larry paused before he knocked at the door. Years ago—was it just a little over three years?—he had stood before the mission house and talked with a black-robed priest concerning Don. He wondered how Don would look. Would the kid have grown as Larry himself had grown? Larry lifted a square-knuckled, tanned hand and rapped against the wood.

After a time a shuffle of feet answered that knock. The door opened and a young man, pleasant faced and black robed, stood in the opening.

"Good morning," greeted the priest. "What can I do for you?"

"I'm looking for Father Paul," Larry answered. "I've come to see him."

The priest shook his head. "Father Paul is gone at present," he announced. "I am Father Robert. Won't you come in?"

Still Larry hesitated. "You got a boy here," he blurted out. "A kid named Don Blue. Is he around?"

Father Robert shook his head. "Don Blue and Father Paul left three days ago," he answered. "Father Paul is taking the boy to the East to put him in school."

Larry's disappointment must have shown in his face. The priest, placing his hand on Larry's arm, urged him to enter. "Come in," invited Father Robert. "Come in."

Reluctantly Larry entered the house.

Sitting stiffly on a straight-backed chair Larry watched the young priest bustle about the parlor. He liked Father Robert. Everyone must have liked the fresh-faced young man, not a great deal older than was Larry himself. Father Robert brought sun-dried raisins and little cakes and put them at Larry's elbow. Then seating himself he leaned forward and addressed the boy.

"You wanted to see Father Paul or Don Blue?"

"Yes, sir," agreed Larry. "You see I . . . well, I'm Don's brother."

Instantly Father Robert's face lighted. "You are Larry Blue!" he exclaimed. "I've heard of you. You have been sending money to Father Paul for Don."

"Yes, sir. I sent some."

"There was quite a search made for you, from what Father Paul tells me."

The priest picked a raisin from its stem and crunched it. "Father Paul wanted you to be here with your brother."

"I had to earn money for Don." Larry's jaw set obstinately. "You say that Father Paul has taken Don back East?"

"To place him in a school," agreed the priest. "Your brother Don is fortunate. Judge Lester interested himself in the boy and is sending him back . . ."

With a single lithe motion Larry came out of his chair. "Judge Lester?" he exclaimed.

"We call him that, although he is no longer on the bench." Father Robert's eyes examined Larry curiously.

"Don can't take nothin' from Judge Lester!" snapped Larry. "He can't."

"Why?"

"Because," Larry took a short turn across the room and back, "Judge Lester was the man that sentenced my dad to hang!"

There was a flat finality in the statement that Father Robert recognized, young as he was. He too got up from where he sat and came to stand beside Larry.

"I didn't know that," said the priest softly.

"Father Paul knew it!" hotly.

Father Robert had no answer for that. He waited.

Larry spoke again. "When will Father Paul be back?"

"I don't know." The young priest shook his head. "I'm not sure. In a month perhaps; perhaps more."

Larry scowled at the floor. "I wisht I knew when he'd be back," he said. "I'll send him money for Don. I want Don to go to school. Don's going to be a lawyer. But Judge Lester's money ain't going to send him." The last words were freighted with fierceness.

"Perhaps," suggested Father Robert, "you will be here when Father Paul returns. You could see him then . . ."

"I don't know." Larry shook his head. "I don't know what Jim's figuring. He wouldn't talk about it. Maybe I'll be here; maybe not. Whereabouts is Don goin' to school?"

"Father Paul is taking him to a school in Boston," answered the priest. "I have the address. I'll give it to you." He crossed the room to a desk, sat down and wrote on a piece of paper. Returning, waving the paper in the air to dry the ink, he handed it to Larry who looked briefly at the scrawl, folded the paper and put it

70

in his pocket.

"Thanks," he said. "I reckon I'll be goin' now. If I'm here when Father Paul gets back I'll see him."

Father Robert smiled. "It is almost noon," he reminded. "You'll stay for lunch?"

For an instant Larry was tempted to refuse. Then he thought of the lonely camp and the long wait until Jim Cardwine's return. Jim did not want Larry in Franklin, the boy knew.

"I can show you Don's room and some of his books," urged Father Robert. "And I made a sketch of him before he left. I'd like to show you that."

"I'm much obliged," said Larry gruffly, and sat down in his chair once more.

It was three o'clock before Larry left Tumac Mission. He had been well fed; Father Robert had taken him over the Mission showing him the room Don had occupied, showing him some of the clothing Don had left behind, and giving him a little pen and ink sketch that exhibited no mean talent. Larry rolled the drawing of that square-faced, stalwart boy, and carried it inside his shirt. It had taken time to do these things and during that time Father Robert had probed the boy, sounding him, trying to soften Larry's grim determination that neither he nor Don should accept anything from John Lester. Father Robert suggested that Larry visit the lawyer, a suggestion that Larry sternly turned aside.

The pinto had been cared for by an Indian who served the Mission. Larry resaddled the little animal, bade Father Robert good-by and thanked him for his kindness. Then with the sun at his back, he rode off toward the river.

It was almost four o'clock when Larry forded the stream. Picking up the tracks he had made that morning, he

71

retraced his trail through the tornillo. Larry was disappointed that he had not seen Don. His brother had been gone and that was a sorrow, but the boy was in good hands. Don was on his road to the East and to school, on the way to the realization of Larry's plans for him. That was good. Still Larry frowned. He had, evidently, not sent enough money for Don. That must be rectified. He would make more money and Don would get it.

Approaching the clearing where stood the rock house, the pinto lifted his head. The motion brought Larry from his thoughts and he was alert when the horse cleared the tornillo. Skirting the rock house Larry stopped the pinto short. The camp was gone! Not a trace. Not a bed or a blanket or a saddle. There remained only the smoldering embers of a fire, and tracks. Larry, sitting the pinto, surveyed those tracks. A wide indentation in sand and weeds showed that something heavy had been dragged to the rock house. With fear and premonition in his voice, Larry called.

"Jim!"

There was no answer. Again the boy called, and then dropping down from his saddle he ran toward the door of the house.

Jim Cardwine lay sprawled on his back just inside the door, his sightless blue eyes staring at the sagging roof. For a long minute Larry Blue could not realize what had happened. Then, swiftly, he stepped inside and knelt beside the body.

Old Jim Cardwine had been shot. There was blood on his buckskin shirt and two bluish holes in the white skin of his chest. His belt was gone and with it his knife and medicine pouch. His pockets had been searched. So much Larry learned in his hasty examination. For a long moment the boy knelt beside the body of his friend, then

72

reaching out he closed the sightless eyes, straightened, and walked out of the house.

Carefully encompassing the camp, Larry saw tracks. There were broad tracks of moccasined or sandaled feet. Jim Cardwine, waiting alone at the camp for the return of his partner, had been ambushed by renegade Apaches. So at first Larry read the sign. He could not believe what he read. Jim Cardwine taken by Indians? It just was not possible. Not Jim Cardwine, who had an extra set of senses, who could hear a chipmunk stir in a thicket and identify the sound. No, Jim Cardwine had not been ambushed!

But how else? Larry could not fathom it. Circling the camp again he saw where horses had gone to the north. Three sets of the tracks he recognized as those of Cardwine's horse and the two pack horses. But there was sign of six animals. Larry looked at the horse tracks, reviewed the sign back at the camp, and then turned back to the horse tracks. Two men had been in the camp, two men besides Jim. Two, who wore moccasins, had stolen all of the possessions of Jim Cardwine and Larry Blue: the furs, the camp outfit, the saddles and the horses. But there had been a third man with them, a man who stayed back from the camp. Larry could not puzzle it out. He went back to the rock house and sitting down beside his friend, looked at Cardwine's placid face. If Jim Cardwine could only talk, just say a word or two. But Jim would never speak again. Sitting there beside his dead friend, something hardened in Larry Blue. Jim Cardwine had fashioned a steel blade and now it was being tempered. Jim Cardwine had given the wolf cub fangs; now was the time to use them. Face grim, eyes blue steel slits, Larry Blue rose to his feet and left the cabin.

73

Over against the hills he found what he sought: a cut bank where an arroyo had changed its course. Here was Jim Cardwine's grave, already dug. Just the sort of burial place that Jim Cardwine would have selected for himself. Returning to the rock house Larry lifted the big body, straining to get its dead weight to his shoulders. It did not occur to the boy to go to Franklin and inform the law of the happenings at the camp. It did not occur to Larry that if renegades had killed Jim Cardwine the thing to do would be to inform the soldiers at the fort outside the town. Just one thing filled the boy's mind, a thing that Jim Cardwine had taught him, a thing that had become so ingrained that it was instinctive. This was Larry's job. This was Larry Blue's duty. He would bury Jim and then set about the task that was before him.

Staggering under his load, Larry carried the body to the cut bank. There he bestowed it, folding the brawny arms across the chest, straightening the legs. His own hat he placed over Cardwine's face and then, standing, he looked at what he had done.

It may have been that, standing there, Larry told his friend good-by. Perhaps in those silent minutes, Larry spoke to Jim Cardwine. Certainly the pinto horse and the birds and the rock squirrel that watched him did not know, and there were no others to see. After a time Larry turned away, climbed the steep cut bank and, reaching the top, averted his face and stamped with moccasined feet upon the crumbling bank. Dirt and rocks tumbled down, rising in a pile. They did not hurt Jim Cardwine.

When the task was done Larry Blue mounted the pinto. He looked once toward the hills where the cut bank now sloped so steeply, and then turning the pinto north, set out through the tornillo. The tracks were plain enough. Men had driven horses before them. Larry followed the tracks and as he followed them the dusk deepened for the sun was already gone. When night came the boy dismounted for he could no longer trail. The pinto grazed and Larry, huddling in the sand as he had done once before, waited for the morning. The air was chilly, nipping through his clothing, but the boy built no fire.

In the morning Larry was up and going again, still following the trail, and as the sun rose, the wind stirred, beginning gently and presaging what was to come. Larry cursed the wind and hurried the pinto.

An hour from his stopping place he found the spot where the men he followed had made camp. There was the pile of ashes and sand where they had made a fire, and there were the marks where their saddles had rested. Two sets of moccasin tracks Larry found, and boot tracks, small and neat and with the toes pointing in. Larry went on.

By ten o'clock the wind was whipping across the valley, erasing the trail which had now taken to the mesa edge. Larry swung the pinto back toward the river, reasoning that the men ahead would have sought the shelter of the growth along its banks. He cut back and forth across the valley but the thing he sought was not there. The trail was gone. Larry stopped the pinto, turned his back to the wind and thought things out.

The men who had killed Jim Cardwine were still going. They would put as much distance as possible between themselves and the scene of their crime, and the wind was not so bad that they could not travel. Accordingly Larry swung the tired pinto north once more.

The sun was a bronze ball high in its southern circle when, riding into a clump of tornillo, Larry stopped short. There, just beyond the growth of brush, was a dun horse. Larry knew that dun: Buck, Jim Cardwine's horse. Buck, sighting the pinto and recognizing a friend, threw up his head and nickered, shrill and high. Larry slid the Sharps out of its sheath under his rosadero, came down from the saddle and let the pinto go. The horse worked along toward the dun.

Beyond the spot where the duo had stood was a rock, a boulder that was strangely out of place in the river valley. Mesquite grew thickly about the boulder and the wind whipped away a little trickle of smoke that came from behind it. Fools! Larry almost said the word. Fools! To kill a man and then stop for a nooning. The breech of the Sharps slid open and the dull brass of the shell in the chamber winked at the boy. He moved forward cautiously. He would have to be sure, but once sure . . .

Working through the growth Larry skirted the rock until he was to its east. Low in the thicket the wind was not so strong, and looking to the west the boy could see the lee side of the rock. Two men crouched there, one bending over a fire, the other squatting against the rock. They were dark-faced and swarthy men, not Apaches, not Indians, but renegades from below the border. Just beyond the shelter three horses stood patiently, and another, back turned to the wind, was to their north. Two horses carried saddles and two carried packs. Larry knew the pack horses. They were his and Jim's. Larry waited there in the thicket, Sharps pushed out ahead of him, waiting with the patience of an Indian. The third man was somewhere near by. He would come.

The third man did not come. Behind the rock the swarthy men ate a meal. They were deliberate, methodical in their movements. Having eaten they set about departing, gathering possessions, food and utensils together. Larry got

76

up from where he lay and walked toward the rock. The third man was not coming. Somewhere to the south the third man had branched off. Larry had moved twenty feet when the men at the rock saw him.

There was no hail of greeting, nothing but swift movement. One of the men behind the rock bent and snatched up a rifle. The other jumped to his left where his weapon leaned against the rock. The man who stooped did not straighten but snapped the gun to his shoulder and fired. Larry felt a sharp plucking at his shoulder. The report of the weapon rolled down the wind, whipped by it. Smoke rose up and was driven away. At Larry's shoulder his Sharps kicked sharply. The man who bent, sprawled falling to the ground. His legs kicked out convulsively and then he was still. Larry, throwing himself flat, rolled swiftly, trying to find cover.

He found cover in a cottonwood log where some aging giant of the valley had been swept down by a flood. Behind the log he reloaded the Sharps, carefully saving the spent shell. That was part of it, Jim had said. Save your shells to reload. Peering over his wooden rampart Larry saw that the horses had moved away from the boulder and that the second man was gone. A bullet ripped through the dead bark beside Larry's head and he ducked hastily. From behind the rock, smoke was whipped away. The second man was behind the rock.

Move or be killed. Move or be killed. Never stay still in a fight, except when you shoot. Larry Blue could almost hear Jim Cardwine's drawling voice in his ears. Pushing the rifle ahead he crawled up the log, reached its end and looked for fresh shelter. A fold of ground, an old cow trail, a tornillo growth, and sand piled about a mesquite; one at a time these shielded Larry Blue. He was to the right of the rock now and could peer behind it. Of course the rock was deserted. That second man was no fool. He had moved, too, but which way? Larry saw a pack horse near by the rock, ears pricked forward and head turned to the right. So that was where the second man had gone!

The Sharps was an impediment for silent stalking. There was a knife with an eight-inch blade in Larry's scabbard. He lifted out the knife, holding it as a man holds a sword, and leaving the rifle, slipped forward. Elbows pulled him along, his knees gave him traction. The wind killed sound but not sight. To Larry's left the pack horse turned his head. The man was moving, moving toward him. Larry gathered himself and waited. The horse's head continued to turn. Larry caught a glimpse of blue cloth then he was on his feet and leaping in!

A gun roared but the distance was too small for work with a rifle. Larry Blue was against a man, his left hand tight about a gun barrel; his right hand, steel-tipped, probing, thrusting in. In Larry's ear a man screamed. Then, suddenly, the boy was no longer striving for the rifle but holding it alone, and at his feet was a contorted, twisting face that, swiftly, was still, the lips drawn up in a grin that showed long yellow teeth. Breathing hard Larry Blue looked down at that face and then turned away.

For a while then the boy leaned against the rock, fighting the retching that possessed him. He struggled against it, fought it down, and was seized again when he looked at the knife he still held. The blade of the knife was not shiny. It was dark. Again conquering nausea the boy went back to get his rifle, carried it to the rock and leaned the gun against it. Then, and not until then, did he wipe the blade of his knife and replace the weapon in its scabbard.

Larry then moved about the camp, skirting the body

that sprawled before the rock, collecting those things which had belonged to himself and to Jim Cardwine. He brought in the horses: the pinto, the dun and the two pack animals. The other horses he left alone. The pack horses held his bed roll and Jim's, the pack of furs, the ax, all the equipment. Larry added the grub sack and the gunny sack that held the cooking utensils. He looked for, but did not find, Cardwine's rifle. He changed his saddle from the pinto to the dun and put Jim's saddle on the pinto. Having done these things he approached the bodies of the men he had killed. Nerving himself, the boy searched those bodies. Money he found and left where he had found it. The few possessions that a man carries—tobacco, matches, cartridges—Larry left in place. He did not find Jim Cardwine's beaded medicine pouch or Jim's knife.

With hands that trembled, Larry tied the two pack horses and the pinto, head to tail. Then, averting his eyes from the rock and the things that lay beside it, he mounted the dun horse and taking the rope of the lead animal, started north. Behind him the wind whistled over the rock and through the mesquite; and sand, fine and powdery, settled down.

# CHAPTER 7

## THE SIDEHILL GOUGER

MR. BART HODGSON, WHO RAN THE OX WAGON, stood beside the cook fire and watched the man riding into the camp. Mr. Hodgson sucked morosely upon the roll of paper and tobacco in his mouth, and made comment. "Granger," said Mr. Hodgson. "Here he comes, him an' two broom tailed mares; goin' to rep with the wagon. Likely his pappy has got ten head of dairy stock scattered out here over the flats an' the kid is goin' to look for 'em."

Having delivered this dictum Mr. Hodgson, who came from Texas, and who, so his crew said, had the disposition of a catamount, turned his back on the approaching figure and surveyed the ridge to the east. The remuda should be coming in from that eastern ridge and if it did not show up within five minutes Mr. Hodgson would be peeved.

"Rides like an Injun," commented Buck Winters, Mr. Hodgson's segundo, who had not turned away. "An' them ain't mares, Bart. That dun geldin' is plumb horse."

"Huh!" snorted Mr. Hodgson, "nester just the same!"

The remuda not having appeared and Bart Hodgson having decided that the day jingler would be looking for another job when it did show up, he turned again and scowled at the approaching rider. That rider had stopped some twenty yards from the fire and was dismounting.

"What's that he's got on his feet?" demanded the OX foreman. "Moccasins, or I'm a shepherd!"

"Sure enough," commented Buck Winters, leaving the question open as to whether or not he meant that Bart Hodgson was a shepherd.

Hodgson looked sharply at his segundo. He was not sure just what Buck meant.

The boy, leaving the horses ground-tied, advanced toward the camp, a long-barreled rifle cocked over his left arm, his right hand hanging loosely at his side. Bart Hodgson and Buck Winters caught a glimpse of level blue eyes set in a square-jawed, tanned face. Then the boy stopped before them.

"My name is Larry Blue," announced the newcomer. "I'm lookin' for a job."

Bart Hodgson grunted. Buck rolled a smoke and eyed it. About the fire the others of the crew sat up or turned, eyeing this new arrival. The cook, old Porky Flynn, came around the tailgate of the wagon and stood wiping his hands on his dirty flour-sack apron.

"What doin'?" demanded Hodgson at length.

" 'Most anything," answered Larry.

"I don't need a man to do 'most anythin'," snapped Hodgson. "Can you ride?"

Larry made a mistake. He said, "Yes, sir." If he had answered, "A little," or if he had shaken his head, the next events would not have transpired.

"Peeler, huh?" grunted Hodgson. "We'll see. Where's that dang' remuda?"

As though in answer to the question, horses appeared upon the ridge and came sweeping down toward the camp. In the rope corral a man made an opening. Other riders moved to where their horses stood. The horses came on, were turned by a mounted man and deftly penned. Coming up from behind the horses a snub-nosed man slid down from a tall bay and walked over to Hodgson.

"They scattered on me," complained the snub-nosed man, hastily forestalling what was coming.

Bart Hodgson grunted, eyeing his day wrangler from battered hat to worn-out boots. "You ain't paid to let 'em scatter," he said succinctly. "You'll draw yore time tonight an' pull yore freight. Cliff, rope out Sunbeam for this fellow that wants a job."

"You mean I'm hired?" demanded Larry Blue.

"If you ride Sunbeam," answered Bart Hodgson enigmatically. "I just fired a man. His job's open."

81

Down by the rope corral Cliff Sparrow gathered up his rope, and swore. He had missed a cast. The second trial settled true over a long bay head, and a fighting, snorting horse was pulled out to the rope barrier.

Larry Blue leaned his rifle against the wheel of the chuck wagon and started toward the dun horse. "I'll get my saddle," he announced.

The bay was hauled out of the corral, still fighting the rope and the men on the end of it. Cliff Sparrow, who rode the rough string for the OX, worked his way up the rope and Larry came back carrying his saddle and his old smooth-bitted bridle.

"There he is. He'p yorese'f," invited Bart Hodgson, waving his hand toward the horse. Larry said nothing but walked in the direction indicated by the hand.

Sparrow, young and lithe and stout as a bull, helped Larry slip the bridle on Sunbeam. When that was done they tied up Sunbeam's left hind foot, hauling it up with a bight of rope. Sunbeam stood shivering and Larry methodically put his blanket in place and tossed up the heavy square-skirted saddle. He cinched it tightly, gathered the reins against the horn, found a stirrup and went half way up, then lowered himself.

"Mount him, kid," urged Sparrow. "You ain't never goin' to ride him 'til yo're on top."

"Leggo his foot," ordered Larry tersely.

"When yore up," agreed Sparrow.

"Now! I don't want no rope to hinder me."

"It's yore neck," said Sparrow and slacked off the rope he held. Buck Winters, deep-chested as an ox, strolled from the little crowd that stood watching, and before Sunbeam's foot hit the ground, possessed himself of the geldings ears. Sparrow snapped the rope free, jerking it away, and Larry went up like lightning.

82

Before Sunbeam could get his head down the boy was in the saddle and had found the off stirrup. Winters jumped away and Sunbeam, with a bawl of pure rage, hung his head between his knees and went to work.

Sunbeam was an artist. He bucked straight through the camp, scattering crowd and fire. He banged Larry's knee against the tailgate of the bed wagon, whirled and kicked the spot where Larry's knee had struck. He plunged and kicked and fence rowed and sunfished, and Larry stayed on top. The boy did not try to kick the horse, he had no spurs. He did not try to fan Sunbeam with his hat, a new hat. He simply rode Sunbeam. For three years Larry had ridden anything that Jim Cardwine put him on, bareback for the most part, and Jim Cardwine had picked anything and everything, from colts around some native plaza, up to and including salty old mustangs that had thrown men and would throw others. Larry rode Sunbeam like an Indian: glued there.

The OX men, hands and reps from other spreads, yelped their approval. Old Bart Hodgson chewed the end of his grizzled mustache and watched the performance. Larry rode Sunbeam out and, ridden out, Sunbeam stopped and sulked. That was Sunbeam's trick. When he could not throw a rider he would balk and no spurs or quirt or doubled rope could move him. Sunbeam stood sullenly, head hung low, sides heaving, and refused to move.

Larry kicked the horse. He beat Sunbeam with his hat. Sunbeam sulked. Labor as he might Larry could not get a movement. Deliberately then the boy dismounted. He strode toward the camp, his blue eyes narrow and his jaw set firmly. Without a glance at Bart Hodgson or any of the others, he took his rifle from where it stood and hauling back the hammer of the Sharps, turned back to Sunbeam. Bart Hodgson stood impassive, but Buck Winters moved swiftly.

"I've felt thataway too, kid," said Buck, reaching out and holding the barrel of the Sharps. "He jolted the hell out of me an' then quit, an' I wanted to kill him. But shucks, he's just a horse."

Slowly the fighting mask dissolved from Larry Blue's face. He turned to Buck Winters and his eyes were wide and blue and there was a sparkle in them. "He's just a horse," agreed Larry.

Old Bart Hodgson grunted. "You rode him," snapped Bart gruffly. "Throw yore bed down an' turn yore horses into the cavvy when you take it out. Graze 'em an' have 'em into camp at supper."

"You mean I'm hired?" demanded Larry Blue.

Bart Hodgson had turned away. He was eyeing the men at the camp and under his baleful stare they moved hurriedly. "Fun's over!" snapped Bart. "Let's git started."

It was Buck Winters that answered Larry's question. "Yo're the day jingler, kid," said Buck. "Don't take 'em too far from camp." With that Buck hurried after the rest, going down to the rope corral where, by now, Cliff Sparrow was roping out mounts. Larry looked after the big man and then, a little unsteady because of the beating Sunbeam had given him, he walked out to that sullen horse and began to remove his saddle. From the rope corral came a call.

"Here's yore horse, kid. Come a-runnin'."

Carrying his saddle Larry answered that call, saddling and bridling the leggy roan that Cliff had roped out. When the OX hands had changed mounts and were riding back toward the camp, Buck Winters dropped back and spoke to the boy. "Run 'em out, kid," he ordered. "I'll go 'long with you a piece."

For answer Larry put his horse out of the gate and the remuda, freed, came pouring out and struck for the ridge at a lope. Larry rode along behind them, Buck at his side.

"Ever wrangle horses?" demanded Buck.

"No, sir."

Buck grunted. "You keep 'em on good grass an' together," he said. "It's a lazy man's job. When we're movin' camp you keep up with it an' if there's a run you got to get to the horses because we'll need 'em. Bart said for you to take that black yonder, for a night horse. So long, kid. Have 'em in when supper's ready." And branching off, Buck loped away to join the crew that was already going out on circle.

There was not much to day-wrangling horses. Larry found that the least riding he did the better he got along. He kept the remuda on good grass and as the OX wagon proceeded upon its way he moved the horses. At night the night hawk, a saturnine man with a perpetual cigarette, took over the work and Larry was free. The OX was branding calves and so there were no herds to hold. Later, when the fall came and the wagon moved back toward headquarters, they would be working beef and gathering and there would be night guards to stand. But not now.

Old Bart Hodgson was a king, an overlord of hard-riding slaves. Bart owned a part of the OX and had run the wagon for years. From his men he demanded unrequiting labor. Two circles a day they made, branding after dinner and after supper. In return he paid good wages, forty dollars a month (which for that time

85

was high); mounted his men on the best horseflesh in the country; fed them like fighting cocks, and when the work was done, let them alone. There was no nagging around the OX wagons. A man pulled his weight or he was fired.

Larry, of course, made mistakes. He went into the rope corral afoot and stampeded the remuda through the thin barrier. In a mistaken idea that he was helping, he roped a cow that was on the prod and, with the cow, went through the camp. One mistake of one kind Bart Hodgson allowed him, but no more. When a thing was shown him, explained to him, Larry committed that thing to memory and shunned the bad as the devil shuns holy water. To the good things that he learned, he clung. Already an adept with the ax, he took most of the wood gathering from the shoulders of the night hawk and he was always ready, as a part of his duties, to help the cook clean out the wrecking pan and wash the dirty dishes. Bart Hodgson watched the boy with an impassive face, saying no word of commendation and but brief words of reproof. Larry learned. Privately Bart opined to Buck Winters that Larry was going to do, which was very high praise.

Being the youngster, Larry came in for a good deal of rawhiding. He took it silently. For the most part the OX crew joshed and told windies and strung the kid good naturedly. There was one exception to that ruling. Cash Dailey, the rep from the 4 Bar, thought that he had the Indian sign on the boy and got nasty with his rawhiding. Larry took that too.

"I'm goin' to have a little talk with Cash about ridin' the kid," announced Buck Winters, speaking to Hodgson inside the little sheepman's tepee the foreman occupied as his own.

"Keep yore mouth shut," grunted Hodgson. "If the kid wants to take it, let him. If he don't he'll say so. You can't go fightin' his battles for him."

Buck kept still.

Cash Dailey, getting meaner and meaner with his kidding, went too far.

Larry had the only rawhide rope in camp, a rawhide that Jim Cardwine had braided from tough bull hide. It was supple as a snake and tender as a child. The rawhide had to be humored. With the tough Manilas that the others carried, tied hard and fast to their saddles, it made but little difference. The whaleline could be wet, it could be dropped to the ground, stepped on, maltreated, and still it would come through. The rawhide was different. A shod hoof set upon it would mar its strength. Wetting stretched it. The rawhide was a thing to be used by an artist. Where the others were tied to what they roped, Larry dallied, taking turns about his saddle horn, feeding out rope when a lunge came from the animal at its end. He had learned from Cardwine and he knew no other way.

Dailey, riding the kid, picked up the rawhide from Larry's saddle one morning and announced that he would use it. Dailey was a good roper, one of the best, but he was a tie man. He carried the rawhide rope over to his horse and tied the end to his saddle horn. Then, taking his own worn-out rope, he tossed it to Larry.

"Here, kid," said Dailey, "this is good enough for a hoss wrangler. Take it an' learn how to tie to what you ketch."

Larry was beside the wagon. At the tailgate Bart Hodgson was standing, talking to Porky Flynn. Buck was in the bedwagon rummaging through the canvas sack that contained his possessions. Larry let Dailey's rope fall to the ground at his feet.

Unhurriedly, his moccasins making no disturbance or sound, he strolled around the fire, came up behind Dailey and spoke gently. "I'll take my rope," said Larry.

Dailey turned. Larry stood there, close to the 4 Bar rider, his left hand outstretched. "I give you my rope," Dailey snapped. "It's good enough for you."

"I'll take the rawhide," Larry answered evenly, his voice level and unhurried. "Hand it over."

Dailey made a mistake. He slapped, open-handed, at the boy. Within the next second he was back against his horse, his face white and his hands shoulder high. There were eight inches of sharp pointed steel at Dailey's belly and behind the steel was a youngster whose eyes were blue flame. "I said I'd take the rawhide," reminded Larry Blue.

With fumbling hands Dailey untied the rope he had fastened to his saddle horn. His eyes still on Larry's face, he passed it over. Unhurriedly Larry took the loops of leather, sheathed his knife and turning casually walked back to the wagon. Dailey's worn rope lay where it had fallen. After a time Dailey came and picked it up. Old Bart Hodgson chewed the corner of his mustache, making a remnant out of the already frazzled wisp. Later, riding out to drop the circle men, Buck Winters spoke to his boss.

"The kid's handy," remarked Buck.

Bart grunted.

"Wonder if Dailey will take it up?" was Buck's next comment.

"Not Dailey," Bart answered gruffly. Buck let it go and the two men rode along at a trot. Suddenly the foreman spoke. "Looks like the kid had been there," he said.

"It does," Buck agreed gravely.

Larry Blue's showdown with Cash Dailey hurt him not a whit with the rest of the OX crew. Dailey carried the thing no further and having finished working out that portion of the range which adjoined the 4 Bar, went his way. Some of the men watched Larry after that incident. They were cowmen and they did not hold with knives. Still the kid had used the thing that was at hand and they let it go. But they did not cease their friendly tormenting just because Larry had called Dailey.

Chief among the tormenters was Cliff Sparrow. Cliff was young and he was full of vinegar. Cliff could tell a tall tale with a straight face and no twinkle in his eyes. Larry liked Cliff Sparrow. He saw Cliff top off a bad one and realized that he himself had been given an easy horse when he was handed Sunbeam on his arrival at camp. He watched Cliff whenever he could, marveling at the ease with which that slim youngster did the things that were required of him. He took Cliff's kidding, listened to and apparently believed his stories, and secretly resolved that he would pull one on Cliff. If he landed Cliff the others would lay off; and, Larry admitted this only to himself, he was getting a little tired of the rough humor.

The opportunity came when the wagon worked the foothill country along the Cimarrons. Cliff, one night when the work was done, began a tall tale of an animal he called a sidehill gouger. According to Cliff the gouger ate limestone as a steady diet and, from working around the mountains, had developed a peculiar deformity in that two legs (those on the same side), were shorter than the opposing members.

"They got short legs on one side so that they can stand level," explained Cliff, watching Larry from the

89

corners of his eyes. "There's right hand ones an' left hand ones. The left hand ones is most fee-rocious."

The tale was old and it was crude. Nobody was expected to believe it. Cliff was delighted and surprised when Larry, seriously, spoke from where he sat. "I'd sure like to catch one," said Larry Blue. "I reckon some of them Eastern folks would pay a heap to have one."

"They sure would," agreed Cliff, throwing out bait. "Tell you what, Larry. I seen where a gouger had been usin' this mornin' when I was on circle. Suppose you go set a trap for him."

Larry got up. "You show me where," he said eagerly. "I'll just do that."

Over by the wagon Buck Winters looked questioningly at Bart Hodgson. Bart made a little motion with his hand. "Let 'em alone," he whispered through his mustache.

Buck relaxed.

"I reckon a big deadfall would do the trick," said Larry. "I'll get the ax."

"You goin' to set that trap tonight?" questioned Cliff. It had not been a part of his plan to be dragged from his bed. Cliff had worked hard that day.

"It's moonlight," said Larry. "We can see good an' we both got to work tomorrow."

Cliff hoisted himself from the ground. "Well, all right," he agreed reluctantly. "Come on." He moved toward his staked night horse.

"You boys'll walk," announced Hodgson from beside the wagon. "Company horses are for cow work, not trappin' gougers."

Cliff Sparrow repressed a groan. Walking was as foreign to him, who lived aboard a horse, as it was commonplace to moccasined Larry Blue. Still Cliff

90

could not back down. "Come on then," he said to Larry again. "It ain't far."

Larry picked up the ax and followed Cliff away from the fire.

They were back in about two hours. Cliff was hobbling and Larry strode along, still carrying the ax and moving easily. Cliff sat down on his bed and with a groan began to pull off his boots. Larry squatted beside him.

"We can set another trap tomorrow night;" said Larry eagerly. "You keep a lookout, Cliff, when you make your circle tomorrow an' see if you can find more sign. I figger about five deadfalls will be just right."

Cliff groaned as his boot came off his aching foot. A sleeping man stirred restlessly, and another not yet asleep said, "Shut up!" peevishly.

Larry went over to his own bed. Beside the wagon old Bart Hodgson chuckled noiselessly. This was going to be good, whatever it was.

Larry lay down and apparently went to sleep. Cliff tossed a while in his blankets and then began to snore. Bart Hodgson waited. Presently Larry got up. Noiselessly he moved to the wagon, and with his knife detached a piece of salt pork from the slab that the cook had on the tailgate. The boy moved on out into the moonlight. Still Hodgson waited.

Larry was gone a long time. When he returned he slipped into his bed and shortly after Bait Hodgson got up from his position under the wagon and sought his little tepee.

Morning broke, gold, blue, and rose. The cook, banging around the camp, made enough racket to awaken twenty men. Not a sleeper stirred except Larry Blue. Larry sat up in his bed, grinned at the cook and got up. He did not wait to make a toilet but started immediately out toward the West.

"Lopes along like a jack rabbit," grunted Porky, watching Larry's smooth stride. "Wonder what he's up to." Porky went on about his work, building the fire, putting on the Dutch ovens. Breakfast was ready and Porky had called, when Larry came running back.

Larry went instantly to the sleepy Cliff, just getting out of bed. "We caught him!" exclaimed Larry. "The deadfall's sprung. Come on, Cliff. Come on!"

Cliff Sparrow rubbed sleep from his eyes and resisted Larry's tugging at his arm. "I'll go after we've ate," said Cliff.

"No, now!" Larry was insistent.

Cliff could not but go. After all, it was his joke and he had to see it through. He winked broadly at Porky, encompassing others of the crew in the grimace, and agreed.

"Wait 'til I put on my boots."

Larry waited.

Bart Hodgson, coming from his tent, ready to get the work started, saw what was going on, hid a grin and ducked back under the canvas. It wouldn't hurt if they were a little late this morning. After all, they had been hitting the ball pretty steady. Cliff and Larry tramped away from the camp. After them floated the tantalizing odor of coffee, and Porky's call: "Come an' get it!"

The two were gone quite a time. The men had finished breakfast and the horses were in the corral when Larry came back to the camp. He was alone. Larry's face was grave when he walked in and stood before Bart Hodgson.

"Where's Cliff?" demanded Hodgson.

Larry waved toward the west. "Out there," he said.

"He wants somebody to bring him out some clothes an' his horse, He's washin' in the creek. You know, Mr. Hodgson, Cliff never told me, but them sidehill gougers are related to a skunk. Anyhow they smell like one."

Hodgson's face never altered in one stern line. Beside the fire Buck Winters, who had with the rest heard Larry's announcement, suddenly threw back his head and roared.

"A skunk," gasped Winters when he could speak. "Cliff done trapped himself a skunk. Oh my Lord!"

The others were convulsed with merriment. Only Larry Blue and Bart Hodgson kept their faces straight.

"I've heard," drawled Hodgson, "that salt pork is right good bait for skunks."

"Yes, sir," agreed Larry soberly.

"We'll take Cliff out some clothes," said Hodgson. "Them an' a horse. You get a bite to eat, Larry, then you go with the remuda. An' don't you go to sleep!"

It was the first time the foreman had called the boy by his given name. Heretofore when speaking Bart Hodgson had said, "Blue," or, "Kid." Larry felt as though an accolade had fallen upon his shoulders.

"Yes, sir," he answered the order, turning toward the line of pots and pans. "I'll get right out with the horses, an' I sure won't go to sleep!"

The OX riders went out on circle that day as usual. Two at a time Bart Hodgson dropped them off. When the last man was gone he turned his horse and rode back toward the camp. His wise old eyes sought and found tracks. In a canyon just where the foothills came down, Bart Hodgson reined in. There before him was a deadfall, a skillfully built deadfall, and just behind it was another, a little pen skillfully built, with a door, now thrown aside, that would fall when the trap was

93

sprung. A hearty odor of skunk hung about the spot. Bart Hodgson sniffed it. Slowly a grin parted his mustache and as he turned to ride away he spoke softly.

"Little devil," said Bart Hodgson. "The little cuss!"

# CHAPTER 8

### WHEN THE WORK'S ALL DONE THIS FALL

IN OCTOBER, WHEN THE OX WAGON CREW DROPPED the beef herd in the big pasture and pulled on in to the headquarters close beside the Cimarron, there was a clear-eyed, tanned youngster handling the remuda. With Buck Winters to pilot him, Larry swung the horses to the horse-pasture gate, put them through and, the work done, turned to Buck.

"Now what?" he asked.

Buck Winters grinned. "Now we shape 'em up, drive over the hill an' ship," he answered. "But first there's a little matter of payday an' a day or so in town. What you goin' to do with all yore money, kid?"

Larry thought that over. "I got to send most of it to Don," he answered. "I sent him quite a bunch a while back, before I hired on." Larry's eyes darkened as he thought of how he had come by that money that he had sent East to Don. Old Jim's pack horses, the furs, the things that he had sold and traded: Larry reviewed them in his mind.

"But you ain't goin' to send it all," persisted Buck. "What you goin' to do with the rest?"

"Buy clothes, I reckon," Larry answered. "I want a pair of boots an' I got to have a coat."

"You better save out enough to get a good outfit,"

94

cautioned Buck. "This can be a tough country to winter in."

That statement was the first intimation to Larry Blue that he had a chance to winter with the OX He had supposed that, like most of the men with the wagon, he would be paid off as soon as the beef was shipped.

"You mean . . . ?" he asked.

"I think that Bart's plannin' a winter job for you," said Buck. "Here we are, kid. Here's home." Buck stopped his horse beside a big corral and stiffly dismounted. Larry, too, climbed down and stood uncertainly beside his mount.

"Jerk off the saddle," commanded Buck. "This is home, I'm tellin' you."

In the morning Bart Hodgson paid off his hands. He piled their wages on the table in the office and one by one they took the money they had earned. Larry's turn came after most of the men were paid. He walked in, facing the grizzled old foreman, and stood waiting. Bart counted money into a pile.

"You got," said Bart, without looking up, "a hundred an' twenty-five dollars comin' to you, Larry. You drawed twenty-five when we was at Cimarron. Remember?"

"Yes, sir," agreed Larry. As wrangler he had been making thirty dollars a month. Twenty of the twenty-five dollars he had drawn had been sent to Don.

"Yo're good to save yore wages," commented Bart, pushing out the pile of coin. "There's yore one-twenty-five."

Larry clinked the gold pieces between his fingers, counted the five silver dollars and half turned. "Wait a minute," commanded Bart. "You got somethin' in mind for this winter?"

95

"No," Larry answered.

"We could mebbe use you." Bart was cautious. "I got to have two, three, riders for line camps an' we keep a little crew here at headquarters. We pay forty an' chuck."

Under his tattered shirt Larry's chest swelled. Forty dollars. That meant that old Bart considered him a full-sized man, a full hand. "I . . ." began Larry Blue.

"You'll want to go to town today," interrupted Hodgson. "Likely there's some stuff you want to buy. We'll get the herd shaped up an' trail 'em to Trinidad in about a week. I'll have a job for you."

That was all, and yet Larry fairly swelled as he walked out of the office. Buck Winters and Cliff Sparrow were down at the corral saddling, and they looked at the kid with friendly, grinning eyes.

"We're goin' to town, kid," said Sparrow. "Throw a saddle on that mangy dun of yores an' come along. I hear yo're goin' to be with us this winter."

Larry tried to be casual but he could not keep the exultation from his voice as he opened the corral gate. "Yeah, I guess I am," he answered.

Springer, the little trading town, was but a short ride from the OX. All the way Larry had to hold the dun down. The dun felt Larry's spirits right through the saddle, it seemed, and wanted to make a display. They rode in, tied their horses to a hitch rail and elaborately stalked down the street.

"First," announced Buck Winters, "we take a drink. Then me, I'm goin' to hit the barber shop. I aim to get shaved a whole lot an' my hair cut, an' mebbe a bath."

"Gettin' soft in yore old age," commented Cliff. "Ain't the creek good enough for you?"

"Not for me," Buck replied grandly.

96

"Come to think of it, it ain't for me neither," said Cliff. "What's yore program, kid?"

"I'll buy a drink," answered Larry slowly, "then I'm goin' to write a letter an' send some money, an' then I'll get some clothes, I guess."

"Well," Cliff stopped before an inviting door, "here we are. Here's the first stop."

There were more OX men inside the saloon and some riders from the Long L and the HT. They greeted the new arrivals boisterously. Larry did not have a chance to buy a drink. There were plenty in the bar who wanted to buy. He took a drink and another, them felt Buck's friendly hand on his arm.

"Make yore next one a cigar, kid," whispered Buck. "They're comin' pretty thick."

Larry, already feeling the two drinks he had taken, nodded his agreement. When the next round came up he modestly spoke his preference and had a box of cigars thrust at him. For the first time since he had entered, he had a chance to survey the barroom.

The bar itself was walnut, well worn and well kept There was a big mirror, banked with glasses, behind the bar, and in front of the mirror two men worked steadily to serve their patrons. Down along the bar was a little group surrounding Cliff Sparrow, and Cliff, face flushed and with a little glass in his fingers, was enjoying himself. Further along were two or three townsmen, friends of the punchers come in to enjoy the festivity that marked the end of the fall work. Still further down the bar was a tall handsome fellow, a pale man with dark eyes that were swift and alert as he scanned the crowd. His black hat was pushed back on his head and across his silk pique waistcoat dangled a gold chain loaded with fobs. The dark-eyed man was smiling, his

97

lips curved under his black mustache, and seemingly he was enjoying the party.

"Who's the tinhorn?" asked Buck of Fran Hartl, a townsman who had come up to greet him.

"Fellow named Truman," answered the townsman. "Royal Truman. He's a pretty good gambler, Buck. Ain't like most of 'em."

"They're all alike, Fran," stated Buck. "We'll likely have a session with him later. Want you to meet a friend of mine, Fran. This is Larry Blue."

Larry found himself shaking hands with the Hartl man and saying "pleased t' meetchu," with embarrassment in his voice.

"Want to talk to you a minute, Buck," said Hartl, and urged Winters away.

Larry, left alone for the moment, leaned against the bar. Wisps of talk drifted to him.

"We worked the Ceinega first an' then went right on to the Salt Flats."

"We had a run down by the Rayado . . ."

"Yeah. I seen him at Tucumcari . . ."

A familiar voice broke into the fragments. "Ride anythin'," stated Cliff Sparrow, his voice thick. "Race horse or bucker; don't make no difference. Ride 'em all. Where is this race horse?"

The crowd about Cliff revolved, pushing him along the bar. Larry found himself moved by the crowd, swept up by its eddy. At the end of the bar Larry could see, by rising on tiptoe, the gambler facing a grizzled cowhand that the others referred to as "Watt."

Watt was talking. "We got us a rider now," he stated. "When do you want to pull off this race, Truman?"

Royal Truman flicked ashes from his cigar. "You can suit yourself," he said evenly. "You set the time and the distance and the course."

Watt turned and looked at the others. Larry saw him wink. "How about after dinner?" asked Watt, turning back. "We'll stake out a quarter of a mile on the flat. How much you want to bet, Truman?"

"You can suit yourself on that too," said Truman. "I'll try to cover what you put up."

"Who you want for stake holder?"

"How will Jake here suit you?" Truman nodded his head toward a perspiring bartender.

"Just fine," Watt gave agreement. "Yo're the easiest fellow to get along with I ever see. Who of you boys wants in on this?"

There were eager voices raised in answer and one or two newcomers had questions to ask. "What is this?" "When's the race?" "Who's goin' to ride?"

Watt, by bellowing, managed to make himself heard and gained some semblance of quiet. "Horse race," he answered. "Goin' to run Stardance against Truman's horse. Cliff's goin' to ride Stardance. Goin' to run it off after dinner out on the flat west of town. Quarter mile race. Now who of you fellows wants in?"

Again the babble broke out. Money grew in a pile before the bald-headed Jake. Some, more cautious, shook their heads. They wanted to see Truman's horse. Larry Blue saw Jake count the money; saw Truman take a roll of bills from his pocket, a wrist-thick roll, and peel bills from it.

"Not hard money, boys," said Truman cheerfully, "but it spends just as easy."

Unnoticed, Larry worked his way out of the saloon.

Larry had some difficulty in finding a way to send Don seventy-five dollars. A clerk in Floersheim's store finally suggested that it might be sent East by his employer, and Larry, after convincing himself of the owner's honesty, made overtures to that amused man of business. Finishing with that transaction and having borrowed paper, pen and ink, and a desk, Larry wrote a letter. There remained only the business of purchasing boots, a coat, shirts and socks and some Levi's. Larry sauntered out. On the street he saw Bart Hodgson going into the town's one hotel, and the odor of food smote his nostrils. Larry decided that he was hungry. The shopping could wait.

He ate a meal in a restaurant, reveling in ham and eggs. Emerging on the street once more Larry saw a crowd of men surrounding a horse. Drawn as by a magnet the boy joined the crowd. The men about the horse dissolved and returned, riding horses. A rider took the racer's halter rope and Larry, getting his own dun, went along. Straight out of town they rode, across the creek and beyond it to a long flat below a hill. Stopping on the flat they were joined presently by Royal Truman and a dark-skinned native leading a chunky roan horse. Truman had a black horse between his knees and there was a flat English saddle on the roan.

"Well, gentlemen," said Truman pleasantly as he dismounted, "are you ready?"

"We got to mark out the distance first," announced Watt.

"When we get that done . . . Where's Cliff?"

Someone said, "Cliff ain't here."

"Our rider ain't here." Watt turned back to Truman.

Truman shrugged. "That's too bad," he said. "You matched a race and the money's put up. We'll run it."

"Not without Cliff we won't. See here . . ."

"You see here: You set the stakes and the course and the time. I'm here and ready. Your horse is here. We'll

100

run the race off." There was quiet insistence in Truman's voice.

"One of you fellows go to town an' git Cliff!" Watt turned from Truman. "Get him out here. He . . . Wait a minute. Who's this comin'?"

A man was coming out from town, spurring his horse to a run.

"Buck!" announced a voice, and another confirmed it. "Buck Winters."

Winters rode up and reined in. Calls of, "Where's Cliff?" greeted him.

Buck was scowling. "Cliff, the damned fool," announced Buck, "is back in town drunk as a hoot owl. We'll have to run this off without him."

From the men about the race horses a protest arose, a steady beat of voices. Royal Truman, imperturbable, smoothed the glossy back of his roan, aloof and unworried.

"Who'll ride?" "We ain't got a rider." "Call it off!"

"It won't be called off, gentlemen," announced Truman when he heard that last remark.

"We can't call it off." Again Watt made himself heard. "We got to run it. Who's goin' to ride?"

Buck Winters, beside Larry, looked down at the boy. He had seen Larry, bareback and riding like a Comanche, circle a running remuda. He had seen Larry get speed out of a horse. "Wait a minute," Buck yelled. "I got you a rider."

"Who?" Watt was facing Buck

Buck put his hand on Larry's shoulder. "The kid here," he answered, grinning.

Larry instantly was the focus of interest. Hard-faced, weathered men stared at him, appraisal in their eyes. Under that scrutiny Larry flushed. "I cant ride," he said

101

to Winters. "I never rode a race."

"You'll ride this one." Buck Winters was confident. "You'll win it, too."

Old Watt, eyes sharp, stood beside Larry. His voice was a dry rasp. "There's got to be a first time," said Watt. "You'll carry a lot of money on yore shoulders, kid."

Watt held Larry's left arm, Buck his right and together they pushed him through the crowd. Men were demanding his identity, asking questions. OX riders in the crowd were answering. They too had seen Larry ride. Suddenly the boy found himself beside the bay racer, Stardance. There was a saddle on Stardance, a light stock saddle. Something stirred in Larry, overcoming his diffidence and fright.

"We'll take that saddle off," said Larry Blue, confidently. Old Watt grunted his approval and moving forward fell to loosening the cinch.

A distance was measured carefully along the flat. Judges were appointed. Jake, the bartender, was on hand, a canvas sack gripped in his fist. On the roan horse the dark-faced native sat the flat saddle, his face confident. Old Watt gave Larry a boost up. Larry's legs gripped a satin bay hide. Under him muscles rippled as Stardance moved.

"Give him a quirt," yelled someone. "He's got no spurs."

"Stardance don't need no quirt," snarled Watt. "Talk to him, kid. Call his name."

Larry said, "Stardance," quietly, and under him the muscles of the bay surged and quivered.

"It's a runnin' start," announced Watt. "You bring yore horse up to the line an' come across even with that Mexican. Even with him, mind! There'll be a shot fired

102

an' you go like hell. If you don't hear the shot, turn an' come back."

Larry nodded his understanding, his voice stifled by his eagerness.

Men gave the riders room, riding off down the course to be at the finish. A veteran cowman, weatherbeaten and grizzled, stood at the starting line, gun in hand pointing toward the ground.

"Ride yore horses back, boys, an' get set," he ordered. "Turn 'em when I call, an' come up a runnin'. If I don't shoot my gun, circle an' come back. You set?"

Again Larry nodded. The Mexican on the roan grinned confidently and said, "*Seguro.*"

"Then let's git at it," snapped the starter.

Larry, riding back of the starting line, kept his eyes on his opponent. Bound not to be caught napping, he watched his rival. A word came from the starter. Larry swung the bay, brought him up, neck and neck with the roan. They were across the line and running, and a shot bellowed. This was the race!

Down at the finish the men watched the horses come in. They saw the native, leaning forward in his flat saddle, urging every ounce of speed that he could get from the roan, rising and falling, bobbing as the roan ran. And they saw a bay horse, a yellow-haired boy glued to him, part of the horse, moving with the horse, flat against the horse's neck, come sweeping past the roan and on to the finish line. Stardance, by a neck. Stardance and Larry Blue!

Guns popped the exuberance of their owners. Men grabbed each other and indulged in a war dance. Larry came riding back to a scene of confusion. Men pulled him from the horse, slapping his back until it stung, pressing money into his hands, thrusting bottles out for him to take. Buck Winters' eyes were gleaming with excitement and Old Watt was doing a little dance all by himself. Somehow Larry had to look to where Royal Truman stood patting the roan, his face calm and expressionless. Presently he left the roan and, walking over, gave Larry his hand.

"Nice race, kid," said Truman evenly. Royal Truman who had just lost a thousand dollars. "You rode him nice."

"Thanks," said Larry and meant it. The gambler's calm, his poise, his perfect sportsmanship, reached out to Larry. This man could win or lose and never turn a hair.

"Come on back to town, kid," urged Buck Winters. "We're goin' to celebrate." Larry allowed himself to be led away.

Back in town men wanted to spend money on Larry Blue. Larry took a drink with the crowd. He had to do that much, he felt, but the whisky burned. Larry did not like whisky. In the saloons the talk was all of the horse race. After the first excitement died down, Larry managed to get out. He wanted to buy the things he needed. The winners had been generous and now he had more money than when he had ridden out to the race course, at least fifty dollars. Larry went to Floersheim's store.

He was looking at some shirts when a quiet voice at his elbow caused him to turn. "You aren't celebrating then?" Royal Truman asked.

Larry shook his head. "I don't want to get drunk," he answered truthfully.

Truman smiled, lips and black eyes echoing each other. "Good idea," he said quietly. "I was afraid . . . I'd like to talk with you, lad."

104

"Why sure," agreed Larry, "I was just buyin' some shirts. I've got to get some Levi's an' some boots too. I..."

"Wait until we talk," urged Truman. "We'll be back." With a smile and nod to the clerk, he led Larry away. Outside the store Truman made for the hotel and in its little lobby he invited Larry to sit down. Seated, the gambler brought a cigar from his pocket, snipped off the end with a knife, and lit a smoke.

"They call you Larry," he said suddenly.

"My name's Larry Blue," said the boy.

"I'm Royal Truman." Truman puffed on his cigar. "I'm a gambler."

"I know that."

Truman scrutinized the tip of his cigar for a moment and then returned it to his mouth. "What are you doing right now?" he asked.

"I'm workin' for the OX." Larry made the announcement proudly. "Goin' to work for them this winter."

"How much do they pay you?"

"Forty a month." Still pride in Larry's voice.

Truman puffed reflectively. "Look here, Larry," he said. "You won that race this afternoon. My roan is a better horse than the bay."

Larry's eyes were wide with astonishment. "Why . . ." he began.

"Emelio is a good rider," Truman disregarded the interruption, "and ordinarily he would have won. You're a better rider."

"Why . . ." said Larry again.

"I've sent Emelio along home," said Truman smiling. "I want the best rider I can get upon Red Bonnet. How would you like to work for me, Larry?"

105

"I don't know," Larry's answer came slowly. "I . . ."

"I'll make you a proposition." Truman's voice was smooth. "I'll pay you seventy dollars a month and I'll give you your board and room. We'll travel and we'll see some of this country. The railroad is in Colorado. We'll go up there and stop at some of the camps. We can make some money, Larry."

It took a long time for the boy to digest that. He looked at Royal Truman. Truman returned that look, black eyes locking with blue eyes and holding them. "And you won't ride a crooked race or pull a crooked play," continued Truman, quietly. "I'll bet on Red Bonnet every time he runs and I'll cut you in for a percentage of what we win. How about it?"

Back in Larry's mind the ever present necessity for money prodded. There was Don back East and there was the need for clothing and . . .

"I'll have to talk to Mr. Hodgson an' get him to turn me loose," said Larry Blue.

Truman nodded, satisfied. "See him," he assented. "It's the right thing to do. And whether you go with me or not I'd like to have you eat supper with me. I'll meet you here at six." The gambler got up then, knocked the ashes from his cigar and, nodding to Larry, trolled out of the lobby. A personable, nonchalant man who knew his work.

Larry sat in his chair for some time after Truman's departure. There were pictures in his mind and ideas to sort. Then he too got up and going to the desk asked the clerk in attendance if Bart Hodgson had a room in the hotel.

Bart was not in his room. Larry went out on the street and after some time found the OX foreman engaged in talk with Buck Winters and several ranchmen. Larry did not break into the conversation, but stood waiting.

Hodgson, glancing up, grunted a question. The boy stated his mission. He wanted to see the OX foreman, he explained. Hodgson detached himself from his friends, stepping aside with Larry.

"I got an offer for a job, Mr. Hodgson," Larry stated bluntly. "There's a man wants me to ride race horses for him."

Hodgson's eyes squinted. "That feller you beat this afternoon?" he asked.

"Yes, sir."

The OX foreman made no comment, but turning, called to Buck and when Winters joined them, nodded toward the hotel. "Let's go up to my room," he suggested. "Larry's got somethin' on his mind."

In Hodgson's room with the foreman sitting on the bed, Larry occupying the edge of the chair, and Buck squatting against the wall, Hodgson spoke again. "Let's have it," he commanded.

Larry took a long breath and plunged in.

"Mr. Truman offered me seventy dollars a month and my keep. He says that we'll go into Colorado up into the railroad camps. He says he'll bet on every race we run and give me some of the winnin's. He says. . ."

Hodgson held up a hand. "Do you want to go, kid?" he asked.

"I got to have the money," Larry answered frankly.

"Why?"

"Because . . . because of Don."

Silence fell for a moment. Larry broke it. "Don's my brother," he explained. "I'm puttin' him through school. Don's got to be a lawyer."

He went on then while the men listened without interruption; talking about Don, telling about what Don was to be, what Don was to do. From that tale the silent listeners learned more than they had ever known about Larry Blue. They learned of Archer Bolton, Old Jim Cardwine, and they learned of Larry too. When he was done Bart Hodgson dropped the dead butt of his cigarette and Buck Winters shifted his position where he squatted against the wall.

"What kind of fellow is Truman?" asked Hodgson.

Buck Winters made slow reply. "I called him a tinhorn and Fran Hartl stood up for him. I reckon Truman is all right."

The OX foreman turned his head and looked squarely at Larry Blue. "It's a chance kid," he stated, "but yore takin' it."

Larry made no reply and Hodgson continued. "Man an' boy," he drawled, "I follered cattle for forty years. I got a little bunch. I make some money. I'd like to keep you with me, but yore yore own boss," He waited then, his eyes and Buck Winters' eyes fixed on the boy on the chair. It was up to Larry.

Larry made his decision. "I got to have the money for Don," he said finally, "Thanks, Mr. Hodgson."

He got up then and going to the door slowly went on out. When the door had closed and the corridor was quiet, old Bart Hodgson spoke. "I hate to lose that kid," he said quietly.

"Why did you turn him loose?" demanded Buck. "If you'd said the word he'd of stayed an' . . ."

"An' fought his head," Bart Hodgson finished. "The kid has got to learn. His job will be waitin' for him when he comes back." He got up then and Buck Winters, too, arose. Buck kicked at an inoffensive chair. "Damn it," said Buck, "I . . . well, damn it!"

108

# CHAPTER 9

## GAMBLIN' MAN

LARRY BLUE CAME BACK TO HIS ROOM IN THE PALACE Hotel through the snow-filled streets of Triton. A year had thickened him, toughened him, but had not added to his height. At seventeen he was five feet eight inches tall and weighed one hundred and sixty pounds. The year had smoothed the boy, added to his knowledge if not his stature. Royal Truman had made no horse boy out of Larry, had not made him a jockey. Instead Truman had done his unconscious best to broaden Larry, to add to his learning. Larry wore good clothes, the best that he could buy. Indeed, as he came now from looking after the comfort of Red Bonnet, he was the picture and height of fashion. On his head he wore a small, roll brimmed derby, and when he removed the fur collared overcoat he displayed a checked suit that was the envy of his associates, immaculate linen and a vest with a chain and string of fobs across it. One concession only did Larry make to his calling. His feet were covered with shopmade boots, high-heeled and fancy stitched. Cliff Sparrow had worn boots like that and Larry had envied Cliff. Now he could wear boots that were better than Cliff's.

Tossing the overcoat on his bed, Larry put his hat aside and sat down. He shared the room with Royal Truman but Truman had not been in it for a day. Truman was playing poker, a big game, and poker to Royal Truman was meat and bread and whisky. Blue eyes squinting a little, Larry sat down and from a vest pocket brought corn husks and tobacco. Jim Cardwine had taught Larry to roll a smoke and Larry unconsciously imitated the old man as he twisted the husks about the brown grains. He wondered when Royal would be in.

During the year they had spent together Larry had learned a good deal about Royal Truman. He knew that for weeks at a time Truman would remain silent, living within himself, and then suddenly break into a flow of talk. Royal Truman had seen a good part of the little world and could tell about it.

With his cigarette held between his fingers, the end smoldering, Larry reached with his free hand into the inner pocket of his coat and brought out a letter from Don. Larry and Truman had been in Triton for two months and mail had caught up with him. Opening the envelope, Larry read the boyish scrawl.

Don wrote thanking him for the last remittance of fifty dollars. He said that he was in the fourth form. He spoke of playing football, mentioning that he had scored a goal in the last match, a statement that left Larry somewhat puzzled. Don was invited to spend the Christmas holidays in Boston with a schoolmate. All these things the letter contained, and one thing more: If Larry could send him a hundred dollars before Christmas, Don would be grateful. He would need the money on his vacation trip. Refolding the letter, Larry put it away. It was a good letter, newsy, and full of interest. But that extra hundred dollars! That bothered Larry, not that Don should ask for the money, but that he, Larry, did not have it to send. The boy on the bed frowned. He wondered when Royal would arrange another race. He wondered too if he would win the race. When Red Bonnet ran and won, Larry had money. Usually he sent it to Don.

Larry possessed himself of a package from the pocket of his coat, cut the string with the big knife which he produced from a sheath inside his trousers, and unwrapped the box, bringing to light a deck of cards and a small contrivance of metal and leather. There was a printed slip in the box and Larry read it through. Then, following the directions he began to adjust the contrivance to his arm.

As he finished, the door of the hotel room opened and Truman came in. Truman showed the effects of his long session at the poker table. His black eyes were sunk in great dark hollows, and his face was thin and lined. With no word to Larry, Truman pulled off his coat and dropped down on the other bed. Larry gave the man no greeting. When Truman came in like this, whether winner or loser, he wanted to be let alone.

Finally the man turned, rolling over on his back. His voice, while weary, held a note of exultation. "Two thousand four hundred dollars," announced Truman. "There were a contractor, two engineers, and a cowman in the game. Some of the best poker I've ever played."

Larry knew now that Truman had won. He asked a question. "Good hands?"

"Poor hands," corrected Truman, "but the others thought that they were good."

Larry grinned. He knew how Royal Truman played poker. It was not the cards but the men that Truman played. The boy got up. "I'll order some coffee," he offered. "You'll want to drink it and then sleep."

"For a week," agreed Truman drowsily, "or a month or a year." The man stirred again, turning so that he faced Larry. Larry was busily removing the contrivance that he had placed on his arm.

Truman suddenly was alert. "What's that?" he

111

demanded, sitting up.

Larry flushed red. "It's a thing I bought," he said evasively. "I just got it. I got a letter from Don today." Royal Truman knew all about Don.

The gambler was not to be sidetracked. "It's a holdout!" he said, rising from the bed and walking across to Larry. "That's what it is!"

Larry's face grew redder. "Yes, sir," he answered honestly.

Truman held out his hand. "Give it here," he ordered. "Whatever possessed you to buy one of those things?"

Larry made no answer. He put the detached contrivance in Truman's hand.

"I've told you," said Royal Truman deliberately, "that you were not to play poker until I had taught you how. I have told you that knowing cards, and the possible chances, and a knowledge of men, were necessary to play poker. And you send off and buy a thing like that. Why, Larry?"

Larry's blue eyes were searching the floor. His voice was muffled when he answered. "Don said that he needed some more money."

"I see." There was anger in Truman's voice. "And you would throw me overboard just because your little brother can't live on the money you send him. You know what I think about cheating, Larry?"

"Yes, sir."

"And you know that I have never pulled a crooked play since you have been with me?"

"Yes, sir."

"Then why . . .?"

"Some of the men down at the stable had a game," answered Larry sullenly.

"How much did you lose?"

"Ten dollars."

Truman laughed harshly. "And I'm not worth ten dollars to you," he said. "Suppose you used that and got caught? Where would they say you learned?"

"From you." Larry's voice was still sullen, like a pupil caught cheating in a school room.

Truman tossed the holdout to the floor. "You had better go out a while," he said to the boy. "Go out and think it over. I'm afraid that I don't want you around me right now."

Larry, head hanging, got up from the bed. Without a word to Royal Truman he pulled on his overcoat, set the derby on his head and stalked out, slamming the door behind him. Left alone, Truman lay down again, squirmed for comfort, sat up and pulled off his coat and then lay down once more. Presently his deep, even breathing told that he slept.

Larry Blue, stamping down the stairs of the Palace Hotel, crossed the lobby and went out on the street. Triton was waking up. The Palace stood on Front Street and across from the hotel the raw lines of the railroad tracks, filled with cars, and the lights of the depot, shone. Larry glared at these. The railroad was Triton's sole reason for being. Triton was almost at the end of steel. Beyond Triton stretched the new track and the grade, and beyond them were the grader camps filled with men. Triton, like some giant nocturnal animal, roared at night. In his year with Royal Truman, Larry had seen several Tritons. Had seen them spring up and grow, and then as the steel pushed on, relapse into tameness and lassitude. But while the Tritons roared, they roared loudly; tonight was paynight and Triton was booming.

Going on down the plank sidewalk covered with

slush that was freezing now that night had come, Larry passed saloons, pool halls, dance halls and bagnios. A restaurant or two added their lights to the many that lit the sidewalk. Striped barber poles advertised the tiny cubicles behind them. Larry passed them by. Front Street was Triton's tenderloin. Above it, toward the close-set hills, stretched the solid town that would remain when Front Street was tamed: the dwellings, the stores and markets, the real Triton. Larry passed a coated man who stood alertly on a corner. The man nodded and Larry returned that nod. That was Bill Carver, the night marshal of Triton.

Further along the street, pausing indecisively, Larry was caught in the flood of light from an open door. Women's voices came shrilly, and a girl, thrusting her head through the door, called to the boy.

"Hello, Larry. When are you coming to see me?"

Turning, Larry caught a glimpse of painted lips, rouged cheeks and eyes that were too bright. "Tonight, maybe," he answered. He knew the girl. She was Grace; the last name an unknown quantity.

"If Royal will let you!" the girl laughed tauntingly. "It's paynight. I won't keep it open for you, kid."

Larry scowled at the laughter the remark brought, and went on along the sidewalk, kicking his boot toes into the freezing slush. "If Royal would let him!" Royal treated him like a baby. Royal . . . Larry stopped at another door, pulled his hands from his pockets and opening the door went into a restaurant.

Sitting at the counter, eating a steak and drinking coffee, Larry bathed in his martyrdom. Nay, he basked in it, every thought bringing his self-sorrow closer to the surface. Royal treated him like a baby, like a punk kid. Royal was glad enough to have him ride Red Bonnet.

Royal liked to have him around to run errands and do chores, but when it came to letting him step out on his own, Royal put down his foot. Royal wouldn't let him go to the house where Grace lived. Time enough for that when he was a man, Royal said. Royal forbade him to play poker or faro or even chuck-a-luck at fifty cents a chance. Dice were taboo. And he bet that he, Larry Blue, knew a whole lot more about dice and cards than any of the fools Royal played with. Royal himself had said that he was smart with the dice and the cards.

Royal wouldn't even let him have a gun. Royal Truman, who carried two of them, a double-barreled derringer and a blue thirty-eight in a holster at his waistband.

"I'll teach you to shoot, kid," Royal said, and then made Larry pop at a target with the thirty-eight! A gambler, Royal Truman? Shucks! He should have been a preacher or . . . or one of those teachers who taught little kids. That was it. A teacher!

Larry got up from his stool, paid his bill and banged out of the restaurant. He'd show Royal Truman. Just because he sent off to a mail-order house and bought a sleeve holdout and a deck of marked cards was no reason for Royal to jump on him. He'd get into a game and clean up and be sitting pretty, then Royal could just go to the devil!

Going back down the street Larry halted before a pool hall and went in. There was a Kelly pool game organizing at the back table: a fireman from the road, a cowpuncher, a conductor and two brakemen. Larry knew one of the brakemen.

"Hi, kid," called his acquaintance. "Come on an' get a stick. I'll give you a pill."

Nonchalantly Larry shoved his derby back on his

head, unbuttoned his overcoat and joined the group. "Kelly'll do 'til somethin' better starts," he announced. "Pour me out a pill."

The brakeman shook the leather bottle.

Larry played Kelly with indifferent luck. When he was not shooting he sat in a high chair close by the table and banged the end of his cue against a tall brass cuspidor until one of his companions made him stop.

"Cut it out, kid, for cripes sake!"

Time wore along. One hour, two hours; eight o'clock, nine o'clock, ten o'clock, with Triton booming out on Front Street and the bald-headed conductor chalking his cue and sighting down it and then stopping to chalk his cue again. Shucks!

Customers ebbed and flowed in the pool hall. Men came back to the wash room, passing the Kelly pool table, and went out again. A party entered, their voices high and excited.

"Way I heard it was that they caught this fellow with a marked deck an' a sleeve holdout. Had it right in his room." Larry heard that and got out of the chair.

"Yeah. He'd been in a big game. Cleaned it up. They went up to his room to get him to play again an' there was the holdout right where he'd took it off an' dropped it."

"He shot ol' man Abner, didn't he?"

"Yeah. . . . What do you want, kid?"

Larry had the speaker's sleeve. "What happened?" demanded Larry hoarsely. "Who you talkin' about?"

"Fellow named Truman. A tinhorn that got caught with a sleeve holdout. He shot the man that caught him an' they're lookin' for him now. What . . ?"

Larry was gone. Overcoat forgotten, still holding the pool cue, he ran toward the front door. At the door he cast the cue from him and ran out into the street.

Front Street at that spot was deserted. Further up the way, toward the Palace Hotel, there was a crowd. Larry ran toward it, boots slipping on the rough ice.

At the outskirts of the crowd he hesitated. There was a constant roar of talk, words intermingling with curses, rising from the crowd.

"Damn' murderer!"

"He killed Abner!"

"Somebody seen him go in the pool hall!"

"Naw, he's in the barber shop."

A man came running, parting the crowd as a ship parts a wave. The runner carried a coil of rope.

"That's the stuff!" came a yell.

And another: "Hang him!"

Larry broke on through the stragglers, making for the Palace Hotel and the saloon below it.

The saloon was deserted. Only a white-aproned bartender stood in front of the bar, looking wistfully out the window. Larry knew the bartender.

"Where's Royal?" he panted. "Where is he, Gus?"

Gus, the bartender, shook his head. "Royal's in trouble, he said morosely. "You better pull out of here, kid. They know yo're his pardner."

"Where is he?"

"He's somplace in the block. Them fellows he was playin' with, come back to get him to play some more. They went up to his room an' found him sleepin'. There was a sleeve holdout on the floor an' a deck of marked cards layin' on the bed. Ol' man Abner accused him of cheatin' an' Royal shot him. They . . . where you goin' kid? Stay out from behind that bar!"

Gus was big and slow footed. Larry Blue was speed itself. The boy eluded the sweeping arm of the bartender, dived behind the bar and came up with the sawed-off, double-barreled shotgun that was kept there for emergencies. He swung the twin muzzles toward Gus, and Gus blanched.

"Easy. That thing's loaded. Easy kid!"

"Where's Royal?" croaked Larry Blue.

"I don't know," wailed the bartender once more. "Put that gun down, Larry. You'll git yoreself killed. Hey, come back here!"

Larry was at the front door. He pushed it open and holding the shotgun waist high went out into Front Street.

The crowd was surging there, pressing against the buildings, roaring now more loudly than before. Larry, holding his weapon, kept close to the wall. No one paid attention to him as he worked his way along. No one heeded him. Little by little he edged in. Then, swiftly, the pressure was released and he was in an entrance way.

"There he is!" yelped a voice. "I see him!"

Larry half turned. The crowd was sweeping back toward him now. Larry confronted angry faces, a raging, seething mass of humanity. He swept the shotgun up and under his thumb the hammers clicked back.

"Stop!" screamed Larry Blue.

In front of Larry men halted, motionless. It is one thing to roar and shout, "Hang him!" It is another to confront a white-faced boy who holds a loaded shotgun at full cock, his finger trembling on the trigger. The men in front of Larry pushed back and those in the rear pushed in. Somewhere in the crowd a man screamed in pain as he went down and was trampled. There were hard men in that crowd, men who could and would

118

shoot, who had before and were ready again to risk their lives. But what man wants to go up against a hare-brained kid with a shotgun?

"Quit shovin'!" yelled a man in front. "Quit shovin'!"

"Hell, he's nothin' but a kid!"

"Go on, take him!"

Voices came from the crowd. In Larry's hands the shotgun described a little weaving circle. He was cold in the pit of his stomach, cold and empty there. His face was a mask, white with eye holes that were simply slots behind which gleamed his eyes.

"I'll kill the man that takes a step," said Larry Blue, and meant it.

The men in front of that crowd believed him. They heaved back, giving way. The open area in front of Larry Blue widened. In the back of the crowd those less hardy spirits moved, easing the pressure. Larry swung the shotgun in little concentric circles, watching, waiting, and as he moved the shotgun he tried to talk, tried to explain.

"That was my holdout. I bought it. Royal never . . ."

Larry might as well have talked to a vacant room. No one heard him, no one heeded him.

It was Gus, the bartender from the Palace Saloon, that saved the day. Gus was fat and he was bald and he had a certain dignity. Gus had issued from the Palace to join the party. Some vagary of movement had put Gus out in front of the crowd and the shift backward had left him alone. Gus tried to preserve his dignity but he wanted to get away from that shotgun. He took a deliberate step backward, slipped as though he had struck a banana peel, and sat down. Still trying to be dignified, Gus attempted to rise. It was too much. There on the slippery planks Gus did a split, and in the crowd a man laughed.

119

That was the signal. That husky, infectious laugh touched off the spark. It spread through the men at the forefront of the crowd, rippled back and back until men who could not see Gus spread out on the wall were laughing heartily at they knew not what. Gus' fresh efforts to rise brought peal after peal of laughter and then, rasping and authoritative, voices broke through the mirth.

"Come on now. Break it up. Move along!"

Larry saw a big man pushing through the crowd. He saw others hustling and shoving men who did not resist them. Bill Carver had arrived and with Carver were his deputies.

Men did not fool with Bill Carver. Carver had earned his job and his reputation, which was tough. Besides, the fight had gone out of the crowd. It had been stopped by a boy with a shotgun and it had laughed itself hoarse at a fat bartender, just now, getting up from the sidewalk.

Carver reached Larry's side. "Where's Royal, kid?" he demanded.

Larry had put down the shotgun. He was shaking now. Still, he managed to answer the officer. "They said he was inside here."

"We'll see," grunted Carver, and to the men who accompanied him: "Keep 'em moving along."

The big man put his hand on Larry's arm and together they stepped back into the entry and opened the door. For the first time Larry saw that this was the barber shop next the Palace. Just that morning Tony, the proprietor, had cut Larry's hair. Tony appeared, face pasty, crawling out from behind the heating stove.

"Truman in here?" demanded Carver.

"In the bathroom," said the barber. "He's hurt."

"Come on, kid," ordered Carver.

The two pushed through the swinging door and into the bathroom that Tony had fitted up. There was a tub of sorts in the room, and a stool. Royal Truman sat on that stool, right arm dangling, blood dripping from his fingers. There was a gun in Truman's left hand. His face was wan but he managed to smile at the big officer.

"What got into you, Royal?" snapped Carver. "What the hell . . ?"

"I didn't think you'd make it, Bill." Truman's voice was weak. "What stopped them?"

"The kid here stopped them with a shotgun," said Carver. "I was up at the jail lockin' up a drunk when ol' man Abner showed up there. He was scared to death. Said he'd shot you. Those galoots out there had it that you'd shot him."

"He did shoot," Truman answered. "He had reason, I guess." The gambler's voice was weary.

"Abner said he'd caught you with a sleeve holdout." Carver was stern. "I thought you run a square game, Royal."

"He does!" Larry, from beside Royal Truman, looked up into Carver's face. "I bought that holdout an' a deck of marked cards. Royal gave me hell for getting them. I was goin' to use them down at the livery barn. I . . ."

Carver looked down at the boy. "You damn' near got yore pardner killed, kid," he said bluntly. "I reckon you evened though. How come you let Abner shoot you, Royal? He never seen the day he could . . ."

"He was right," said Royal Truman. "I didn't want . . ."

"Didn't want to kill the old fool," finished Carver. "I got to get you out of town, Royal. They're quiet now, but this is pay-night an' if they get a little more

121

liquor . . ."

Truman nodded wearily. "Whatever you say, Bill," he agreed.

Bill Carver scowled. "There's a freight leavin' pretty quick," he announced. "I'll get you on that. It's kind of tough . . ."

"I'm lucky to be living," Royal interrupted the officer. "I see your side of it, Bill. I'll go."

Carver grunted his relief. "I'll get you on the freight," he said. "You'll have to leave yore stuff, I guess. We won't have time to get that."

Larry had been tying a handkerchief about Truman's shoulder. There was a nasty wound in the shoulder and the boy had laid it bare. He stood up now.

"The kid, too," said Carver. "He'll have to go."

"Larry stopped them with a shotgun, you say?" Royal Truman had regained his voice.

"Yeah. Held the bunch. Come on if yo're ready."

Carver helped Truman to his feet, one big hand supporting the weakened man. Larry gathered up the shotgun. His hands trembled a little as he raised it. Royal Truman smiled at the boy and from that smile Larry gained confidence. His hands ceased their trembling.

Outside the barber shop Carver's deputies closed around the three, a compact little group. The men who still loitered on Front Street gave way before the marshal and his men. Across the walk they went, and across the street to the yards. There an engine puffed and couplings clanked as the cars were moved. Carver leading the way, the men went along the line of cars to where a lighted caboose stood. From the door of the caboose the conductor poked his head.

"Passenger for you, Henry," said Carver. "You'll take 'em out of town an' wherever they want to go."

"We ain't supposed to carry passengers," complained Henry. "This here train is goin' East empty an' we ain't no passenger train."

"You'll take these passengers," Carver announced grimly. "Get aboard, Royal." His big hands hoisted Royal Truman up the steps. Larry, still clutching the shotgun, followed.

"Mebbe you can come back sometime," said Carver, on the ground. "I'll kind of get yore stuff together an' look after it for you. But don't hurry back, Royal."

"I won't," said Royal Truman. "So long, and thanks, Bill."

Larry supported Truman. On the ground Bill Carver stood watching the two in the caboose door. Up ahead a whistle sounded questioningly. The conductor, pushing past the two in the doorway, waved a lantern. Again the whistle sounded and a rumbling came as the engineer took up his slack.

"So long," called Bill Carver.

Later, sitting on the seat of the caboose, while the freight train climbed steadily, Larry Blue looked at Royal Truman. Truman lay outstretched on the seat, his right arm resting on his chest.

Tears were very close behind the blue of Larry's eyes. "I got you into it," said Larry, a tremor in his voice. "I made you lose Red Bonnet an' all your clothes an' . . ."

"You kept a rope off my neck, too," reminded Truman. "Don't forget that."

Larry said nothing in answer. His eyes were those of a whipped collie pup, whipped and knowing the reason for the punishment. Royal Truman saw those eyes. He smiled under his mustache. "We're not broke, Larry," said Truman. "Don't forget that I cleaned up in that game. I've got that money, and I've got a partner that I can bank on now."

# CHAPTER 10

## DOCUMENTS AND CLIPPINGS

AN EDITORIAL FROM THE *FRANKLIN CHRONICLE,* UNDER the date line, August 20, 188— and entitled, "HOW LONG?"

How long are the good citizens of this community to be preyed upon by *vultures* and *fiends in human form?* The Editor of the CHRONICLE names no names but in company with the others of this community we *know* the perpetrators of the series of dastardly *murders* and *hold-ups* that have been committed in this vicinity within the last three months. *Human patience* is short and we warn the law enforcement officers of this town that unless steps are taken the law will *revert* to the hands of those who gave it, and there will be a *necktie party* of the *first magnitude.*

From the *Franklin Chronicle,* a clipping under the date September 13, 188—

ARREST MADE IN STAGE HOLD-UP

Yesterday afternoon ye Editor of the CHRONICLE was called from his sanctum by United States Deputy Marshal Bert Rutherford and informed by that official that George Whiteman had been apprehended in the act of stopping the west-bound stage in Apache Gap.

124

Acting on information received from a source that he declined to disclose, Marshal Rutherford and his men rode into the gap and found the stage stopped. Pursuing the bandit the officers were engaged in a running gun battle for a distance of perhaps four miles, when a well-aimed shot brought down the miscreant's horse. The rider was stunned by the fall of his horse and Marshal Rutherford had no trouble in arresting him.

Whiteman has been taken to La Mesa for safe keeping, as feeling in Franklin is running high. He will be arraigned in the fall term of court under charges of armed robbery. Marshal Rutherford and his men are to be congratulated on their prompt action. If Franklin was endowed with other officers of the Marshal's caliber there would be a general exodus of undesirable characters from our fair city.

News item from the *Franklin Chronicle* under the date line of November 19, 188—

SENTENCES PASSED

Judge Parsons, sitting in the United States Circuit Court, today pronounced sentence upon a number of malefactors. Among those sentenced were: George Whiteman for a period of seven to fourteen years for Armed Robbery; Amedeo Vincente, Smuggling, five to ten years . . .

From the *Franklin Chronicle,* an editorial under the date line January 1, 188—

Today the CHRONICLE goes under new management. As is customary it is the desire of the editor to state the policy that will be pursued by this paper. It is our desire to publish news, untinctured by personal prejudice or animosity. We feel that this will be a welcome relief to those subscribers who have come to feel that the former proprietor was too militant and prejudiced. With the railroad shortly to enter our city, and with the possibility of another connecting line coming to Franklin from the north, the time has come to lay aside personal likes and dislikes and for all the good citizens of Franklin to pull together and boost our city.

A letter from Don Blue to his brother Larry, subscribed Boston, Massachusetts, July 26, 188—

Dear Brother Larry:

I received your letter of June 30 a week ago and I hasten to answer it. Let me thank you for the draft for $200.00 which you enclosed. It was timely and much needed.

At present I am living with the Potter family, as I did last summer, and am reading law in the office of Crotchford and Sutherland, an old and reputable firm. I am enjoying my studies very much except that I find Mr. Sutherland a strict task master.

He gives me time for myself and is very stormy when I fail no to finish the reading he prescribes. I find myself wishing that I could be with you and that you were not so determined that I should become a lawyer. However, another year will see me finished with my education and Mr. Sutherland grumpily informed me that, even slow as I am, within two years after I graduate if I apply myself I should be ready to take my Bar examinations.

A letter from Father Paul has arrived. I am afraid that the dear old man is aging rapidly. His handwriting shakes and scrawls across a page until it is almost illegible. He has indeed been a father to me and I dread the time which I know must come.

Would it be too much to ask you to increase the next remittance you send me, to some extent? I find that my wardrobe is lacking in several details and now that summer has come and there is boating I feel that I should have the proper costume.

I will write to you again shortly and report my progress. In the interim believe me to be,

Your obedient, loving brother,

Don.

To Mr. Larry Blue,
Los Animas, Colorado

From the *Franklin Chronicle*. A news item dated December 30, 188—

## EXECUTION IN LOMA

Yesterday in our neighboring city across the river, a bandit, one Tomaso Patron, was executed by the military authorities. Patron, one of those outlaws who have been preying upon the commerce of our Sister Republic, was apprehended at the Casa Estevan Rancho twenty-two miles east of Loma while in the act of raiding the ranch. He would have escaped and been free to continue his nefarious career, but for the fact that when the rurales descended upon Casa Estevan, Patron, who had already stolen the valuables from the house, returned to get a box of jewelry overlooked in the room of Senorita Amanda Estevan.

Brought to Loma, Patron was speedily tried and

executed by a firing squad. Under the Diaz administration banditry is becoming an unprofitable pursuit below the border, and it is hoped that the execution of Patron will serve as a warning to those other enterprising gentry who follow his trade.

A letter from Larry Blue to his brother, Don, subscribed Tonopah, Nevada, August 15, 188—

Dear Don,

Your letter of July 26th followed me here. I am sending you a draft for $400.00. If that is not enough I expect you to write me. I am sorry that I did not write sooner, but was on the move.

You don't need a boating costume. That sounds like you had a girl and you don't need a girl; not yet. Keep your mind on the law.

Things are very good here as there is a fresh strike and the town is booming. I will send you more money within a day or two.

Your affectionate brother,
Larry.

A letter from John Lester to Alexander Sutherland of the firm of Crotchford and Sutherland in Boston, Massachusetts, subscribed Franklin,—, September 3, 188—

My dear Alexander:

I was indeed glad to receive your letter concerning my protégé, Donald Blue, and to learn that the boy is doing so well under your tutelage. He is a good boy and came to my notice, as I wrote you, under a most remarkable set of circumstances. I feel that I am in duty bound to aid him in whatever way that I can, but I must act anonymously.

I plan, as soon as Don finishes college and a few months in your office, to bring him West. I am growing old and find that I need youth about me. As you know I have an interesting and lucrative practice here and I plan that Don shall fall heir to it when I go to join my dear wife. In the meantime I am asking you to advance him small amounts of money, saying that it is remuneration for copying briefs, or any other work that a clerk in your office would normally perform. I want the boy to have every opportunity for advancement, socially as well as mentally, and I know that you will see that he receives every advantage.

With kindest regards to yourself and family, I am

Sincerely and respectfully yours,

John A. Lester

An obituary notice in the *Boston Transcript* under the date of October 5, 189—

ARCHER J. BOLTON

After a long and lingering illness, Archer J. Bolton passed away in his home on Prospect Avenue the night of October 4, 189—.

As a young man Mr. Bolton graduated from Harvard University and immediately enlisted in the Fourth Massachusetts Volunteer Cavalry, in which organization he served through the last year of the War between the States. After returning from the army he read law, but in company with many another, he found that civil life was trying and went West.

After a number of years' residence in the western

territory, Mr. Bolton returned and a year after his arrival back in Boston, married Josephine DeWitt Bolton, the widow of his brother, Thomas J. Bolton.

Mrs. Josephine Bolton passed away within a year after her marriage.

Archer Bolton is survived by a sister, Mrs. Clark Andrews of Franklin, — and by two stepchildren, DeWitt W. and Constance A. Bolton.

Funeral services will be held at the home, Friday, October 6, at 3 o'clock, the Rev. Domican Fevrel officiating. Interment will be made in the Fairview Cemetery.

A portion of a letter written by the Warden of the Fort Leavenworth Federal Penitentiary, to the President of the United States, Feb. 11, 189—

The Pardon Board has recommended to your Excellency that George Whiteman be granted a full pardon and returned to his citizenship. I wish at this time to add my humble voice to that of the Board.

George Whiteman has been an exemplary prisoner during my term as Warden. He has applied himself diligently and I am informed has so studied that he is capable of passing the Bar examinations. During the recent outbreak in the prison Whiteman refused to join with the conspirators and conducted himself admirably. When the prisoners were rioting in the mess hall and the life of Guard Williams was endangered, Whiteman, by an exhibition of personal bravery, brought the guard from the hall. I believe him to be worthy in every way, of a pardon, and I sincerely pray that your Excellency will see fit to grant it him.

His law studies will enable him to make a place for

himself in the world and I believe that he will be a living example of the reform which we wish to instill in our prisoners . . .

A headline from the *Franklin Chronicle,* June 14, 189—

## NORTHERN CONNECTION ASSURED
## FRANKLIN

*Atlantic and Pacific to Build Branchline South*

A letter from Alexander Sutherland of the firm of Crotchford and Sutherland, Boston, Massachusetts, to John Lester of Franklin, subscribed Boston, Mass., August 7, 189—

My dear John:

I have neglected writing to you for some time due, in part, to the press of work now prevalent in the office. The offense is inexcusable, I know, and yet I beg that you will forgive me and even go further and undertake a piece of work for me.

A client of the firm, Archer J. Bolton, died recently in this city, and in undertaking to clear up the estate we find that he was intestate. Why, John, will men believe that they are immortal?

Examination of the estate leads us to believe that the only property of value that Mr. Bolton possessed was some sections of land bordering the Rio Grande near by Franklin. To be frank with you, our client was a drinking man and before his death squandered considerable wealth inherited from his brother. Further to complicate matters, Archer Bolton married his brother's widow who had two children: a girl,

Constance, and a boy, DeWitt. He stood then in a double relationship, that of stepfather and also of uncle to these two. Beside the boy and the girl as heirs, we find another: a half sister, Mrs. Clark Andrews, who resides near by Franklin. We would like very much to turn the legal business connected with this estate over to you, to have you act as our Western representative as it were. I hope that you will consent, and when I receive word from you I shall forward all papers, etc., connected with the matter, to you for examination.

I have already taken the liberty of giving Constance and DeWitt your name as a reliable party to consult in the matter. The children tell me (I call them children, but the boy is twenty-six and the girl a year or two younger), that they are coming West to Franklin within a short time. As I understand it they have a dual purpose in their visit; they wish to be with their aunt, whom they have not seen for a number of years, and they also want to look at the property they have inherited. DeWitt is enthusiastic and from what he tells me would like to become a Western ranchman.

Please write me immediately concerning your wishes in this matter.

Your protégé, young Blue, is doing nicely. At times he exhibits a desire for more activity than we are able to afford him here in Boston, but since his graduation he has been diligently pursuing the study of law with us and shows commendable advancement. Indeed, I believe him ready for his Bar examinations and he will take them within the next few weeks,

Knowing your plans for him, I suggest that we send young Blue to you as a messenger, carrying the documents in this Bolton matter. You will have opportunity then to see him for yourself and discuss the situation.

Mrs. Sutherland joins me in kindest personal wishes. I am, sincerely your respectful, obedient servant,

Alexander Sutherland.

A headline from the *Franklin Chronicle,* dated April 5, 189—

SEEMANS ELECTED MAYOR

*Popular Franklinite given 342 plurality*

A letter written in Austin, Texas, to Abe Seemans of Franklin, dated May 1, 189—

Dear Abe:

Your letter received and I suppose that congratulations are in order on your election. You ought to have things about where you want them now. I have been pardoned as you know, and came down here to take the Bar examinations which I passed with flying colors. Now it seems to me that you need some help there in Franklin and I am coming to give it. I know you will be glad to see me, so glad that you will have an office furnished and awaiting my arrival. I could use and would appreciate a little money placed to my account in the bank also.

I will wait here in Austin for a few days until I hear from you. This is a very interesting town and the Ranger headquarters are here. So far I have not talked with any of the Rangers but I know several of them. In fact, I know a number of things but have kept them to myself for seven years and will continue to do so, providing I think it worth while.

I should hear from you within a week or ten days at most, don't you think so? Until that time I remain your tight-mouthed friend,

George Whiteman.

From the *Franklin Chronicle,* July 12, 189—

ARRIVALS:
At the Plaza Hotel: DeWitt Bolton, Boston, Mass.; Constance Bolton, Boston, Mass.; Turner J. Consadine, Austin, Texas . . .

An advertisement in the *Franklin Chronicle*, July 15, 189—

AT THE EMPIRE OPERA HOUSE
SAMUEL J. LEVINE PRESENTS

"The Coward's Revenge,"
*or*
"Maid, Wife, and Widow"
A Tragedy in Three Acts
-And-
The Swiss Yodelers
A Musical Light Comedy

With

ANNETTE BONDREAUX
(The French Canary)

20 Ladies of the Ensemble 20
Box Seats, $10.00; Orchestra, $8.00; Balcony, $4.00
At the Empire Opera House Tonight
8 o'clock P.M.

A letter written by Royal Truman and addressed to Donald Blue, care of John Lester, at Franklin.

Denver, Colo.

July 5, 189—

Dear Mr. Blue:

Your letter to your brother was given to me to read as I am taking care of all of Larry's business at present. Larry is in a hotel here with a wound in his side which he got when a gang of toughs tried to hold up our card rooms. He is doing very well and will be out and around pretty quick and I will send him on down to Franklin to visit you for he needs a vacation. He had made all arrangements to meet you at La Junta as you wanted him to, when this matter came up, and the fact that he could not travel fretted him a good deal. If you had wanted to see him as badly as you said, you would have come over to Denver in place of going on to Franklin. However, Larry will come to see you in about three weeks, I should judge, as he wants very much to see you.

You need not worry about Larry's being all right as this wound is not serious. He was alone when the trouble started. Any two men he would have taken care of and did, but the third man was one too man many. However, I came in in time to take care of the third man, being just a minute late, so Larry was shot in the side. I regret this because I did my best, but was a little slow.

A telegram will reach Larry here but you had better send your telegram to me because I do not want to fret him at present. He will come to Franklin as soon as able and I have explained to him that the reason you did not come to see him was probably business. As I have said there is no need for you to worry, for Larry was too quick for two of them and only me being late caused him to get hurt.

Respectfully yours,<br>Royal Truman

A news item from the *Franklin Chronicle,* July 1, 189—

## UNITED IN MARRIAGE

The CHRONICLE learns from Austin that Mrs. Luella Andrews, former owner of the Cross C Land & Cattle Company, and our popular mayor, Abraham Seemans, were united in marriage in Austin, Tuesday, August 20th. The ceremony was performed by the Rev. Will Eastoan of the First Baptist Church of Austin.

The happy couple are spending a brief honeymoon in the Capitol, following which they will return to Franklin. While their plans are not known it is thought that Mr. and Mrs. Seemans will probably make their home in town where Mr. Seemans can look after his official duties.

The CHRONICLE joins with all of Franklin in wishing the Mayor and his bride, happiness and prosperity.

# CHAPTER 11

### REUNION

LARRY BLUE GOT OFF THE PALACE CAR AT THE Franklin depot, alighting on the cinders of the platform. He held himself a little stiffly and his face beneath the blond hair and above the dark mustache, was pale. The trip down the river valley and across the baked plain of the Jornado del Muerte had been one long delirium of heat and more heat. There was no relief from it here on this sun-assaulted cinder platform. Behind Larry, the brakeman, sweating in his shirt sleeves and with his uniform cap pushed back on his head, put two grips on the cinders and spoke:

"Here you are, Mr. Blue."

Larry said, "Thanks," absently, his blue eyes searching the platform for his brother. Surely Don would be at the depot. Surely Don would come to meet him. With a start Larry realized that he would not know Don. He had not seen Don for fifteen years. Don was twenty-five, a man grown, just as he, Larry Blue, was a man grown. Would Don recognize him? Would . . ?

A man came hurrying through the crowd that had descended from the train, a young blond fellow who anxiously scanned the faces of the men he passed. Don! Larry almost laughed aloud. He had thought that he would not recognize Don. Not recognize that blond replica of himself that came hurrying along? It was funny! Larry half raised his arm to attract the attention of the hurrying youngster and at that moment Don saw him.

Don Blue finished his journey down the platform at a run. "Larry!" His voice was a shout. Instantly, it seemed, he was beside Larry, Larry's hand in his, his arm about Larry's shoulders. "Larry . . . ! I didn't know . . . I thought . . ."

"That you wouldn't know me," Larry finished, grinning. "I was thinking the same thing. Easy, kid, take it a little easy. That side is still a little sore."

Instantly Don was contrite. He dropped his arm from Larry's shoulders but retained his grip on the hand. "You don't know how good it is to see you," Don said.

137

"I forgot all about your being hurt, I was so excited. I forgot all about everything. How is your side? Does it pain you badly?"

"I forgot it, too, kid," Larry answered. "It doesn't hurt. By George. . . . Stand off and let me look at you."

Don, relinquishing his grip, stood back. There were spots of color on his cheeks and his eyes blazed with excitement. Larry, looking at his brother, saw a well set-up young fellow, a trifle thin perhaps, but with a healthful thinness, broad-shouldered, narrow-hipped, dressed in a modish suit and with a stylish, narrow-brimmed, low-crowned derby hat set on blond hair that was inclined to curl. Don was clean shaven and there were not as yet the lines that would give his face character.

On his part Don Blue looked at the brother that he had not seen for so long. Larry Blue was as tall as Don. His shoulders were thicker than Don's, but his hips were as lean and narrow. Larry held himself stiffly because of his wound. A black slouch hat of finest felt was pulled over his eyes; the square skirts of his long black broadcloth coat hung over gray trousers. Larry wore boots, singularly small for so big a man; his hands were long, the fingers promising dexterity. His mustache was small and dark, and about his eyes and at the corners of his mouth were little firm creases. Here was a man who seldom smiled, but whose whole face was lighted when he did smile.

The two brothers were sober as they inspected each other and then suddenly they laughed and each took a step forward.

"Kid!" said Larry.

"Larry," exclaimed Don.

Again their hands met to grasp firmly.

138

"I've got to get you in out of this sun," Don announced, after a moment. "I've a carriage here. We'll get your luggage . . ."

Larry, stepping back, bent for the grips. Don forestalled him.

"I'll take those," he said, picking up the grips. "Come on, Larry. Come on!"

Don had a barouche waiting in front of the depot, the top up and a driver sitting stiffly on the seat. He put Larry's bags into the carriage, helped Larry in with a solicitous hand, and got in himself. The driver, a dark-faced native, looked around for orders.

"Just take me to the hotel," directed Larry. "Then you can send your buggy along to the livery and you and me will visit."

Don laughed. "This is no livery stable rig," he informed. "Judge Lester . . . What's the matter, Larry?"

Larry Blue had started to arise. "You know what I think of Lester," he stated, his face stormy. "If this belongs to Lester . . ."

"Sit down," Don commanded. "Judge Lester is expecting us. I'm staying with him and he has had a room made ready for you. Surely, Larry . . ."

"You and me have got to talk, Don," interrupted Larry. "I'll ride in this rig but I don't like it. Take me to the hotel, driver."

The driver, face impassive, looked at Don for directions. Don nodded, and turning, the coachman started his team.

As the barouche rolled along from the depot up Franklin's busy thoroughfare, Larry Blue kept his eyes straight ahead. He was scowling, not noticing the buildings on either side or the people on the sidewalks. Don, too, kept silent and it was not until the horses

139

stopped that he spoke.

"Here's the hotel, Larry."

Larry got out of the barouche, Don following him. A porter coming from the door, took the grips and the two men entered the hotel, Larry making straight for the desk. He registered in the book the clerk turned toward him, nodding impatiently at the mention of accommodations and rates, and taking the key that was offered, turned to his brother. "Come on up," Larry commanded. "We're going to talk."

Nothing loath, Don followed as Larry led the way toward the stairs, the porter carrying the grips, brushing past to precede them.

There were three stories in the Plaza Hotel. The porter led the way along the upper hall, took the key from Larry and unlocked a door and let the two men enter the room. Larry tipped the boy, then, crossing to the bed, took off his hat and sat down. Don Blue, standing beside the door, also removed his hat and put it on the table, but he did not seat himself. It was Don who began the conversation.

"You're acting foolishly, Larry," said Don bluntly. "I'm in partnership with Judge Lester. Everything I have I owe to him. He got me into Sutherland's office back in Boston; he helped me when I was in school. Now he's given me this chance to come in with him here. You may have some idea concerning him . . ."

"Some idea . . . !" Larry snapped the words. "Lester is the man that sentenced our father to hang! You say he's done everything for you! How about me? I suppose that I . . . ?"

"Of course you helped me," Don interposed swiftly. "I would be the last one to say that you didn't. You sent me money and you kept me in clothing and you did everything that you could do. I know that and I appreciate it. Don't think that I don't appreciate it. Just the same, if it hadn't been for John Lester . . . Why, Larry, he's done everything for me: Given me the entrée into circles that I could never have reached alone; given me a chance that any young lawyer would jump at. I tell you, Larry . . ."

Larry Blue looked up and smiled ruefully. "I reckon I wasn't so much as I thought I was," he said softly. "Somehow I had the idea . . . . Well, you needn't be beholden to Lester any more. I'm here and I've got enough money with me to do almost anything you want. Would fifteen thousand let you cut loose from Lester, Don? Because if it would . . ."

Larry got up from the bed and, unfastening his silk pique vest and opening his shirt, fell to fumbling with a buckle. Don watched him. Larry pulled out a soft leather belt of finest cordovan, with flapped pockets along its length.

"I've got fifteen thousand here," Larry said, holding out the money belt, "and a telegram to Royal will bring that much more or more if we need it. Here, Don, you take this and . . ."

Don made a little gesture as though he pushed away the proffered belt. "You don't understand, Larry," he said. "I can't take your money. You've sent me a lot of money, more than I needed sometimes. I can't take money and go to John Lester and say that I'm done with him. It goes deeper than that. You don't understand. . . ."

Larry Blue sat back on the bed, his money belt across his lap. Larry's coat was open and Don could see, peeping out from beneath Larry's right arm, the dull blue and brown of a gun butt.

141

"I reckon I don't understand," Larry Blue drawled slowly. "It's going to take a heap of understanding for me to see how you could hook up with the man that hung your daddy."

"But he didn't hang him. He . . . Oh you don't understand, Larry. Why do we have to quarrel when you've just got here, when we haven't seen each other for fifteen years? Why can't we be friends? I always thought that you were the finest ever, Larry. Remember how I used to tag you around when we were kids and how you'd cook for me and look after me when father was off on a spree? Remember . . ?"

Larry Blue's face softened under the words. "We won't quarrel, kid," he said softly. "I'll say no more about it. If you want to hook up with Lester I won't like it, but I won't say a word. Only don't ask me to tie up with him. Don't ask me that!"

Don Blue had won a partial victory. He was shrewd enough to go no further with it at the moment. "How did you get hurt, Larry?" he asked. "I'd counted on your meeting me at La Junta and coming on down to Franklin with me. What happened? I had a letter from Truman . . . . ."

"Couple or three fellows got bad one night," Larry's tone was evasive. "Tried to hold up the place. We'd had an extra good clay and I didn't want to see it all go out, so I tried to stop them. One of them got me in the side before Royal came in."

"But the other two? What happened to them? Truman said that you took care of them. He said . . . did you kill them, Larry?"

"How come you didn't come over to Denver when I couldn't meet you at La Junta, kid?" asked Larry. "I kind of looked for you over there. I couldn't travel, but I

142

thought that you'd . . ."

"I was carrying some papers from Mr. Sutherland to Judge Lester," Don answered. "I had to get them down here right away or I'd have come to Denver. Of course I was disappointed when you didn't meet me, but having those documents; and there being a hurry about their getting here, I just came on."

Larry nodded at the explanation and Don amplified it. "You remember the Cross C, Larry? The big ranch north of town? Clark Andrews owned it. His wife inherited the property when he died. Well, Mrs. Andrews had a half brother named Archer Bolton. She had two half brothers, in fact: one in Boston and the other, Archer, here. The brother that lived in Boston died and Archer Bolton went back there and married his widow. She had two children, a girl, Constance, and a boy named DeWitt. Archer Bolton died in Boston not long ago and his stepchildren inherited his property. Mrs. Andrews is trying to get some of it. She has married again, a man named Seemans who is mayor here. I've been trying to help Judge Lester save the property for the children. I had a number of documents that pertained to the case and . . . What's the matter, Larry?"

Larry Blue's eyes were blank, as though he looked into distance. Indeed, he did look into distance, back over a period of years to a woodpile beside which he leaned on an ax, and where stood a thin-faced, handsome woman and two black-haired children.

"Nothing," answered Larry. "Go on, Don."

"Archer Bolton died intestate," said Don, resuming his story. "If he had made a will Mrs. Andrews— Seemans I suppose I should call her—would have no claim to the property at all."

143

"Is there much of an estate?" Larry asked curiously.

Don shook his head. "Not a great deal," he answered. "Bolton ran through a considerable amount that he inherited from his brother. In fact the only thing of value left is some river bottom land that lies along the railroad tracks north of Franklin here."

Larry's eyes widened. That would be the tract of land that had the rock house upon it where he had lived with Archer Bolton. He had ridden past it that afternoon and looked out at the waste of tornillo, sand and mesquite. Value in that land?

Don answered Larry's unspoken question. "A smelter company wants to buy the tract," he said. "There is limestone there, and some clay deposits. It is adjacent to the railroad. A number of mines west of here are concentrating their ore and shipping it. If the smelter can locate here at Franklin it will be a great thing. They have offered a hundred thousand dollars for the tract but it is in litigation and . . ."

"And they won't buy unless it's clear," completed Larry. "And you're helping get title to it for the Bolton kids?"

Don nodded. "Did you know any of them when you were here?" he asked. "Archer Bolton or Constance or DeWitt or Mrs. Seemans?"

"I might have known some of them a little," said Larry cautiously.

Don, removing a watch from his vest pocket, looked at it uneasily. "I think . . ." he began, "Judge Lester is expecting us to dinner and . . ."

"You go on and tell him I won't be there," directed Larry. "You can come back and eat with me. We've got a lot of visiting to do, Don. A whole lot."

"If you won't mind . . ." began Don. "I really ought to

144

tell the Judge that you won't be there. He was expecting you, Larry; looking forward to meeting you."

Larry shrugged. "You run along and tell him," he commanded. "And come back, Don."

"I'll be back," Don promised, and opening the door, smiled at Larry and went on out of the room.

When the door had closed behind his brother Larry Blue removed his coat and vest and unfastened his collar and tie. Then he lay back on the bed and stared at the ceiling. There were many things for Larry Blue to think about. Don's allying himself with Judge Lester, for instance. Larry did not like that, he did not like it at all. If he had his way. . . . He scowled at the ceiling. Perhaps after a while he might have his way, but it would take time. And then there were the Boltons: Archer Bolton dead, and the girl Constance, and the boy DeWitt. Larry remembered them, remembered them well. And Mrs. Andrews with the thin, handsome face, and Clark Andrews who would have liked to help a homeless waif and dared not; and old Duck Bunn and . . . Larry lay on his back for a long time while the shadows lengthened outside the Plaza Hotel, and Franklin sent up a drowsy humming through the open window.

Presently Larry roused himself. Rising from the bed he removed his shoulder harness and his shirt, casually inspected the wide bandage that swathed his middle, and then, going to the wash stand beside the window, poured the basin full of tepid water from the pitcher and began to remove the stains of travel. He had completed his toilet and was putting on a fresh shirt of fine white linen when there came a knock on the door.

"Yes?" Larry called.

"Gentleman down in the lobby to see you, Mr. Blue

came the answer.

"I'll be right down," called Larry, working with the bow of his tie. Footsteps receded down the corridor and Larry finished with his tie. Resuming his shoulder harness, setting the short-barreled, heavy Smith & Wesson in place under his arm, Larry donned vest and coat. Picking up his hat he brushed it carefully, used a towel on his boots, and then as clean as possible and cool once more, went out of his room and locked the door.

Don was waiting in the lobby. With him was a girl dressed in cool gray silk who stood laughing up at him. Larry reached the bottom of the stairs and, crossing the lobby, approached Don and his companion. The girl turned with a smile as Larry arrived and Don, bowing, made introduction.

"Constance, may I present my brother, Larry? Larry, this is Miss Bolton. She . . ."

"I returned with Don to insist that you come with us." The girl laid one gloved hand on Larry's arm, her black eyes meeting his blue ones. "Don said that you were tired and that you needed rest, but I insisted that he bring me. We have all heard so much about Don's brother Larry and have had your praises sung to us so that we just can't wait to know you better. You will come, won't you?"

"I . . ." began Larry.

"I know that you are tired after your journey and I know that you have been hurt, but please come." Constance Bolton was insistent. She had been denied little in her life and she did not now expect refusal. Larry stared at her. Under his scrutiny the color flooded her cheeks and she looked away.

"I can't refuse so pressing an invitation, Miss

146

Bolton," Larry said slowly. "If it will please you then I'll come."

The girl looked back at him. "Of course it pleases me," she said. "I knew that Don and I could persuade you. Shall we go?"

The girl turned to leave and Larry followed her and his brother out of the lobby. In the barouche the girl settled herself, Don beside her. Larry, taking the front seat, back to the driver, held himself bolt upright as the carriage rolled along toward the northern end of the town.

"Do you find Franklin changed, Mr. Blue?" questioned Constance. "Don says that he didn't remember it at all when he came back. I suppose there is a great deal of difference?"

"A good deal," Larry agreed gravely.

The barouche climbed a hill, wheeled before a long adobe house and stopped. Alighting from the seat the driver opened a wooden gate that gave egress to a patio. Don was on the ground helping Constance Bolton from the carriage, and Larry, when the girl had alighted, came down stiffly. As he walked toward the open gate, Don beside him and Constance Bolton on his other side, a man appeared, a gray-haired man, clean-shaven, deep lines etched in his face but with a pair of the steadiest blue eyes that Larry had ever seen.

"We brought him, Uncle Judge," Constance announced. "I knew that he couldn't resist us," she added gaily.

John Lester held out a fine, blue-veined hand. "I'm glad that you have come, Mr. Blue," he said courteously. "More than glad."

Perforce Larry took the extended hand, held it briefly and relinquished it. Constance went on through the gate

147

and the three men followed her, walking slowly. Candles flickered on the table set in the patio, for dusk had come. Judge Lester gravely indicated a chair.

"Won't you sit down, Mr. Blue?" he invited. "Don tells me that you are recovering from a wound. Did your trip tire you?"

Larry found himself in the chair, his hat taken by a soft footed servant who appeared and retired into the shadows. "I am not tired," he said. "Thank you for asking me to come, Judge Lester."

Lester waved away the thanks. Constance came from the house, her silk dress rustling softly, and from a door in the rear of the patio a servant appeared bearing a tray and glasses. "DeWitt will be here in a moment," announced the girl.

There was sherry, good sherry, in the thin glasses on the tray. While the servant passed the wine, a man, tall, dark haired, handsome in the candlelight, came from the house. He took a glass from the tray as he passed, and joined the others. Larry rose from his chair.

"Mr. Bolton, Mr. Blue," Judge Lester made the introductions.

DeWitt Bolton nodded and smiled at Larry, making no motion toward Larry's half-extended hand. Larry lowered the hand and turning slightly, lifted his glass. As he sipped the sherry he watched the others of the group.

"You are going out, DeWitt?" asked Judge Lester.

"I have an engagement," DeWitt answered carelessly.

"I'm sorry," Lester said, "I had hoped . . . ."

Without waiting for Lester to complete his sentence DeWitt crossed the patio and placing his glass on a small table, spoke to the servant who had once more appeared. "Is dinner served, Juan?"

"Come, Mr. Blue," directed Lester, turning from DeWitt. "I had dinner served in the patio. I thought it would be cooler and here on the hill we have no mosquitoes. Come, Constance. Come, Donald."

Seated at Judge Lester's right, with Constance Bolton across the table from the host and Don beside him, Larry looked at his companions. DeWitt was boldly handsome, echoing his sister's features and coloring. His forehead was good, broad and intelligent; his eyes were well placed, but there was a touch of petulance, a little weakness about the mouth and chin. Constance looked at Don, smiling at him, and Don, returning that look, fell into conversation with the girl. Judge Lester, gravely courteous, spoke to Larry, asking him questions concerning Denver and its vicinity that Larry answered somewhat absently.

When the meal was finished DeWitt excused himself and went into the house. Constance, after a moment, announced that she would leave the men with their cigars in the patio, and she also went in. Larry could hear her voice drifting out and DeWitt's deeper voice answering her. Presently a door closed and the voices ceased. Don rose from the table and put his hand on Larry's shoulder.

"I'll be back in a moment," he said. "Excuse me." Don too went into the house. Larry, turning back to Judge Lester, found the elderly man holding out a cigar.

"Thank you," said Larry. "I'll smoke a cigarette."

He rolled a thin cigarette, lit it from the candle that Lester held out to him, and puffed reflectively.

Judge Lester spoke softly. "You don't like me, Mr. Blue." Not a question, simply a statement of fact.

"No," Larry agreed, "I don't."

"I am sorry." Lester, having lighted his cigar, held it

in his long fingers. "I had hoped that you would."

"It makes no difference to you," stated Larry.

"You are wrong. It does make a difference."

There was quiet in the patio, then Larry said: "Why?"

"Because of Don," Lester answered. "And because...perhaps . . ."

"You sentenced my father to hang." Larry took a deep inhalation from his cigarette. "That was your duty maybe. I don't know. I've always thought that if he had had a smart lawyer he would have got off. My father was no good, I guess. He drank and he didn't look after his boys, but . . ."

"Still he was your father," finished Lester evenly.

"Yes."

"And so you wanted Don to be a lawyer?"

"Yes, I did. I don't know why exactly. I suppose I had some idea of his coming back here and putting it over on you. I don't know. I was a kid and kids have wild ideas."

"And now Don has come back and gone into partnership with me."

"And I don't like it."

Again silence interposed. Then Lester spoke again. "Are you going to try to take Don?" he asked.

"What would you do?" Larry asked.

Lester looked at the glowing end of his cigar. "I don't know," he answered. "I can give Don . . ."

"Don says he owes everything to you now." There was a trace of bitterness in Larry's voice.

The cigar end made a little glowing arc as Lester waved it. "That is not true, of course," he said. "He owes what he is to you. I have tried to help Don . . ."

"Why?"

"Because I felt that I should help him." Lester's voice

150

was strained. "When I was on the bench, Mr. Blue, I believed that the Law was right. I believed that I should cleave to the letter of the Law. Then my wife . . ." the voice softened, ". . . died. I learned that there was no mercy in the law; either the man-made law or the Higher Law. Since that time I have tried to temper the laws as I met them, tried to make them fit the facts and the occasion. Father Paul, as long as he lived, helped me. The law, through me, had deprived you and your brother of your father. I tried, as I could, to make amends. I did what I could for Don and I searched for you. I had hoped . . ."

"What did you want of me?"

"I didn't find you. Does it matter?"

"No," Larry agreed, after a moment, "it doesn't matter now."

The candles guttered in a little vagrant breeze. The night air was soft. "And so . . . ?" said Larry.

"And so Don has come to be with me, a partner in my business and my heir when I die," Lester finished.

"Have you told him that?"

"About the business, yes; the other no."

"Are you going to tell him?"

"I intended to," answered Lester after a momentary pause. "Now I don't think I shall. I want you to take Don with you, Mr. Blue."

Larry was shocked to silence. After a moment he got out one word: "Why?"

"Because . . ." Lester's voice was a drawl, "I . . . you saw Don with Constance, Mr. Blue?"

Instantly Larry jumped to conclusions. "You don't think Don is good enough for her," he challenged.

Lester shook his head. "That is not true," he refuted. "If you could take them both I would be pleased. I have come to love Constance as my own daughter, but if she and . . .Don . . ." He let the words trail off.

"Then what is it?" Larry snapped,

"This trouble over the Bolton estate," said Lester slowly. "Mrs. Seemans is trying to get a share of the estate. Archer Bolton died intestate and Constance and DeWitt are his heirs. I . . ."

"Don said something about it," Larry interrupted. "Why would you like Don to pull out?"

"Because Mrs. Seemans has engaged George Whiteman as her attorney," Lester stated positively. "I am afraid for Don."

"Why?"

"You don't know George Whiteman," answered Lester. "Whiteman is dangerous, Mr. Blue. He came here a few months ago and already he has acquired a reputation. Whiteman was a thief, a road agent, and a murderer. He was arrested for robbing the mails from a stage and sent to Leavenworth. While there he studied law. Somehow he was pardoned. When he got out he took the examinations in Austin and was admitted to the Bar. He came back here and joined Seemans. Seemans is a politician of the worst type. He is our mayor. He controls the marshal's office, the city council, and the police force. Franklin is wide open, Mr. Blue. The gambling dens, the brothels, every form of vice that exists, pay tribute to Seemans and when there is trouble Whiteman defends the case. He lost a case, his first one. Two days later he killed the man that opposed him. That cannot be proved but it is common knowledge. There is not a lawyer in Franklin or in this judicial district that will take a case against Whiteman. A jury cannot be impaneled that will bring in a verdict against him. And that is not all: Seemans has had Whiteman appointed as

152

prosecutor."

"It seems to me that you would do something about that," drawled Larry. "A town that has enough backbone to stand up for what's right can be decent if it wants to be."

In the dusk Larry could not see Lester flush. "We have done something," the lawyer said presently. "We have a citizens' committee here but so far we have not accomplished much. Personally I wrote to the Attorney General and to the Governor. I know them both. I asked that the Rangers be sent in to clean up the town. I received letters thanking me for my information and promising an investigation; but the matter has gone no further.

"Seemans is a politician. He controls a good many votes and of course the Governor and the Attorney General are elected officials." The old man's voice was bitter as he spoke the last sentence. It was an indictment.

"And the Federal people?" Larry asked. "How about them?"

"Seemans and Whiteman do not commit Federal offenses," Lester answered. "They stay clear. Why should they get into trouble when there is a rich field for them to work without that?"

Larry nodded. "Seemans runs the police and helps elect the district judge and he and Whiteman sit back and skim the cream," he recounted slowly. "I've seen it done. My pardner and I pay out considerable in Denver just for that sort of thing. We have to. It's part of our business."

The slow motion of Lester's head was Larry's only answer and Larry went on: "And you'd like me to get Don out of it," he said. "Don is all wrapped up in this girl and he'll go through with this case, and you're

153

afraid that Whiteman will come down on him. Is that it?"

Again Lester nodded.

"What would you do if Don left? Throw up the case?"

"No." Lester shook his head. "I wouldn't do that."

"You'd let Whiteman come down on you then?"

"Perhaps. I wish that you could get Don to go back to Denver with you, Mr. Blue. At least for a while. I think . . ."

Constance Bolton's voice came from the door. "Uncle Judge, will you and Mr. Blue come in now? Don has promised to sing if I play for him. We are in the music room."

Judge Lester arose. "Shall we go in, Mr. Blue?" he asked courteously.

# CHAPTER 12

### WHERE THERE'S A WILL . . .

IT WAS TWELVE O'CLOCK BEFORE JUDGE LESTER'S carriage delivered Larry Blue and his brother at the door of the Plaza Hotel. Larry, descending to the sidewalk, spoke to Don.

"Come on up a while," he urged. "We've hardly got to talk yet."

Don looked at the driver. "What about . . .?" he began.

"You can take a cab home," said Larry. "Come on in."

Telling the Judge's driver that he need not wait, Don accompanied his brother into the Plaza's lobby. In

154

Larry's room, the lamp lighted and a little night wind fluttering the curtains, Don took a chair and Larry relaxed upon the bed. Propped up by pillows and with his hands locked behind his blond head, he looked at Don. Don was good to look at, Larry thought; young, keen, handsome. Don's lips were curved in a half-smile as he watched his brother with bright blue eyes.

"You've come a long ways, Don," Larry said suddenly. "A mighty long ways. You always were a good kid, though. Remember our last talk when I took you out to Father Paul's?"

Don nodded. "Father Paul," he said, a tinge of reverence in his voice. "I owe a lot to that old man, Larry. He wrote me regularly before he died. He was . . ."

"A mighty fine man," Larry said softly.

"Did you know that he looked for you?" Don asked. "He came to town to find you. Asked the sheriff and the marshal both to make a search, and looked all over town himself. He wanted to adopt you when he adopted me."

Larry nodded absently. "I didn't know at the time," he said. "You wrote me about it. Remember?" Larry smiled and then chuckled softly. "That was what Seemans wanted of me, I reckon," he said. "I wasn't letting Seemans find me though. I'd rolled some beer barrels down on Seemans when he was laying for a man, and I was scared plumb to death of him. I surely hid out." He laughed freely at the recollection and Don joined in the mirth.

"You must have covered some country after you left here," said Don when the laughter was spent. "I never did know just where you went. For a while Father Paul got letters from you and then I went East and . . ."

"I went around," Larry said slowly. "I stayed close to

155

here for a time and then I picked up with a trapper. I stayed with him until he was killed. . . ." A momentary savageness crossed Larry's face. Don, watching closely, caught that glimpse of ferocity and almost recoiled from it. It was as though suddenly a mask had been stripped away and the grim elemental force beneath it exposed. Then Larry's face was smooth once more and his voice, passionless, went on. "I tied up with a cow outfit," he continued.

"Punched cattle for a while and then got to riding race horses and then into cards. I've been with them ever since."

"Your partner, Mr. Truman, wrote to me," announced Don. "I have his letter at the office. He must be quite a man."

Larry Blue nodded. "Royal will do," he said, and then, more slowly, "Royal will do to take along."

Don Blue did not realize it but he had just heard spoken the highest approbation that Larry was capable of giving. The tone had been casual, the words prosaic, a miracle of understatement. Don, Eastern-raised although Western-born, seized what he thought was his moment.

"Why don't you sell out up there?" he asked, easily. "Why don't you get your money out of your partnership and come down here? You and I could be together then. I know of a dozen chances where a man could invest his capital in good, respectable business ventures. How much could you put into a business, Larry?"

Larry caught that word, "respectable," and a glint of amusement showed on his face, then was erased. "I suppose I've got a hundred thousand," he drawled. "I own a piece in a mine or two. Royal and I have a livery barn in Denver that does pretty well. We own two

156

saloons and a restaurant, and then of course," Larry spoke slowly, "there's the card rooms."

"Why . . ." Don was flustered. "I had no idea, Larry. I had no idea that you were engaged in so many things. I thought that you were . . ."

"A gambler?" finished Larry. "I am. That's what makes me money."

"But these other ventures. Surely they . . ."

"They're side lines," Larry said succinctly. "I gamble for a living. You want me to sell out and come down here. I can't quite see it that way. Royal and I make a pretty good team. Royal has put me on my feet and in a way I've put Royal on his. You see, Royal thought that he had to look after me."

There was the explanation, simple enough as it stood. Nothing said about the bond of friendship between the two, Royal Truman and Larry Blue. Nothing mentioned of the lean times, the hard sledding, the tough days. Simply: "Royal thought he had to look after me." And to look after Larry Blue, Royal Truman had sunk every dollar that he could into sound hard business ventures and gone back to the card tables, the faro layouts, and the roulette wheels to make more. And Larry? Larry had looked after Royal, too.

Don digested Larry's statement in silence. Larry gave him time to think and then spoke again. "You've made your proposition," he said gently. "Are you ashamed of me because I'm a gambler, Don?"

"No!" Don's answer came quickly, almost fiercely; perhaps too quickly and too fiercely, Larry did not notice that. "No," was answer enough and it pleased him.

"Now I'll make you one," Larry drawled. "You come back with me. Shake this two-bit business here. Come

157

on back to Denver. Things are stirring in Denver, and I'm in them. You come back with me. You'll have all the law you can practice in thirty days. In a year you can run for office if you want to. County attorney or maybe the state legislature. I know the right people and Royal knows those I don't. How would you like to be Governor or a United States Senator some day, kid?"

Here was temptation. Don Blue was an ambitious young man. There lolling on the bed was his brother, a brother that he had not seen for a long time and a man who held out those things that any ambitious young man might crave. And, looking at Larry, Don knew that Larry's proposal was no idle talk. Larry Blue would go through. Larry would give him those things he held out, would make them possible. All Don had to do was say, "Yes."

Don shook his head. "I can't, Larry," he answered.

"Not good enough for you?" Larry's eyes narrowed.

Again Don's blond head was shaken. "You don't understand," he said. "It isn't that I don't want the things you've talked about. It isn't that. But you were at Judge Lester's tonight, Larry."

Larry caught the meaning of his brother's words. He flushed a little. "It's not good enough," he repeated. "Let me tell you, Don, Royal and I have sat at the Governor's table. The Mayor of Denver calls me Larry. His wife invites me to their home. You think . . ."

Again Don shook his head. "No," he said and a touch of the fierceness that lay under Larry's eyes was echoed in Don's. "I've got to make this myself. I've got to . . ."

"Young lawyers don't make it themselves," Larry said cynically. "What you mean is that you'll take from Lester what you won't take from me."

Silence fell upon the two. Don broke it. "You're
158

unfair," he said hotly. "You're unfair to me and to Judge Lester. I won't take anything from him that I wouldn't take from you, but I've come down here to help in this Bolton matter. I . . ."

"If the Bolton matter was cleaned up you'd go with me?" Larry's eyes were hard and shrewd and keen.

Don made a little, petulant gesture. "You make it hard, Larry," he said. "I'm here. Judge Lester has taken me in as his partner. A while ago when I suggested that you come down here you turned me down short enough. Now you want me to give up what I have and come with you. . . ."

"To have more," Larry said, implacably. "What is it, kid? Out with it! Are you ashamed of me?"

"No! It's just that I . . . Damn it, Larry, won't you see?"

On the bed Larry stirred, bringing his hands from behind his head and reaching into his vest pockets for corn husks and tobacco. He twisted a thin smoke and held out the makings to Don. Don shook his head and pulled out a cigar. Both men lit their smokes.

"I'm kind of dumb," said Larry. "I guess I'm kind of dumb. Well kid, we won't press it. I'll be here a few days and visit with you and you come up to Denver and visit with me. Some way we'll get together."

Relief flooded Don's face, "That's the talk," he said. "You come to the office tomorrow, Larry. We'll have lunch together and then take half a day off and go around and look up all the places that we used to know when we were kids. Come about ten o'clock."

"I'll do that," Larry agreed.

"I've got to go now." Don got up from his chair. "Constance is sitting up waiting for DeWitt. DeWitt has an affair with a show girl and it worries Constance. I generally . . ."

"You like her a heap, don't you?" Larry swung his feet over the edge of the bed and sat up.

Don colored. "I like her," he agreed.

Larry made a little humming "Mmm" under his breath. "Who is DeWitt tied up with?" he asked.

"A girl named Bondreaux," answered Don. "She is the prima donna (God save the mark!) with that traveling theatrical troupe here. From what I learn, half of the gamblers and highbinders in town are following her. She . . ." Don stopped and colored, realizing what he had said.

Larry laughed. "You go on home to your girl, kid," he commanded gently. "You and me will get together tomorrow."

The two shook hands at the door in parting and Larry watched Don as he passed down the corridor to the stairs. When Don was gone Larry closed the door and, as a matter of habit, placed a chair under the knob. He undressed slowly and when the light was out and he lay in bed, he stared up at the velvety blackness above him, his mind busy.

He had offered Don a good deal and Don had turned it down. In a way that pleased Larry. Don was a man and wanted to stand on his own two feet. When Judge Lester put in his word perhaps Don would change. Perhaps he would go back to Denver, at least to look the place over. There was that possibility.

But Don was proud and despite his protestations Don was a little ashamed of Larry. Larry knew men and he believed that he knew Don. There was still some Eastern stiffness in Don. Give him a little time. That was the medicine: time. And what was it Don had said about DeWitt? DeWitt was having an affair with a girl

160

named Bondreaux. Into Larry Blue's mind that name brought a recollection of a blond-headed sprite of a girl with dark eyes. A girl that followed him like a shadow. Annette Bondreaux! Larry wondered if this girl, this girl that DeWitt was pursuing, could possibly be Annette. Thinking of her he drowsed off.

Larry Blue awakened at the leisurely hour of eight. He stretched, yawned, and presently got up. When his toilet was made, freshly shaven and immaculate in clean linen, he went down the stairs and to the dining room of the Plaza.

After breakfast, with a cigarette sending up blue spirals, he walked out into Franklin's sunlit street. Following directions he had gained from the clerk at the desk, he made his leisurely way north and east and presently came to the two-story brick building that housed, so the sign said, the law offices of John Lester.

Larry went up stairs, along a hall, and entered an anteroom. Two rooms led off the anteroom and from one of these came voices. Larry, standing in the waiting room, heard Don's deep voice and the quieter, lighter voice of Lester. Presently Don came out, saw Larry, and crossing to him, shook hands and gave a greeting.

"I have some business to talk over with the Judge," he said. "Come into my office and wait for me. I won't be long."

To this Larry agreed, and followed Don into the second of the two rooms. Don took a file of papers from the desk, excused himself and entered Lester's office. Larry sat down behind the desk. Through the open doors of the next office the voices resumed their humming.

Larry had nothing to do but wait. He rolled a cigarette and lit it. He toyed with the letter opener and the paper weights on Don's desk. Still the voices hummed on.

Looking about, Larry's eyes fell upon a letter on the desk. Here was a letter to Don in Larry's own handwriting. Larry picked up the letter and scanned it. The first few words told him that this was not of his writing. Larry turned the sheet and on the back saw the signature, "Archer Bolton."

An amused smile crossed Larry's face. Pulling a sheet of blank foolscap toward him, Larry dipped a pen and wrote a sentence, then held up the letter and what he had written, for comparison. They were identical. Larry wrote another line and again made comparison. Word for word, letter for letter, flourish for flourish, the words on the two sheets echoed each other. Archer Bolton! Archer Bolton had taught him to write. Larry's mind flashed back to those days in the rock house, to the weary hours of meticulous copying there, to the days when old Jim Cardwine had bent down over his shoulder as Larry strove to copy the exercises that Archer Bolton had set. How careful Jim had been that Larry make an exact duplicate. Nothing but perfection would suit the old trapper! Larry tapped the desk top with his pen. The letter and the sheet of paper were forgotten. Steps sounded in the anteroom and hastily, almost guiltily, Larry put down the pen and swung in the swivel chair so that he looked out the window.

"Tired of waiting?" asked Don from the door. "I won't be long now, Larry. Judge Lester wants some papers from the Bolton file. Tell me: Why will a man as smart as Archer Bolton be fool enough not to make a will?"

"I don't know," Larry answered. "Maybe he did. Have you been through everything he left?"

"Time and again." Don was going through a thick envelope. "If he made a will we would not have missed it."

"But you might have," said Larry, casually, hiding the gleam in his eyes. "It might be inside something that you hadn't unfolded or . . ."

"Not a chance," Don laughed. "I'll be back in a few minutes, Larry." He went out of the office and Larry swung swiftly to the desk.

Pulling a fresh sheet of paper to him he dipped his pen and scratched busily, signing a name with a flourish at the bottom of what he wrote. Then reading it over, he shook his head. This was not right; this was too hasty. He must try again. Larry crumpled the sheets he had written, thrust them into the side pocket of his coat and again essayed his task. Once more he wrote across the sheet, his hand moving rapidly and without hesitation:

Boston, Mass.,
Jan. 1, 18—

"Being of sound mind and desiring to dispose of my worldly goods," Larry was remembering his own will now, the will that he had made in Don's favor, and with Royal Truman as executor, "I hereby leave all my worldly possessions to my two children, Constance and DeWitt Bolton, to be shared by them equally."

Larry paused. Who should be executor of this will? Don? No, that would not do. Judge Lester? No again, for Archer Bolton would not appoint a man he did not know. The lawyer back in Boston! What was his name? "I hereby appoint Alexander Sutherland to be executor with this will attached," Larry wrote on, and then once more he signed a name: "Archer Bolton."

Larry waved the paper in the air. Time was short. Disregarding the fact that the ink might not have dried perfectly, he folded the document, got up from the chair, and thrust it into the envelope file from which Don had

163

just removed documents. He had scarcely regained his chair before Don came in.

"Finished," exclaimed Don. "Wouldn't you like to visit the Judge a moment?" He was tucking documents back in the file as he spoke.

Larry shook his head. "I don't suppose the Judge is very keen to see me," he answered. "Why don't you go through that file again, Don? There is a chance that you've overlooked that will. I knew Archer Bolton when I was just a kid."

Don laughed. "I tell you I've been through it twenty times."

"Twenty-one won't hurt," Larry drawled. "We've got plenty of time."

"There's no use wasting it," Don replied. Still his fingers toyed with the file even as he spoke. "I know exactly what's in there. Know it by heart. Here is a deed to the property here. Here is a certificate for some worthless stock that Bolton bought. Here is a letter that he wrote to Clark Andrews, his brother-in-law, and another to his half-sister, Luella. She is Mrs. Seemans now. Here is a . . . what's this?" Don pulled a sheet of paper from the file. There was no superscription on the sheet. Larry had not had time for that. Don looked at the paper and slowly, almost mechanically, unfolded it. "Why . . ." he said. "Why . . . my God, Larry!"

With no further word he wheeled and started hastily toward the door, then stopped, turned and slowly came back to the desk. "Do you know what this is?" he demanded.

Larry's face was the impassive, expressionless mask of the professional gambler. "What is it?" he asked.

"It's a will." Don's voice was vibrant. "A holograph will. Here against the back of the file. Stuck under the

164

flap. Do you suppose . . ?"

He walked over to a chair and sat down, staring at the paper he held. "This leaves everything to Constance and DeWitt," he announced, not lifting his eyes from the paper. "It appoints Sutherland executor. Why . . . why . . . this is wonderful. This . . . why, this doesn't leave Seemans a leg to stand on."

"It always pays to look," drawled Larry.

"But how did you know?" Don's eyes were two bright slits leveled at Larry above the paper. "How did you . . ?"

"Hunch," Larry stated flatly. "Gamblers play hunches, kid. You better take that in to Lester. That cleans this up, doesn't it? There's nothin' tying you here now."

Don got up from where he sat and crossed slowly to the desk, looking down at his brother. "Larry," he said slowly, "I've seen your writing and for the last few months I have examined a good deal of Archer Bolton's. There's a similarity between them. A great deal of similarity."

"That so?" Larry drawled.

"Yes. You want me to go north with you. You want me . . . Larry, take a pen and a piece of paper and write what I tell you."

"Sure." Larry reached out and took a pen and paper.

"Being of sound mind and desiring to dispose of my worldly goods," Don dictated. Larry's pen scratched busily. No tremor in his hand, no attempt to change or disguise a letter or a word.

"Now give that here," Don commanded.

Larry held out the paper. Don took it, held the two sheets up before him, looked from one to the other, looked at Larry and back again. "They are identical," he announced. "Larry, you wrote that will."

Not a muscle stirred in Larry Blue's impassive face. His eyes met Don's, locked with them, and held. "If you think so, tear it up," directed Larry Blue.

Don put the papers on the desk, face up, looked at them, and looked back at Larry. "Did you write that?" he demanded.

Larry could hardly repress a smile. Don was between the devil and the deep blue sea. Don was in a hard spot. Larry could almost see what was going on in his brother's mind. He believed, Don did, that Larry had written that document, that will lying on the desk before him. He believed it and yet he could not be sure. The will had come from the file of papers containing all the documents pertaining to the Bolton case. It had been back underneath an envelope flap. It might have been overlooked in the many times those documents had been surveyed. If it was authentic, if it was truly Archer Bolton's will, then it was precious beyond belief. And if it were not; if Larry had written it, why then, what? Don did not know. Don did not tear up the will.

"Did you write that?" Don demanded again.

"Suppose I did," Larry asked, "then what?"

"Then I'll tear it up," Don flared. "I won't be crooked, not for you, not for . . ."

"And suppose I didn't?" Larry drawled again.

Don hung his head. He could not meet Larry's eyes and through his own expose the turmoil of his mind.

Steps sounded in the anteroom and Judge Lester stood in the doorway. He nodded and spoke pleasantly to Larry. "Good morning, Mr. Blue. Don said that you were here. I thought that I . . . What is the matter, Don?"

Don looked up, his face strained.

Larry answered the question. "Don's coppered a bet,"

166

he said gently. "He's found a will."

"What!" The exclamation was fairly jerked from Lester. Two swift steps and he had pushed Don aside and reached the desk. Snatching up the paper he read it through and as he read, first incredulity, then surprise, and finally a great relief showed on his face. "Why, Don," exclaimed the judge. "Why . . . where did you find this?"

Don gestured toward the Manila file. "There," he said. "In the back under a flap."

"And we've overlooked it all this time!" Lester exclaimed. "My boy, do you realize what this means? Do you realize what this does? He leaves everything to Constance and DeWitt. Sutherland is appointed Executor and I hold Sutherland's power of attorney. A holograph may not be witnessed. This . . . why this is perfect!" Lester's hand was on Don's shoulder now. Almost he embraced the boy.

Beneath Larry Blue's dark mustache a smile flickered briefly.

"When I show this to George Whiteman and to Luella Seemans," said John Lester, "our difficulties will be over. The smelter company will buy that river property immediately. Constance and DeWitt will have their due. Don, this, this is perfect." The Judge could not keep the exultation from his voice.

Larry Blue got up from behind the desk. "I reckon," he drawled pleasantly, "that you and Don will have plenty to do now, Judge. I reckon you'll be busy. Don and I will postpone our little visit. I'll be at the hotel, Don, when you get through." He paused and smiled at his brother. "And make up your own mind, kid," he said softly.

Don followed Larry to the door. "I want to talk to

167

you," he snapped. "I've got to talk to you, Larry. I'll come to the hotel."

"Come along," Larry urged. "We'll visit:' He grinned sardonically at his brother. "And don't try to tell Lester that I wrote that will," he murmured. "He won't believe you, kid."

Don opened his mouth to speak but Larry did not wait for the words. He swung away from his brother and went on out.

# CHAPTER 13

## THE PRIMA DONNA

LARRY BLUE, EMERGING INTO THE BRILLIANT SUN-light of Franklin's street, settled his black hat a little lower over his eyes and glanced at his watch. It was just past eleven o'clock. Not time enough to do anything of importance before lunch and still time that would hang heavily. Turning east on the board sidewalk that stretched before the office building, Larry walked along smiling to himself. He had just put it up to Don. He wondered, as he walked, what Don would do. Larry shrugged. Judge Lester would probably govern Don's actions and Larry had no doubt as to how the Judge would proceed. That will, forgery that it was, was as good as probated right now!

The sun directly overhead beat down hotly. The black hat and black broadcloth coat that Larry wore were not the coolest garments in the world. Larry slowed his brisk pace and looked up and down the street. As though in answer to that look a cab rounded the corner and came toward him. This was not a new cab, nor were the horses particularly spirited. The driver, a portly figure, had laid aside his coat, and suspenders were outlined against a none too clean white shirt. The driver's hair was gray under his plug hat. His nose was bulbous and shining with something other than sunburn. From cheeks and chin a stubble of gray beard sprouted.

The driver swung the vehicle toward the curb. "Cab?" he asked.

In answer Larry opened the door and climbed in. Half of the cab top was rolled back, giving from the back seat a view of the driver's perspiring neck and his soiled collar. Larry, settling back on the worn cushions, automatically avoiding a broken spring, looked up through the opening.

"I'll go to the Plaza," he said.

For answer the driver grunted and the horses moved ahead.

Larry surveyed the neck and collar before him. They were familiar; oddly reminiscent. Another cab passing to the left rattled by, its driver hailing Larry's coachman. "Hi, Duck."

Larry's driver raised his whip in response.

"Are you Duck Bunn?" Larry asked, leaning forward.

Upon the seat the neck wrinkled as it turned. "What if I am?" demanded a gruff voice.

Larry Blue smiled. "Not a thing," he returned. "You cooked for the Cross C one time, didn't you?"

"And if I did?" Antagonism in the question.

"Did Archer Bolton ever come back?" Larry pursued.

The driver said, "Whoa!" squirmed around on the seat and peered through the open cab top. "Who," he demanded, "in the hell are you?"

Larry chuckled. "The last time I saw you you were riding an English saddle and swearing because there

169

wasn't anything under you. Remember, Duck?"

Duck Bunn's bewhiskered face disappeared. The cab creaked and rocked as he came down from his seat; then eyes wide with incredulity, the face was thrust into the open window beside Larry.

"Damned if you ain't Larry Blue!" ejaculated Duck Bunn.

Larry held out his hand. Duck took it after wiping his own palm on the seat of his pants. They shook hands solemnly and gradually Duck's wrinkled face creased into a smile that echoed Larry's own.

"By gosh," said Duck, "you made it, didn't you? I figgered you'd been hung or somethin'. How are you, Larry?"

"Pretty good, Duck," Larry answered. "And you?"

"I make out," Duck said. "I eat pretty regular an' sleep good. What's brung you back to Franklin?"

"A little business. Have you been here all the time, Duck? When did you leave the Cross C?"

"When Clark Andrews died. I couldn't stand that damn' hellcat of a wife he had, so I pulled out. Then she sold the ranch and the new man had his own crew."

"Been driving a hack since then?"

"Not all the time. I've been here an' there. Been in Franklin since the railroads come in. Yo're lookin' prosperous, Larry."

"I've made a little."

Duck pulled a plug of chewing tobacco from a pocket, eyed it, brushed it off and offered it to Larry. When Larry shook his head, Duck gnawed off a corner, got the chew under control, and spat.

"Didja ever see old Jim Cardwine again?" he asked, returning the plug to his pocket. "Old Jim thought a lot of you, kid."

"I saw him." Larry's answer was brief. "I lived with him a couple of years. He's dead. What happened to Bolton, Duck? Did he ever come back?"

Duck shook his head and spat again. "Naw, he never come back," he said. "How long you goin' to be here, Larry?"

"For a while. I don't know just how long for sure. I'm stopping at the Plaza."

Duck nodded. "An' I better be takin' you there," he stated. "If you want a cab while yore in town, Larry, I got a place in that cab rack up by the corner close to the hotel. I ain't got the best cab in town, but . . ."

"It's plenty good enough for me," stated Larry Blue, "and I want you to drive me."

Duck nodded his satisfaction, grinned at Larry, and climbed back up on the seat. "Giddap!" he ordered. And then turning, looked back through the open top. "Any time or anywhere, Larry," he announced, "I'll be on hand."

At the hotel, asking Duck to call for him that afternoon, Larry watched the cab roll away, lifting his hand as a parting salute to Duck.

In his room Larry removed his coat and as he did so a paper crackled in his pocket. With a grin he reached in a hand and produced the crumpled sheets. Lighting a match he touched the flame to the papers and held them until the heat burned his fingers. Then hanging his coat over the back of a chair he crossed the room to the bed and sat down. He had, he believed, done a good stroke of business.

Passing the desk on his way to the dining room that noon a thought struck Larry and he addressed the clerk. 'I heard there's a show in town. Is it any good?" he asked.

The clerk, a sleek-haired young man with an incipient mustache that he tried vainly to curl, nodded emphatically. "Best show that's been in Franklin," he stated. "They built the opera house here two years ago and had Madame Patti an' some more here to open it. But this girl they've got there now has got Patti backed right off the boards. I'll tell you, Mr. Blue, she's all right."

Larry smiled. Evidently Annette had an admirer in the clerk. "What's her name?" he inquired.

"Annette Bondreaux. Sing? Say! An' looks! An'. . ." He winked broadly at Larry.

"Ummmmm," said Larry. "That way, is it?"

The clerk leaned forward earnestly. "I don't know, you understand," he confided, "but they say that she's got half the men in town on her string. This young Bolton that lives up at Judge Lester's and George Whiteman, and I guess the Mayor himself, only he's afraid of his wife."

"You don't say!" said Larry. "Where does she stay? Here?"

"No." The clerk shook his head. "The whole troupe stays down at the Oxford. It's a kind of cheap dump down by the station. I told the boss when they came, I said, 'Mr. Carmichael, it would be good advertising for the Plaza if we had that theatre troupe up here. We could give them rates and they'd bring business to the house.' But he couldn't see it that way. Seems like I never make a suggestion but what he turns it down." The clerk's voice took on a plaintive tone.

Larry was in no mood for adolescent confidence. He said "Thanks" briefly, nodded to the clerk, and went on to the dining room.

When Duck Bunn halted his cab before the Plaza

Hotel at two o'clock, Larry was waiting for him. He nodded to Duck, and climbing into the cab, gave directions. "I want to go down to the Oxford, Duck," he said. "I'll stop there a while. You wait for me."

Duck nodded his understanding and the cab moved away from the sidewalk.

The Oxford Hotel was not particularly pretentious. Where the Plaza was brick and three stories tall, the Oxford was frame and its third story was a false front. The Plaza was; the Oxford had been. Leaving the cab at the curb Larry went into the tawdry lobby.

The clerk at the desk was a native who stared long and hard at Larry Blue. Larry paid no particular attention to the stare but asked if he might see Miss Bondreaux. At that question several women in the lobby giggled and resumed the conversation they had interrupted at Larry's entrance. The clerk was bland, polite, and adamant. Miss Bondreaux was in her room and had asked not to be disturbed.

Larry knew how to deal with such situations. "You tell her that there's an old friend of hers in the lobby," he ordered. "Just tell her that." The green edge of the bill showed under the hand that Larry placed on the counter.

"For an ol' friend Mees Bondreaux ees een," the clerk beamed, his hand sliding out toward the bill. "I weel tell her. She ees esleep most of the afternoon . . ."

"You get that when you come back," stated Larry. "I want to see Miss Bondreaux."

The clerk's smile changed to a frown, returned with renewed force, and he scurried out from behind the desk. Larry leaned against the counter, waiting. In the lobby the women chattered low voiced. Several looked toward him and smiled half-invitations. Larry did not return the smiles. The clerk came back down the stairs, reached for the bill and said: "Numero twenty-two, señor."

Larry released the bill, nodded, and turned toward the stairs.

Upstairs he went along the corridor, stopped at a numbered door and knocked. A voice said: "Come in," and turning the knob Larry entered. Annette Bondreaux sat on a chair across the room, beside the opened window. The room was stifling hot and only the tiny fluttering of the dingy curtain told of stirring air. Just inside the door Larry stopped.

Annette had drawn her long silken robe close about her when the summons came at the door, and now holding it closed with one small hand, she stared at her visitor. The robe did not completely conceal the softly rounded curves of shoulders and breasts, and opened at the throat, exposing the ivory pillar of the girl's throat. Annette's blond hair was cut short and curled in damp ringlets, making a golden frame for her face. Larry, looking at that face, met the deep darkness of the girl's eyes and looked no further.

"Larry!" There was wonderment in Annette's voice. "Larry Blue!" She made a little gesture with her free hand as one will who brushes aside an apparition, and then very slowly she came to her feet. "Larry!" she exclaimed again.

Larry Blue found that there was a choke in his throat as he tried to speak. The words he wanted would not come. He took a step toward the girl, his hand automatically pushing shut the door behind him. Annette, great, dark eyes staring, stood motionless.

Larry got out words. "Annette! It's me. I'm . . ." He got no further. With one swift motion the girl was across the room, her hands on Larry's shoulders, her head against his chest.

"Larry," she sobbed. "Larry!"

For an instant Larry Blue felt the soft warmth of her body against him, felt the silken smoothness of her shoulders at his arms went up and his hands rested on them. Then the girl pushed herself back, tilted her face up to his and looked into his eyes. "I . . ." she began. "Why, Larry, I never thought it would be you. I never thought I would see you again. The clerk said that there was a gambler in the lobby that wanted to see me, a man who said that he was an old friend. I . . . It is you, Larry? You're really Larry Blue?"

Larry pushed the girl away now and holding her by her shoulders smiled down into her upturned face. "It's really me," he assured. "Larry Blue. But I never thought that I'd find you, Annette. I heard that there was an Annette Bondreaux in town with the theatrical troupe. Just on the chance that it might be you, I came . . ."

"And found me!" Now that she had regained her poise Annette freed herself from Larry's hands, standing clear of him. "Sit down, Larry. It has been a long time since we saw each other. A long time." She laughed, a treble, tinkling trill. "Remember," she continued, "remember the last time I saw you, and how we ran?"

Larry smiled. He took the chair the girl indicated, sat down and placed his hat upon his knees. Annette, crossing the room from him, sat down upon the bed, arranged her robe about her and swung one small, slippered foot. "How you have changed," she said. "I remember . . . Did you do all the things that you planned, Larry? Did you send Don to school and make a lawyer of him? Did you . . ?"

"I did some of the things," Larry interrupted the flow

175

of questions. "Some I didn't do. And you, Annette? How do you come to be here? What has happened to you? How have you been?"

Annette shrugged. Her wide, mobile mouth made a small grimace that was instantly erased. "I am here because I am the singer with Sam Levine's troupe," she said. "We are on tour. As for what has happened to me . . ." Again she shrugged.

Larry looked about the little room. It was typical of the Oxford and of a thousand hotels like the Oxford. Larry Blue knew the room well. With Royal Truman, in the lean years, he had been in many such another. Annette, following his eyes, spoke the thing that he was thinking.

"Not very fine, Larry. But good enough for a singer in a fourth-rate troupe."

The bitterness in her voice was a shock to Larry. Again he looked closely at the girl, his eyes a little narrowed. "Tell me about it, Annette," commanded Larry suddenly. "Tell me."

Something in the words, some force of tone or inflection, reached through the hardness that the girl had momentarily thrown about herself. The dark eyes softened. "You can see," she said with a small gesture of her white hand. "My father was killed. Maman," Larry started as he recalled how Annette had always used that word in reference to her mother, "took me to Chicago where we had relatives. We lived there. I worked in a cafe for a while after I was old enough. Then Maman died. My aunt . . ." Again a shrug expressed more than words. "Well, I was young and I had a little voice. I thought that I could sing. I went into a chorus in a burlesque show. One of the principals became ill and I took her place. Since then I have . . .

But why are we talking about me, Larry? What of you?"

"How long have you been with this outfit?" Larry demanded, disregarding the question. "Do they treat you all right? Are you getting along all right?"

Again the little gesture with the hands, and a shrug. "I am the principal with the troupe," Annette answered. "I sing and I dance a little and I am paid for it. I live well enough. Now, Larry! What are you doing here? Why are you in Franklin? What has happened to you since that night that we ran?"

Larry grinned. Mentally he resolved that he would make things easier for Annette. Principal with the company or not, he did not like these surroundings. Annette was . . . Annette deserved better than this. He, Larry Blue, would see that she had it. "There's nothing much to tell about me," he drawled. "I left Franklin that night we got caught out behind your father's place. I drifted around some. Wound up gambling. I've done pretty well at it."

Annette's eyes traveled over Larry, surveying him from the crown of his blond head to the tips of his expensive, shop-made boots. She nodded. "You have done well," she agreed. "And why did you come to Franklin?"

"To see Don," Larry answered frankly. "Don's come down here and gone into business. He's a lawyer. I want to get him to go back to Denver with me."

"And he won't go?"

"No." Larry shook his head. "He won't go. You see, Annette, there's a girl . . ."

"And Don will not give her up for his brother," Annette finished. "Men are foolish, Larry. I see many men and know how foolish they are."

"I'd take the girl back with him," Larry stated. "What

177

I want is Don. I've spent most of my life trying to get Don where he is. Now I want him and he won't come."

"Have you talked with the girl?" Annette asked, colorlessly.

"No, I haven't."

"You might try, Larry," the words came slowly. "Women understand things, sometimes. I believe that a woman would understand your wanting Don. Sometimes a woman . . . Why don't you talk with her, Larry?"

"I'm going to," answered Larry, strongly. "Thanks, Annette. I . . ."

A knock on the door interrupted the rest of his sentence. Annette, rising from the bed, crossed to the door and opened it. From the hall a voice said, "Thees letter, señorita, ees give me for deliver. I . . ."

Annette said, "Thanks," and closing the door, came back into the room. "You will forgive me?" she asked, looking at Larry.

"Go ahead," said Larry Blue.

The girl opened the note, read it through swiftly, and then crumpling the written page, tossed it to the bed. Her eyes were preoccupied with some inner thought as she turned to Larry again. Larry caught that expression.

"I've got to go now, Annette," he said, rising. "I wanted to find out if it was my Annette Bondreaux here in Franklin, and I've found out. Can you have dinner with me, or supper after the show? I . . ."

"Not tonight," Annette said quickly. "I have an engagement for tonight."

"No, not tonight," Larry agreed. "Don is coming to see me tonight. We'll make it another time. You set the date."

Annette hesitated. Larry thought that he understood

178

that hesitation. He smiled. "You can get hold of me any time," he said. "I'm at the Plaza Hotel. You find out when you'll be free and drop me a note. We'll go out and look the old town over and have some fun. Good-by, Annette."

"I'll make it soon, Larry," Annette assured. "Good-by now, and I'll surely see you."

"Unless you're blind," Larry answered, and smiling to the girl, went down the stairs.

# CHAPTER 14

### RUNAWAY

THERE WAS A NOTE FOR LARRY AT THE PLAZA DESK, A square envelope addressed in the fine legal script that Larry had come to recognize as Don Blue's handwriting. Don was curt and precise. Larry could not repress a smile when he read the missive. Don was angry. Larry could see the anger bristling from every word and phrase. Yet the note was pleasant reading. Don wrote that he was busy and would be engaged throughout the afternoon. Larry would understand. Larry's grin broadened. He did understand. The will that he had written had given Don something to work on. Still, the note continued, Don wanted to see his brother and would be at the Plaza Hotel at seven.

Having finished reading Don's note, Larry unfolded the second sheet of paper that had been in the envelope. His eyes widened as he read what was written. Constance Bolton hoped that Mr. Blue would drive with her that afternoon. She would call with the carriage at four, when the sun was less inclement. Larry, after a

179

hasty glance at his watch, fairly ran up the stairs to his room.

He was back in the lobby at four, freshly shaved for the second time that day, linen immaculate, boots shined to perfection, coat and trousers brushed and furbished. Larry's eyes were on the windows and when Judge Lester's barouche drew up before the Plaza he was at the entrance, ready to step into the street.

Still he waited until the coachman had dismounted from the seat and come into the hotel before he stepped out. Something restrained his eagerness. Larry followed the dark-skinned native out to the carriage and removing his hat, stood beside the vehicle.

Constance Bolton was a vision, in yellow silk, bonnet coquettishly hiding one eye, a small black curl making a soft tendril against the rich color of her cheeks.

The girl smiled at Larry Blue. "I was afraid that you could not come, Mr. Blue," she said, looking out at Larry from beneath the bonnet brim. "Don said that you would not care to drive and did not want me to ask you, but I thought that you would like to see some of Franklin."

"I am delighted." Larry recalled the courtly manners of some of his friends and impressed them for service. "There is nothing that would make me happier, Miss Bolton."

Constance made a little gesture, drawing her skirts more closely so that there was room for Larry on the seat beside her. "Then get in," she invited, "The river road, Felipe."

Larry climbed into the barouche and settled himself beside the girl. Felipe clucked to the team of matched bays, and the barouche moved away from the hotel.

At first the equipage threaded Franklin's dusty

streets. Leaving the Plaza they wound past the railroad tracks and on toward the depot. Not a particularly beautiful part of the town or one that was prepossessing. Constance Bolton, while they drove, talked to Larry, keeping her eyes upon him; and Larry, for his part, watched the girl. He did not note it when they passed the Oxford Hotel, nor did he see the little party of women that stood on the walk before the hotel. One of the group, blond-haired and dark-eyed, half raised her hand and then stood with turning head to watch the barouche out of sight. To that blond-haired girl another spoke.

"You don't keep your men, Annette. Wasn't that fellow here this afternoon?"

To the speaker Annette turned with flashing eyes. "Keep your tongue, Mae," she snapped.

Mae, blowsily past her beauty, made swift retort and for a moment a wordy war raged in front of the Oxford. Of all of this Larry was blissfully unaware. Felipe had turned the team into a drive, a road that led between towering cottonwoods and that wound peacefully beside the muddy Rio. Constance, relaxing, leaned back against the soft cushions of the barouche and sighed.

"I love it here," she said. "It is so cool and the sun coming through the trees is like the sunlight in a cathedral."

Larry, too, leaned back. He did not note the beauty of the drive but looked still at his companion. The girl, catching that gaze, flushed rosily.

"You must think a great deal of Don, Mr. Blue," she said suddenly. "Coming down here from Denver to see him. Don says that you are in business in Denver. He is very proud of you."

"I'm proud of Don," said Larry quietly.

181

Constance Bolton turned so that she faced Larry. "I want to thank you," she said. "Don told us at noon that it was your insistence that led him to make a last search in our stepfather's papers. It was then that he found the will that was left. If it had not been for you . . ."

"He would have found it," Larry made interruption. "It was just a question of time anyhow. I was riding a hunch, that's all."

"But DeWitt and I are grateful," persisted Constance. "It means a great deal to us, of course. Tell me: Why were you so sure that stepfather had left a will?"

Larry felt himself on dangerous ground. He sought to escape it. "I suppose that Don told you I am a gambler," he said. "Gamblers play their hunches. I just felt that there was a will there and I came out right, that's all. What are Don and Judge Lester going to do with it?"

The girl turned away and Larry had a view of her profile. "They have an engagement with my aunt and Mr. Seemans this afternoon," she replied. "Don says that they will tell them about the will and show it to them, and then the legal business will be finished. I do not like my aunt, Mr. Blue. When we first came here, we stayed with her. She and DeWitt quarreled, and of course I took DeWitt's part. We moved then to Judge Lester's home."

Larry nodded. "Mrs. Seemans will drop her claim when she sees the will," he observed sagely. "That will clean up all the legal business."

Constance nodded thoughtfully.

The barouche rolled into an opening among the cottonwoods and then back among the trees again. "I'd like Don to go back to Denver with me," said Larry bluntly. "I want him there. I can do things for Don in Denver."

182

Constance looked searchingly at Larry, then glanced away. "You have been doing things for Don all your life," she said softly. "Don has told me about some of them."

Larry brushed that aside. "Don's all I have," he said. "Who else would I do things for?"

Again that swift sidelong glance. "You might do some things for Larry Blue," reminded the girl. "It seems to me . . ." she let the words trail off.

"I have done things for myself." Larry's words were sturdy. "I've come along. I'm . . . well, I'm not much, but I have come along." The finish of the speech was almost apologetic, almost a plea to the girl to see that Larry Blue had advanced.

Turning now so that she faced him fully Constance smiled at the man. "Tell me," she commanded. "Tell me about what you have done. I have heard Don talk, and Judge Lester. Tell me."

"There isn't much to tell," Larry said awkwardly. "I've done what I had to do, that's all."

The girl made a little grimace of impatience. "I want to hear," she said. "You say that you are a gambler. What do you do? What does a gambler do? I have never met a gambler. I never knew a man that would admit he was a gambler. What do gamblers do, Mr. Blue?"

Larry's hand sought his dark mustache and brushed it nervously. His voice was constrained as he answered. "Mostly," said Larry, "they gamble."

The girl was not satisfied with that reply. With soft feminine persistence she pursued her questioning. Larry made answer. Presently he forgot his constraint, his awkwardness. Gradually, little by little, Constance Bolton uncovered Larry Blue, removed the overburden of reticence and revealed the man that lay beneath. To

183

her Larry Blue talked as he had never talked to another and, enthralled, the girl listened.

The road had left the river bed and climbing now, emerged upon the mesa. There, following the ridges, it wound snakelike back toward Franklin. The sun was low, hovering over the blue hills west of the river, touching the tops of the Cantandos and bathing them with gold. With a last wild burst of glory the sun was gone and only the pale aftermath remained. Larry Blue stopped talking.

"And you did that for Don?" Constance's voice held a touch of awe, of incredulity as she asked the question.

"Don is my brother," Larry said simply.

The girl was thoughtful. "You must love him deeply," she said, after a moment's pause. "You must . . ." Her dark eyes, wide and bright, and still touched with the wonder of the things she had heard, met Larry's. Constance's lips were parted and in her throat a pulse beat. She had been sheltered all her life. Like many another girl she had received attention, the prosaic, accustomed attentions of prosaic and busy men. Here, for the first time, she had encountered a man who was not prosaic, but elemental; a man who was a raw, ungoverned force. A man who in following the thing he believed right would kill or be killed cheerfully because of the force within him. Larry had told his story in the parsimonious, understated phrases of the Westerner, but Constance Bolton, listening, had heard the wild song of the frontier beating through the mundane sentences. Almost instinctively her hand went out toward the man beside her.

"You want Don," she said softly. "You would stop at nothing to have him with you. I . . .ah . . .what do I matter? I . . ."

This girl was Don's! Larry remembered that. Larry Blue kept his hands upon his knees, his fingers tight-clenched. Don loved her! Don . . .

The barouche lurched. On the seat Felipe yelled. Something, perhaps a snake in the road, perhaps some vagrant shadow, had frightened the team of trotters. The horses, curvetting, reared as one and left the road. Felipe had been paying no attention to his horses. Now inattention was repaid. The reins were jerked from his hands. The horses, out of the road, lunged forward. A front wheel struck a rock. With the lurch Felipe was thrown from the seat and the bays, uncontrolled went wildly out across the sagebrush flat.

With that first lurch and yell Larry's muscles tensed. He came to his feet, holding to the iron arm rest of the seat. Constance Bolton, clutching wildly, found a hold, was thrown loose from it and caught at another.

"Hang on!" yelled Larry Blue, and giving to the rocking lurches of the barouche, went up, catlike, over the back of the driver's seat.

The reins were gone. Larry did not even try to retrieve them. He looked back, swiftly, saw that Constance was in the bottom of the barouche, holding fast to the little edge of the body, and then, leaning forward, Larry caught the dashboard with his hands, swung his body and like some circus acrobat rehearsing a simple act, went down to the bounding tongue. His hands, releasing their hold on the dashboard, caught at back-strap and crouper on either side. A flying hoof brushed his leg, almost upsetting him. Then Larry was on the lunging back of the nigh bay, legs locked, body giving to the horses' lunges. Now hands went out to catch the flying reins; now Larry leaned forward and caught at the bit of the off horse. His voice, steady,

185

calm, more controlling than the hands, was in the ears of the bay team.

"Whoa, whoa, you damned fools. Think this is a time to run away? Whoa, whoa, now!"

Voice and pulling hands had their effect. The bays were gentle as kittens. They had been frightened, they had run, they were running, but now that mad gallop was controlled. Under voice and hands they swung into the road. Steadily the hands pulled in, steadily the voice, softly cursing but not angry, soothed them. From run to lope, from lope to trot to walk and then to panting stop, the bays came. Larry Blue slipped down from his impromptu mount, reached the side of the barouche and his strong arms gathered up the girl who lay, eyes closed, on the floor. He held her against his chest.

The face was pale. Long eyelashes lay against colorless cheek. The jaunty tendril of hair beneath the coquettish bonnet, now disheveled, was like the curl of some little girlchild asleep in a man's arms. Larry, looking down into that face, feeling the soft body in his arms, was filled with sudden rage and fright and something else. This girl was Don's! This woman, desirable, beautiful, in his arms, was the woman his brother loved. All his life he had done for Don, had given to Don. His every move and thought had been for Don. But why?

"You might do something for Larry Blue . . ." It seemed to Larry that the girl's voice spoke again. Why should he give up for Don? Why should he . . . ?

The bays stood panting in the road. Felipe, face bloody from an encounter with mesa rocks, coat torn, came running up. Larry Blue, lifting Constance Bolton, stepped up and into the barouche.

"Señor," panted Felipe. "Señor . . . !"

186

"Damn you," swore Larry Blue fiercely. "Damn you, drive home!"

Constance had recovered her senses before they reached Judge Lester's house. The girl shuddered, sighed, and opening her eyes, saw where she was. Larry, releasing her from his arms, helped her to sit up. The color flooded back into the girl's cheeks and she looked, wide-eyed, at Larry.

"It's all right, Miss Bolton," Larry assured. "It's all right now. They just got scared and ran. They're all right now. Gentle enough."

"I saw you go up over the seat," said the girl, her voice faint, "I saw you and then you were gone and I thought . . . I couldn't see you and I thought . . ."

"I had 'em to stop,—said Larry earnestly. "It's all right now."

The girl said no more. As she calmed she began to arrange her disheveled dress, to straighten her bonnet, and with sundry small pats to order her hair. Larry watched Felipe's back and did not look at Constance. When they reached Judge Lester's he helped the girl to alight, holding her small, mittened hand in his stronger, broader palm.

"I can't thank you now," said Constance, her voice small. "But you . . . you saved my life. You must come back, Mr. Blue. You must come so that I . . ."

Larry smiled reassuringly. "I'll come to see that you have no bad effects from your fright," he said. "Of course I'll do that; but you mustn't say I saved your life. The team would have stopped running anyhow and . . ."

"Come soon," urged Constance, interrupting. "You must come soon, Mr. Blue. I . . ." Her voice faltered.

"I'm keeping you standing here." Larry was contrite. "You go in and lie down. You'll feel all right pretty soon. I'll come back tomorrow and see you." He led the girl to the door, opened it and saw her inside. Felipe was still sitting on the seat of the barouche. Larry walked back to him.

"You better take that team to the barn," he said sternly. "And next time don't go to sleep!" With that admonition he left Felipe and walked slowly down the hill toward the center of town.

It was late when Larry reached his hotel, almost seven o'clock. Don's note had said that he would come at seven, and so going to his room and making a hasty toilet, Larry returned to the lobby to wait for his brother. Seven o'clock, and no Don! At half past seven Larry went out of the hotel and walked along the boardwalk in front of it. Going back into the lobby at eight he sat down and tried to compose himself. Don was late, but then Don was busy and had not been able to get away. It was as not until eight-thirty that Don appeared. He came through the door, resplendent in full dress, and Larry rising to meet his brother, was sorry that he had dressed so hastily himself. Don took Larry's extended hand briefly. He was frowning and he broke brusquely into Larry's greeting.

"Where can we talk?" he asked.

"I thought that we'd have dinner together," Larry said, "then we can do whatever you want."

"I haven't time for that." Don glanced at a watch that he took from a vest pocket. "Can we go to your room?"

"Why, sure." Larry, surprised, turned and led the way to the stairs.

In Larry's room, the door closed and the lamp burning brightly, Don refused a seat but stood beside the door. The frown he had worn when he came into the hotel was a scowl now, directed at Larry.

188

"We're all very grateful to you for what you did this afternoon," Don announced abruptly. "DeWitt and Judge Lester and I. Constance fairly sings your praises."

"Pshaw!" Larry waved that aside. "The fool coachman wasn't watching and the team ran. It wasn't much of a trick to stop 'em."

"Nevertheless we're grateful." Don's language was precise, his tone formal. "I haven't much time, Larry. Constance and the Judge are waiting for me. We are going to the theater. Constance has a foolish idea that she wants to see this woman with whom DeWitt is so enamored."

"Oh?" said Larry, his eyebrows lifting a trifle. He waited for Don to continue. It seemed logical to Larry that Don should ask him to join the party. After all, the Boltons were scarcely strangers to Larry and surely his brother would want his company.

Don gave no invitation. "I wanted to talk with you about that will," he announced. "I kept Judge Lester from probating it. I talked him out of that idea, but I couldn't keep him from showing it to Mrs. Seemans and her husband. Larry, did you write that will?"

Larry was hurt because Don had not asked him to join his party. He was hurt that Don preferred the company of others to his own, and he was just a little angry. Don was acting as though Larry had committed a crime. Don had a chip on his shoulder and Larry Blue in all his life had never failed to knock off an offered chip.

"You can make up your own mind about that," he snapped. "What do you think?"

"I think you did."

"Then why didn't you tear it up?"

"Because if you did not write it, I would be doing Constance a great injury."

189

"What about her brother? Don't he count?" Larry was deliberately rubbing a raw spot.

"Of course he counts. But Constance . . ."

"You're stuck on the girl." Larry grinned at Don.

Don flushed darkly. "I want to know about that will," he insisted obstinately.

"And you can't find out," Larry drawled.

Don spoke, his tone conciliating, and in speaking made matters worse. "There is no use of our quarreling, Larry. I came to ask you a question. You won't answer it. You place me in a difficult situation."

"Never," Larry was sententious, "look a gift horse in the mouth, kid. You might find out something that you don't want to know."

Don drew himself up. "I'll tell you this," he said. "If you did write that will, if you committed a forgery, then you are directly responsible for whatever comes of it."

"All right," Larry made casual agreement. "If I wrote it I'm responsible. Then what?"

"Then . . . then . . . Judge Lester is going ahead. He will probate the will. He thinks that Archer Bolton wrote it. Judge Lester is the soul of honor. He . . ."

"And I'm not!" Larry snapped the words. "I'm your no-account gambler brother that you're ashamed of. You'd better trot along to your friends. It won't do to keep 'em waiting. After all, they gave you everything, remember? Everything except a backbone. You think you're in a tight spot and you come to me. Grow up, boy. Do your own deciding for once. And don't be so high and mighty. Take what's given to you, like you've done all your life, and be thankful for it."

The instant that the words were out of his mouth Larry Blue was sorry he had spoken hem. He had not meant to hurt Don, had not meant to quarrel with him.

190

Don was his brother, his kid brother, and Don was more precious than anything in the world to him. Anger had made Larry speak, anger that Don had no more regard for him, that Don would not include him with Lester and with the Boltons. A childish jealousy, a hurt that was picayunish.

Larry came to his feet. "Don," he began, "Don . . ."

But Don Blue was gone, the door slamming shut behind him.

Larry reached the door, put ut his hand to open it and stopped. After all, there was no recalling what was said.

Larry's momentary contrition was lost. Let Don go! Let him go with the people that he thought of so highly. He, Larry, was not good enough for Don's society. He would, lacking an invitation to his brother's party, have a little party of his own. Snatching up his hat from the bed where he had tossed it, Larry pulled it on savagely and blowing out the light, stamped out of his room and down the stairs.

When Larry reached the cab rank at the corner his searching eyes found Duck Bunn. Duck was leaning against his hack, his battered plug hat tilted down over his nose. He woke with a start when Larry shook his arm, his hat remaining in place only by some miracle of equilibrium.

"Huh?" grunted Duck. "What . . .?" Then, seeing who had awakened him, "What you want, Larry?"

"We're moving out a little," Larry stated crisply. "You and me, Duck. We're going to see the bright lights and hear the eagle scream and the owl hoot. Come on!"

"What do you mean?" demanded Duck. "Whats got into yore craw?"

"There's nothing in my craw that a little liquor won't help," Larry snapped. "You're my company tonight,

Duck. You and me are going to prop up Franklin and put a chunk under part of it. Come on, shake a leg! I've got a thirst and I've got the money to do something about it. Come on!"

Duck looked searchingly at Larry Blue. Duck had seen men like Larry before this, men with a wild light in their eyes, men with something eating into the mind behind the eyes. Larry was upset, Larry was overwrought. It would never do to turn Larry Blue loose alone, not when he felt like this.

"You want to get drunk, huh?" asked Duck Bum "Come on then. I'm your huckleberry!"

# CHAPTER 15

## LET'S SEE THE TOWN

As MAYOR OF FRANKLIN IT WAS LOGICAL THAT Abraham Seemans should live in the best house in town. That he did not own the house or the blooded team he used, or any of the various appurtenances of wealth that he displayed, bothered Seemans not at all. He had their use and if his wife Luella was in actuality the owner, still Abe Seemans was the front. Now, in a chair in the parlor of the house, Luella Seemans sat stiffly upright and spoke to George Whiteman while Abe took his ease upon a horsehair sofa.

"I will not be cheated," stated Luella, her eyes agate hard. "What is mine is justly mine and I want it."

Still a handsome woman, Abe thought, looking at his wife. She might begrudge him money, might be so parsimonious as to border upon the miser, but still she was handsome. And she did not spare money upon

192

herself. Her dress was heavy silk; her shoes, the toes discreetly peeping out from beneath the dress, were the finest that money could buy. Her hair, with only the single streak of gray, was arranged in style. Only the wrinkling skin of her neck betrayed her age, and only the harsh lines about her nose and the corners of her mouth, betrayed her disposition. If Luella would only be more free with her money, if she did not force him to subterfuge in rendering her the accounts of the Crystal Palace and of the other houses on San Sebastian street, he would be happy. Abe glanced almost fondly toward George Whiteman. Whiteman had engineered the marriage and hoped to profit by it. After all, Whiteman had his uses. Whiteman had come chiseling in on Abe Seemans, but (Abe reluctantly admitted this) he had profited by Whiteman's chiseling.

"You can't go against a will," Whiteman said flatly. "You had a claim as long as Bolton was intestate, but now that a will has turned up you've lost out."

That was another thing that Abe Seemans envied. George was not afraid of Luella. He showed his lack of fear in the very deliberation with which he loaded his pipe from the beaded buckskin tobacco pouch.

"I used that property for years when I owned the ranch," Luella stated. "Surely that gives me some claim upon it."

Whiteman lighted his pipe, disregarding Luella's frown. She did not like tobacco smoke to scent her curtains and drapes. "That only gives them a claim on you if they want to push it," he drawled. "I take it you didn't pay Archer Bolton a lease?"

"I did not!" Luella was fuming now. She loved a dollar, did Luella, almost more than life itself. "I tell you, George, I want my money from that river land."

Whiteman grunted. "Try to get it," he growled.

There was silence in the parlor. Abe Seemans stirred uneasily. He did not like silence. Usually it presaged trouble. At his motion his wife turned. "You might suggest something!" she snapped. "So far your contribution has been that you and George have a drink."

Under his wife's stare Abe twisted. His eyes strayed from Luella's face to a picture on the wall. There was a small safe imbedded behind that picture. Abe had never seen the inside of the safe. He lacked the nerve to open it. Long ago he had possessed himself of the combination but he had never tampered. "We might trade something." he ventured. "Maybe you have something that you could trade to Lester . . ."

"Why should I trade anything?" Luella's voice was harsh. "I want what is mine. There is one hundred thousand dollars tied up in that river land. The smelter company will buy it tomorrow. They want the clay for a brick yard and the limestone for something in their process. You can sit there and let me lose thirty thousand dollars and not offer a suggestion. Trade something indeed!"

Whiteman puffed on his pipe, his long front teeth showing when he removed the pipe from his lips, and his eyes colorless slits as his mind revolved the question. "I'm not sure that Abe isn't right, Luella," drawled George Whiteman after an interval. "You might work up a trade."

"And what is your bright idea?" she asked.

Whiteman put the pipe back, puffed once more and drawled an answer. "Just suppose that young Bolton got into trouble, Luella. Don't you think that Lester would be willing to trade any interest in that property to keep

194

DeWitt from being hanged?"

Luella leaned back in her chair. She had been sitting primly upright in the position she always assumed when laying down the law. Now she wanted to think, and so relaxed. "Hmm," she said slowly. "Just what do you suggest, George?"

Whiteman shrugged. "Suppose that your dear nephew was in jail for . . . let's say, murder. Don't you think you could get a quit-claim deed to that river land if you got him out?"

"I won't spend a cent on it," Luella warned. I won't . . ."

"Abe would come in handy here," Whiteman continued. "It seems to me that Abe would help a lot. He has political connections, you know. Judge Goshan would listen to him."

Luella, turning to observe her husband, sniffed. "It would be the first time he was useful," she stated. "Go on, George. Speak what's on your mind."

"You might not like it," said Whiteman slyly. "After all they are your niece and nephew. You know blood is thicker than water."

"Tell me what you're planning and stop trying to be sentimental," Luella snapped.

Whiteman touched the tips of his fingers together and eyed them, the pipe forgotten in his mouth. "Well then," he said, "suppose that DeWitt killed someone. He is arrested for the killing. We are in a position to get him off with a light sentence or to set him free. Wouldn't that be something to trade?"

Luella proceeded to pick holes in the scheme. "In the first place," she objected, "DeWitt would probably be killed instead of anyone else. He is a child in arms. In the next place we must have witnesses we can depend

195

upon . . ."

"There's Fernald and Morton," Abe Seemans suggested sleepily. "You remember I caught them knocking down on us at the Crystal Palace. I think we could depend on them. And DeWitt's stuck on that Bondreaux girl. If he killed her because he was jealous . . ."

"No," Whiteman's objection came swiftly. "We could never get him off if he killed a woman. Besides . . ."

"Besides you want that girl yourself," said Luella shrewdly. "I'll grant that Morton and Fernald might do, but who would do the real work? Whom can we trust?"

She looked at George Whiteman as she spoke. Seemans too looked at the lounging man. Whiteman shrugged. "If it was worth while . . ." he purred.

"It would be worth while," Luella stated. She was a business woman, Luella Seemans, despite the fact that she allowed her husband to steal from the receipts of her various enterprises. She knew that he stole but he dared not take too much. "After all, we would get the whole amount for the river land in place of just a third. I would trade a third for two thirds."

"Thirty thousand dollars," said Whiteman musingly. "That would make the thing worth while Yes, Luella, I think that you could count on me for thirty thousand dollars."

Luella got up from her chair. "I'll leave you two to settle the details," she announced. "After all, you are men. But there must be no slips, George. No mistakes. I won't spend a penny on either of you if things go wrong." She rustled out of the room following that statement, Whiteman following her with admiring eyes. When the door had closed he relit his dead pipe and puffed in into life.

196

"Sometimes," Whiteman said musingly, "I wish I'd married her myself, Abe. She's a fine figure of a woman and she has a brain."

Abe. Seemans nodded. He too was often surprised at his wife. She was smart and unscrupulous and Abe knew it. Still he believed that he was as clever as she was. "Who have you got picked out, George?" he asked. "How you going to frame it?"

Whiteman puffed upon the pipe "I tell you," he said, not answering Seemans, "she's smart. She hired me to get the Deaf Smith tanks for the Cross C when Andrews had it. I got 'em and the tanks made the ranch. The only fool thing I ever knew her to do was marry you, and I got her to do that." Smoke trickled up from his lips.

"I had a little to do with it," snapped Seemans. "Don't take all the credit, George. Now go ahead. How do you plan to do this?"

Whiteman, pursing his lips, removed the pipe. "Wayne Justice is getting pretty big for his pants. He's moving around a lot and . . . ."

"And he's got an inside track with Annette," Seemans grinned.

"Yes, and he's got an inside track with Annette," agreed Whiteman unruffled. "Now I can use Annette to get Justice and young Bolton together. One of them could give a party for her and invite the other. That would be the best way. Have it upstairs in the Crystal Palace, in that private room. Then . . . ."

"You could be around," said Seemans, sitting up on the couch.

Whiteman scratched his ear with the stem of his pipe. "I would be around," he agreed quietly. "You'll have to handle some of it, Abe. You're the mayor . . . ."

"I can have Morton and Fernald on hand," said

197

Seemans, "and two or three of the boys from the police force. I think they'd do about what I wanted them to." His voice carried satisfaction. "I can throw a bug into Levine's ear if you say so. He owes me a favor."

Whiteman nodded. "We'll work it out," he said. "Abe, when are you going to give me some money?"

"I haven't any money," said Sccmans defensively. "Luella . . ."

"But you know where she keeps it," Whiteman interrupted. "You and I had a bargain, Abe. Suppose I went back on it? Suppose I talked about the city funds and a few other things I know about?"

"You don't bluff me, George." Called upon, Abe Seemans could be as hard as Whiteman. "I can talk some too, How about that Haslip thing that old Tom Blue was hung for, and how about you and those half-breeds downing old Cardwine when he started checking up on you? You've even got Cardwine's pouch in your pocket, full of tobacco. Suppose I spoke up about them?"

"Then I'd kill you," Whiteman stated placidly.

"If you had the chance," Seemans retorted. He stared steadily at Whiteman; Whiteman met the look. Abe Seemans was not as smart as George Whiteman; he lacked Whiteman's cleverness, but he was every bit as unscrupulous. He lacked Whiteman's cold-blooded willingness to kill, lacked Whiteman's nerve, still he had a sort of cunning that stood him in good stead.

"Don't forget that you helped out in the Haslip affair," said Whiteman. "Don't forget . . ."

"We've got too much on each other to be sitting around makin' threats," Seemans stated placatingly. "You know I'm with you, George, an' you know I'll get you some cash as soon as I can. Haven't I always

198

divvied up?"

"And you'll keep on!" threatened Whiteman. "All right, Abe, we'll drop it. Now about this other thing."

Duck Bunn was disappointed in Larry Blue. Larry drank in saloon after saloon but it seemed to have no effect upon him save to increase the high, keen edge of his unrest. A good comfortable drunk and a headache the next morning would fix Larry about right, Duck thought. He had seen that prescription work before. The trouble was that Larry would not get drunk.

"And now where?" Duck demanded when they came out of the sixth saloon and went to the cab. "Now what's the next thing? This is the last saloon in this block."

Larry considered gravely. "We'll go to the show," he announced. "Drive to the theater."

At the Empire Opera House Duck waited, ill at ease, in the foyer while Larry bought tickets. The show was more than half done, the ticket seller informed. If the gentlemen wanted to see the drammer . . .

Larry said to hell with the drama, he wanted to see the music show. The ticket seller shrugged. That was what most gentlemen came to see, he intimated and his eyes on the roll of bills that Larry produced—if the gent would like to go back stage he, the ticket man, knew all the members of the troupe and would . . .

Larry took the tickets and walking away from the window, joined Duck.

Larry had paid enough for his seats to assure that they would be well down in front. He and Duck disturbed a number of people in gaining their seats, settled into them and Duck asked, loud enough to cause heads to turn in his direction, what he should do with his hat.

Larry advised him to sit on it and someone behind advised them both to shut up. They settled back, preparing to enjoy the last act of the play. When the curtain had fallen, lights were lit in various places in the building, and Larry had a chance to look around. He saw, in a box to his right, the familiar figure of his brother. Beside Don was Constance Bolton; and Judge Lester, the pleated white bosom of his shirt gleaming, stood further back in the box. The anger in Larry and the liquor surged for control. He stared steadily at the box.

Constance saw him, Larry knew. She smiled and touched Don's arm. Don turned his head, saw Larry and turned away.

Ushers extinguished the lights, curtains parted, and from the stage a number of raucous voices informed that:

"We are merry, merry maids; we play and sing all day . . ."

Larry morosely watched the stage. He saw the chorus, plump thighed and waists laced to thinness—hourglasses as far as torso went, and highly painted as to face—perform various evolutions that might charitably have been called a military drill or a dance. Then Annette Bondreaux came on stage and Larry forgot the chorus.

Annette sang. She had a voice, not strong but true and sweet. She danced, Larry watching her flashing feet and ankles as her big skirt swirled. He saw Annette smile at the boxes; saw her coquette with men in the front row, heard their guffaws. The liquor in Larry Blue began to take hold. That was little Annette Bondreaux up there. That was the little kid he had played with so long ago.

"It's a damned shame!" anounced Larry, loud enough so that people about him turned to look. "A downright, damned shame."

Duck Bunn put his hand on Larry's arm. He knew the symptoms, did Duck. When men who held as much liquor as Larry held began to talk about things being a damned shame then they generally decided to do something about it. Duck wanted no crusader on his hands.

"Hot in here," Duck whispered. "Let's get out."

"I'm not goin' out," Larry stated. "I'm staying here."

Duck shrugged. He was in no position to enforce his desires.

"What do you mean, 'a damned shame,' neighbor?" the bald man on Larry's other side demanded. "Don't you like the show?"

Larry stared at the speaker. The man who sat next to him was burly and what he lacked in hair on top of his head he made up with the hirsute adornments on his face. It was a glorious growth.

Larry did not like the man who sat next to him. "Walrus," he observed. "Damned shame that she's got to sing to a walrus like you." It was a witty comment, Larry thought, and he laughed.

Larry's neighbor did not see the humor. His breath was heavy with liquor and he was a surly drinker. "Lissen, squirt," said the bald-headed man, "anytime I got to take talk offen a guy like you . . ."

Larry reached over and seized one handlebar mustache. With a sigh Duck Bunn reached back for the life preserver in his hip pocket. Hacking in Franklin was no peaceful pursuit and Duck went prepared.

The Empire Opera House of Franklin catered to all classes. The Empire was prepared to handle emergencies of all kinds. There were already three burly ushers and the house manager coming down the aisle when Larry pulled that mustache. They had reached the row of seats by the time Duck swung his life preserver and they were evacuating the noncombatants when Larry hit the man beyond the handlebarred gentleman. The ushers were trained and their teamwork was perfect. They had no trouble with Duck who went peacefully, but they carried Larry up the aisle. On the stage the show had stopped, to resume haltingly when the turmoil died.

In her box Constance Bolton caught at Don Blue's arm.

"That was . . ." she began.

"That was my brother," Don finished, scorn in his voice.

"Will they hurt him?" Constance gasped. "You had better go, Don. You had better . . ."

"He can look out for himself," snapped Don. "Haven't you had enough of this, Constance? Don't you want to go home?"

Judge Lester leaned over the girl. "We had better leave, my dear," he urged.

A mixture of emotions on her face, Constance arose from her chair. "I . . ." she began and then, swiftly, "yes, I'll go. I've had enough."

# CHAPTER 16

### COYOTES YAP

AT MID-MORNING OF THE FOLLOWING DAY, LARRY Blue groaned and opened one eye a trifle. Duck Bunn, sitting beside a table, head in his hands, straightened and walked over to the bed. "Comin' to life, are you?" growled Duck. "It's about time."

With an effort Larry got the other eye open. His surroundings were totally strange to him. Adobe walls, roughly plastered with mud, were on four sides, and through an open doorway the sun streamed in. Somewhere close-by an engine bell was clanging, every stroke of the clapper finding an echo in Larry's head. "Where . . .?" demanded Larry thickly.

"My place," said Duck. "Here's part of the dawg that bit you. Lord, what a night!"

Taking the little glass of liquor, Larry drank and grimaced. "Tastes like a bucket of soap," he complimented. "What happened last night?"

"I'll give you one more little drink," announced Duck, squinting at the glass. "Last night? Oh yeah. You remember gettin' throwed out of the opery house?"

Larry nodded glumly and flinched as the engine's whistle sounded. "I can go that far back," he affirmed. "We got mixed up some after that."

"You got mixed up," corrected Duck. "I stayed sober. After we got throwed out of the theayter, we went places an' done things."

"I feel like it," Larry agreed ruefully. His two small drinks had taken hold; his head was clearing, and now he swung his feet over the edge of the bed and sat up.

"About one o'clock," Duck spoke with unction, "you was buyin' wine in the Crystal Palace. There was some disturbance upstairs an' the po-lice come. I got you out of there an' poured you in the hack an' brung you home. I wasn't goin' to take you to no hotel."

Larry nodded. "I made a first-class fool of myself," he said. "Thanks for playing nursemaid, Duck."

"You got a talent for makin' a damned fool of yoresef," Duck agreed, disregarding the thanks. "Yore brother an' a girl seen you in the show. I reckon they

203

thought highly of you. Anyhow yore brother didn't show up none."

"No reason for him to." Larry was terse. "I'll get dressed, Duck." He suited his actions to his declaration, standing up a little unsteadily and reaching for his trousers. Duck watched him narrowly and when he saw that Larry could negotiate it alone, spoke again.

"I took care of the team," Duck said. "Now I'll go harness up an' take you to the hotel. "You'll want to clean up a little an' eat."

Larry groaned at the mention of food. "I won't eat for a week" he promised. "You go ahead and hook up your team, Duck."

The old hack driver waddled out and Larry finished with his hasty dressing. He felt like hell and from what he could see of himself in Duck's fly-specked mirror, he looked like the wrath of God. Duck came back in, whistling cheerily, and announced that he was ready to go. Larry flinched from the whistle and followed Duck out of the adobe. The hack, with the team harnessed, stood beside the shack. Larry looked around.

Duck's home was on the far western edge of Franklin. The railroad yards were at his front door and only a little below the house. There was an engine puffing importantly about the yards, making up a train. Over beyond the railroad was the river. "Nice place you got, Duck," Larry commented. "Nice an' quiet. A man can sleep good."

"You didn't complain none last night," grunted Duck. "Git in. You look like hell after a hard winter."

The ride to town refreshed Larry. The air cleared his head and when he alighted from the he cab in front of the Plaza Hotel he felt a great deal better. Duck, with other duties to attend, said that he would come back

204

later on, and Larry went in through the lobby, passing the clerk's curious glances.

In his room Larry made his toilet and adjusted his clip holster under his right arm. As a matter of habit he removed the short-barreled gun from the holster and inspected it. The gun, a Smith & Wesson tip-up model, had been altered by the best gunsmith in the Rockies. The barrel was cut off so that but two inches remained. the butt rounded, and the front of the trigger guard cut away. Larry was proud of the gun for it embodied his own ideas. He had trained himself to shoot left-handed because he knew that in a tight spot an opponent would watch his right hand. Satisfied with the condition of his armament he put the gun away and slipped into his coat.

Larry was ashamed of himself. He had blown off steam the night before and, along with his headache, a natural reaction had set in. Larry sat down in a chair in his room and considered the opposite wall. He remembered the things that Duck had said, and particularly he remembered that Don and Constance had been present during the display at the Empire Opera House. The fact that Constance had seen him expelled from the theater hurt. Thinking it over, Larry decided that he had better set matters to rights. He could go to Constance and apologize for his acts but before he did that he had better see if Constance would receive him. He owed Don an apology too. Larry flushed when he thought of what he had said to Don. He would have to make that right with Don if he crawled to do it. So resolved he got up from the chair and left his room, locking the door behind him.

It was fully noon when he went down the stairs and the odor of food, coming from the dining room, was almost too much for Larry. He did not care if he never

205

ate again. Leaving the hotel Larry went east along the side of the Plaza, turned, and taking another street, set off toward Judge Lester's office.

When he reached the brick building he climbed the stairs and found the door to Lester's anteroom open. Larry went in. He wondered if Don was in his office and he wondered too just what he would say to Don, how he should begin his apology. Standing in the doorway of the anteroom he saw that Don's door was closed. Larry advanced a step and Judge Lester appeared at the door way of his office.

Larry was shocked at the man's appearance. Lester was old, old and wasted. His face was deeply lined about mouth and nose, and the skin clung, skeleton-like, to his cheek bones. The eyes were deeply sunken under the white eyebrows, and Lester's voice was hoarse when he spoke.

"Good morning, Mr. Blue."

Larry said, "Good morning," and waited.

"You have come to see Don?" asked Lester.

"Yes," said Larry. "I want to see him. It strikes me that I made kind of a fool of myself last night and I wanted to tell him so."

"Don will be here soon," Lester said. "He is busy now. He. . . A terrible thing happened last night, Mr. Blue. DeWitt killed a man."

Larry's eyes narrowed at the announcement, otherwise his face gave no sign that he had heard it. "Yes?" he asked evenly.

Lester nodded, and walking across the anteroom sank down wearily into a chair. "He killed a man named Justice," announced the old lawyer.

Larry nodded.

"DeWitt was with Mr. Justice and the Bondreaux

206

woman and Mr. Whiteman and some others," Lester continued, his voice lifeless. "They had a party at the Crystal Palace. It seems that DeWitt and Justice quarreled and DeWitt shot him. He had been drinking, of course. They had all been drinking."

"Who saw the shooting?" asked Larry crisply. "Annette?"

Judge Lester shook his head. "She was out of the room at the time it happened," he said. "So was Mr. Whiteman, I understand. The men who saw the actual shooting were a Mr. Fernald and a Mr. Morton. Mr. Morton is the proprietor of the Crystal Palace."

"They were in the restaurant?" Larry asked.

Lester shook his head. "Upstairs in a private room," he answered. "DeWitt remembers nothing about it. He had a weapon, a gun that he bought shortly after he came to Franklin. That was beside him on the table with one cartridge discharged. They are holding DeWitt without bond pending hearing."

"And Don . . ?"

"Don is with DeWitt and Constance now." Still that lifeless lassitude in Lester's voice "Constance insisted upon seeing her brother, and Don . . ."

"I guess I'll wait for Don to come in," Larry announced.

The Judge remained, a small, sunken shape in his chair. Presently he raised his head. "Don had an engagement with you last night," he said. "I am sorry that he did not stay with you. Constance insisted upon seeing this woman with whom DeWitt is infatuated, and of course Don and I could not let her go alone."

"Of course not," Larry agreed. Walking over to the old lawyer, Larry stood before him. "You said one time that Whiteman and Seemans were pretty bad," he observed. "Will this get Don into a tight spot?"

"I don't know," answered Lester, wearily. "I wish that Don had gone with you. I wish that he were away from Franklin."

Larry shrugged. "If wishes were horses . . ." Don was here and Don was in this, and if Larry knew anything about his brother, Don would stay in it. The thing was, of course, to protect Don. Instinctively, Larry's left hand slid up under his coat and touched the butt of the gun that hung beneath his arm. The cool wood of the grip was reassuring.

Steps sounded in the corridor and Don Blue came into the anteroom. He looked at Larry and through him, no recognition in his eyes, and spoke to Judge Lester. "Constance is downstairs in the carriage," he said. "Why don't you take her home, Judge? Take her home and get some rest. There is nothing that we can do now." Don's voice was gentle with consideration for the older man.

"I believe I will," agreed Lester, wearily. "Are you coming, Don?"

Don shook his head. "Not right now," he returned. "I'll get a bite to eat and then talk to some of the witnesses. You go alone, Judge."

Lester was courteous. He bowed to Larry and taking his hat from the rack went to the door. "If you learn anything, Don, you had better come to the house," he said, pausing beside the door. I will be back here later, of course."

"I'll come out, Judge," promised Don. The judge went on out to the street. When he was as gone Don turned to Larry, apparently seeing him for the first time. "Well," he said bitterly, "why have you come here?"

Larry was frank. "I made a fool of myself last night,"

he answered. "I talked like a fool and I acted one. I'm sorry."

Don's face softened momentarily, and then hardened again.

"You know what happened?" he asked.

Larry nodded.

"As dirty a frame-up as I've ever seen," Don continued. "DeWitt did not kill that man. DeWitt was too drunk to talk when Judge Lester and I were called to the jail this morning. I'm going to get to the bottom of this if it is the last thing I do."

"Let me help," Larry offered eagerly. "I kind of know about things like this, Don. I've seen the inside of some pretty seamy deals."

"I have no doubt of it." Don's voice was curt. "Odd, isn't it, that this happened as soon as that will turned up?"

Larry started to speak, then decided to remain silent.

Don was not finished.

"I think, Larry," Don went on, "that you've done enough damage. Constance saw you last night in the theater. Naturally, it gives her greater consideration for me to know that my brother is a drunken rowdy. If it is just the same to you I'd rather that you kept hands off. I thank you for your offer, but I believe that I can handle this without your help."

Again Larry made ready to speak, and again he stopped.

There were steps on the stairs, several men ascending. They came on toward the office and both Don and Larry turned so that they faced the door. Abe Seemans entered, a flamboyantly dressed Abe Seemans, with puffy jowls and beady eyes almost hidden by fat. Behind Seemans came a long-faced, buck-toothed man

209

with eyes so light a color as to seem almost white. Judge Lester followed the long-faced man. It was Lester who spoke.

"I met Mr. Seemans and Mr. Whiteman coming to the office, Don," he explained. "They want to talk with us about DeWitt." Lester saw Larry Blue and stopped. "If you are busy . . ." he began after a moment's hesitation.

"I'm not busy," said Don. "Come into the Judge's office, gentlemen."

Seemans and Whiteman, obeying that invitation, walked past Larry. Seemans nodded as though Larry were an acquaintance, but Whiteman gave Larry only a long, hard stare. Lester followed them, and Don, turning from Larry without another word, went into the office and closed the door. For an instant Larry eyed that closed portal, then with a shrug he walked toward the corridor.

When Larry Blue looked at the closed door of Judge Lester's office and then went out, he had no idea of the turmoil he left. Behind that closed portal were four men, two of them sure of their position, with a deal to offer; and two who were distraught. Abe Seemans took a chair beside Lester's desk, Whiteman sat in another chair against the wall, and Lester lowered his tired body into the seat behind the desk. Only Don Blue remained upon his feet, standing beside the door and eyeing the visitors.

"George and I thought that we had better come to you, Judge Lester," Seemans began. "We wanted to talk to you concerning that affair last night. It is very bad."

Don watched the speaker, and Judge Lester nodded. "Very bad," he echoed.

"Of course we don't want to be too hard on young Bolton," Seemans continued, his voice fat and unctuous.

"In a way he is my nephew. His aunt is very much distressed over the whole thing."

Lester said, "I can imagine," his voice dry. Under pressure the old man was rallying from his shock and fatigue.

"Now George and I have come here to make what arrangements we can," Seemans went on. "Feeling as I do, of course I will help all that I can. Still, you understand my official position." He cleared his throat ponderously.

"Yes," said Lester.

"George and I know that the young man was very deeply enamored of Miss Bondreaux," continued Seemans. "We understand that jealousy led to the difficulty which resulted in DeWitt's shooting Mr. Justice. In fact George here heard the quarrel start."

"They fought over the girl," Whiteman said bluntly. "That's where the trouble started."

"We appreciate your concern, gentlemen." Don took a hand in the talk. "Now if we can come to business . . ?"

"Ahem!" Seemans cleared his throat again. "As you know, Mr. Morton and Mr. Fernald were witnesses to the actual shooting. They have already testified before the coroner. Miss Bondreaux was spared that ordeal and Mr. Whiteman, as prosecutor, could not . . ."

"Mr. Whiteman's being a witness automatically disqualifies him from taking any part in the prosecution," Don broke in. "Certainly in defending DeWitt I shall call on Mr. Whiteman to testify."

Whiteman started to speak but Seemans interposed. "And very properly, too," he agreed. "However, there is a possibility that it will not be necessary to defend DeWitt."

"What do you mean?" Don snapped the question.

Seemans cleared his throat again . "I . . . ah . . . I have certain connections, as you know," he said. "I am acquainted with Mr. Morton and with Mr. Fernald. Now if they were to testify that DeWitt shot in self-defense there would be no case and no prosecution. You gentlemen can see that."

"Yes," Judge Lester took up the burden of answering, once more. "We can see that."

"Mr. Morton and Mr. Fernald might be approached," continued Seemans. "They . . . ah . . . they . . ."

Whiteman was tired of this beating around the bush. His voice was direct and blunt and bespoke his weariness with diplomacy. "Abe means that Morton and Fernald can be reached," he said. "But it'll take a lot of money."

"I won't . . ." Don began.

Judge Lester stopped him. "What is the proposition, gentlemen?" he asked.

"Just this." Whiteman gave Seemans no chance to answer. "If Morton and Fernald are seen by the right party and paid enough they would change their testimony."

"This is . . ." Don began.

Again Lester interposed. "How much money?"

"A good deal." Seemans spoke now, Whiteman having brought the business to the climax. "I am afraid more than you or than Mrs. Seemans and I can raise. Now I had this in mind: There is that property of Archer Bolton's. Both the children and my wife have a claim upon it. I thought . . ."

"You forget that Archer Bolton left a will giving that property to Constance and DeWitt," Lester spoke crisply.

212

Seemans coughed. "A will which we will protest," he announced. "Mrs. Seemans has very legal claim upon that property as you well know. However, let that pass. If Constance and DeWitt sign a quit-claim deed to that property I am sure that I can raise sufficient money to satisfy the demands of Mr. Morton and Mr. Fernald. I dislike anything so smacking of bribery, but there it is. Surely DeWitt's life is more valuable than . . ."

"I'll be damned if we will!" There was a ring in Don's voice. "We won't turn that property over to anyone. If these men can be bribed they can be discredited in court. I intend to fight this case. I'll use every legal method to protect DeWitt, but if DeWitt killed that man he is guilty and should be punished. I strongly suspect, however, that he did not kill Justice. This visit . . ."

"Don!" Lester's voice, raised and sharp, stopped the younger man.

"What were you going to say, Blue?" That was Whiteman, ominous and sinister.

"I was going to say . . ." Don began.

"Gentlemen," Lester spoke swiftly in interruption, "you must forgive Mr. Blue. He is overwrought and young. No . . . Not a word, Don! I . . ."

Again Whiteman spoke, low-toned like the growling of a dangerous dog. "I hope that Mr. Blue will live long enough to recover from being so young. Witness or not, I'm going to prosecute this case. We've done what we can for you. You can take this offer or . . ."

"Or what?" Don flared.

"You'll find a wolf turned loose," Whiteman concluded. "Let's go, Abe."

Seemans was still oily, still unctuous. "We will give you time to think the matter over, Judge," he said. "You

213

can get word to me. Good day, Mr. Blue."

When Larry Blue reached the street after leaving Don's office, he turned left and started back toward the Plaza. He had taken but a few steps when his name was called. Glancing up from his study of the board sidewalk, Larry saw Constance Bolton sitting in Lester's barouche beside the curb. She was looking at Larry and as their eyes met she beckoned. Removing his hat, Larry approached the girl.

"You are walking, Mr. Blue," Constance said when Larry came up. "Can't I take you to your hotel?"

Larry hesitated. He knew that Constance had seen him making a fool of himself at the Empire. Don had been very direct in what he had said. The idea had been conveyed and clung in Larry's mind, that the less he was seen, the less he had to do with Constance Bolton, with Judge Lester, even with his brother, the better pleased all parties would be. Yet here was the girl offering friendly aid.

"Why . . . thank you," said Larry.

"Get in." Constance moved on the seat. "We will go to the Plaza Hotel, Felipe."

As the barouche moved along the street Larry looked at the girl beside him. He could see that Constance had been weeping. Her face was drained of its normally rich color and the suspicious pink of her nostrils told of tears having been shed. Larry wanted to offer solace to the girl, but did not know how to begin. Constance came to his aid.

"You know about DeWitt?" she asked.

Larry nodded. "I heard," he answered hesitantly. "If I . . . if there is anything . . ."

"DeWitt has always been wild." Apparently

214

Constance had not heard the offer Larry began, "He . . . I thought that if we came to Franklin he might change. He is my brother and I love him, but . . ."

"He's pretty young," Larry apologized.

"He is as old as you are. He is older than Don, and Don doesn't . . ."

"Don's got reasons to behave," aid Larry, eyeing the girl. She flushed pink under his scrutiny. "Me . . . I'm not an angel,' he continued. "Sometimes I . . ."

With a movement of her hand Constance checked Larry's self-accusation. "DeWitt is weak," she said. "You . . . you are not weak, Larry."

The name fell softly from her lips. Larry realized that she used it unconsciously. She had been thinking of him as Larry, not as "Mr. Blue." There was a thrill in that and more than a thrill in the soft voice, husky with unshed tears, that spoke on. "You . . . you have been our good genius, Larry. Don found the will my stepfather left because you asked him to look again. You . . ."

That will! Larry turned from the girl, not hearing her words. He knew why DeWitt Bolton was in jail, accused of murder. He knew why Constance was weeping and troubled. It was because of the will he had written. He had thought to bring things to a head when he scrawled those sentences upon foolscap in Don's office and signed Archer Bolton's name. He had thought that the document would clear the way for this girl beside him and for her brother. But that had not been the real reason for his forgery: He had wanted Don, wanted his brother. And now, because of his action, Constance was troubled, DeWitt was accused of murder, and Don . . . Don was alienated. And still . . . still Constance sat beside him, her very presence a joy, her eyes soft and lighting when he looked into them, her

215

voice sweet when she spoke his name: "Larry."

"Don said that you would go back to Denver after . . . after last night." Once more Larry caught the thread of the girl's words. "Don't go. Don't go, Larry. I . . . we need you here."

"I'm not going back to Denver yet a while," said Larry strongly, and then, the words odd to the girl because apparently they had no relevance: "I stand by what I do. My bets stick."

Felipe pulled the carriage in to the sidewalk in front of the Plaza, stopped his team and turned and looked at his passengers. Constance Bolton's hand lay over Larry's and her voice was very earnest when she said two words, "I'm glad."

Larry realized that they could not sit there in the barouche talking. He pressed the girl's hand where it lay in his palm, and rising, got out of the carriage. "You will stay and help us, Larry?" Constance asked, seeking final confirmation.

"I'll be here and help all that I can," Larry assured her. "But . . . Don won't take it kindly."

"I am disgusted with Don." The girl flushed again. "Last night I wanted him to help you and he would not. He thinks . . ."

"Don't quarrel with Don about me," said Larry. "I'm not worth it."

The girl's eyes were veiled by her long lashes. "Perhaps . . . perhaps I don't feel that way," she said, then blushing at what she had implied: "I will see you soon, Larry. I . . . I must go now. Drive home, Felipe!"

Larry watched the barouche roll away, then turning, he went into the hotel. He wanted time to think and a quiet place to do his thinking.

When he had made himself comfortable upon the bed

216

in his room, his feet propped up and a cigarette rolled, Larry squinted up through the smoke and let his mind work. He was responsible for this trouble, he knew. It all led back to Larry Blue. He had wanted Don to be a lawyer. Very good. Don was a lawyer and something of a snob, too. Larry was responsible for that. Don was pretty much of a kid and Don was in love. Don . . . Don was not the only one in love. What about Larry? That girl, Constance Bolton, with her rose petal lips and the dusky color in her cheeks and her soft voice . . . what about her? What did she mean to Larry Blue?

A man lying on a bed, smoking a cigarette and thinking about a girl, can build air castles. Larry Blue built them. There was Denver where he amounted to something. In Denver Larry could build a house, set up an establishment. He could quit the gambling. Royal would never say a word except perhaps: "Play your hand out, kid." It would be all right with Royal. In Denver . . . But what was he doing thinking about Denver? He was in Franklin and there were things to be done. Don . . . It always came back to Don. All his life things had centered about Don. Why shouldn't he let Don go, let him hoe his own row? Because Don was his brother and because Don was in love with Constance Bolton and because he had to think of Don. All right, he would think about Don and this trouble. It was his place to think about it. By forging that will Larry had caused the trouble and he would finish it or else he wouldn't be here. Now to business and let the day dreams go.

There were three witnesses against DeWitt Bolton. Annette Bondreaux was one of them. He must see Annette. The other two witnesses were planted. Who had Lester said? A man named Fernald and another named Morton. Annette was a showgirl. Her reputation

217

was none too good if the clerk's wink had meant anything. She might, perhaps, be discounted a little. The other two . . . Larry began to get ideas about the other two, ideas that crystallized into movement. He swung his feet down from the bed, got up and slipped into his coat. He would talk with Duck Bunn and then perhaps he could get some action.

Duck's hack was not in the cab rank at the corner. The other drivers, interrogated, did not know Duck's whereabouts. Larry was angry. It was late afternoon, he had not eaten all day, he was irascible and Duck was not on hand when he was needed. Larry glanced up at the sun. He had no time to waste.

"You tell Bunn to come to the Oxford for me when he gets back," Larry instructed the driver he had questioned. "Here. Here's for your trouble. Tell him to get down there."

The driver looked at the bill. He grinned. "Yes, sir," the driver agreed. "I'll tell him. Want me to take you down there?"

"I'll walk," Larry answered, and swung off toward the Oxford.

At the hotel the clerk greeted him obsequiously. The clerk remembered the other visit and the tip. Miss Bondreaux was in her room and the gent could go right up. Larry swung away from the desk. The clerk was disappointed. Then he shrugged philosophically. After all it was too much to expect a five spot every time.

At Annette's door Larry rapped impatiently and when Annette answered, called his name. Within seconds the was opened and he went in.

Annette was dressing. There were toilet articles on the dresser and her hair was fluffy about her head. She had, evidently, thrown on a robe when Larry called, and

218

her eyes were eager and bright when she looked at her visitor.

"I was hoping that you would come, Larry," she said. "I had meant to send you a note. I wanted to see you."

"I wanted to see you, Annette," said Larry briskly. His voice was commonplace, no meaning note in it. Annette's eyes lost some of their sparkle. "I want to talk to you about last night."

"Oh," Annette said slowly, "last night. It was an awful night, Larry. It seems like a nightmare."

"Pretty tough, all right." There was no sympathy in Larry's tone. "I imagine it upset you. You were pretty sweet on young Bolton?"

Sudden anger flared in Annette. "I hated him," she answered. "He was always . . . he tried to . . ."

Larry stopped the girl. "He's just a kid," he apologized for DeWitt. "You've got to make allowances for him. Don's going to defend him, Annette, and I came over to see if you could help any. I'd like to know what happened last night."

"It's always Don." Annette's voice was bitter. "When we were kids it was Don . . . Don . . Don . . . I'm sick of Don. Let him look out for himself!"

"But confound it, Annette," Larry's temper was short, "Don's my brother. This young Bolton . . ."

"He killed the only decent man in Franklin, as far as I'm concerned," Annette flared. "I came back into that room and there he sat, drunk, with his gun on the table beside him and Wayne. . ."

The girl turned, flung herself down on the bed and sobs shook her slim body. Larry, helpless, looked at the disaster he had wrought.

"Now wait a minute, Annette," he beseeched. "Now don't get upset. I just wanted . . ."

219

"You're like all the rest." The girl turned, sat up, her eyes flashing. "You want. You want! All I ever hear from men is what they want! How big they are. What they will do for me! The only man that didn't follow after me like a bloodhound was Wayne Justice, and your precious brother's client killed him."

This would never do. This would never do at all. Larry knew that he was off on the wrong foot. Knew it and did not know what to do about it. He tried another course.

"DeWitt's sister is about crazy over this thing," he said, softening his voice. "She's crying her eyes out over her brother. You're a girl, Annette and . . ."

"And I have cried my eyes out over a man too," Annette flung the words at him. "Larry . . ." She checked. Her eyes lost their hard look and became questioning. "Do you like her?" Annette asked.

Larry nodded. "She's a lady," he said, and unknowingly cut deeply with his words. "She . . . she doesn't belong to the same kind of people that we do, Annette. I . . . well, I like her." His conclusion was awkward, saying more than the words themselves expressed.

"Are you in love with her?" Annette's eyes were searching.

Larry flushed. "Don's in love with her," he equivocated. "I didn't mean to talk about Constance. I just wanted to know if there was anything that would help Don. He'll put you on the witness stand, Annette, and he'll make it pretty tough, I'm afraid." There was a warning in that.

Annette's face hardened. "I'm used to things that are tough," she said. "Do you think working in a show like this one is a bed of roses?" Her laugh was high and unnatural.

Larry blundered on. "I just didn't want you to get hurt, kid," he said. "I know that you've had it tough. Maybe I could make it easier for you. I'll talk to Don."

"I don't need your help!" Annette threw the proffered kindness back into Larry's face, "You can tell your brother that I don't know a thing that will help him get that murderer off and I'll go on the witness stand and swear that as far as I know, Bolton killed Wayne Justice. You come here talking about helping Don and all the time you're thinking about that girl. You're in love with her. Get out and leave me alone. Get out. Get out!"

Annette flung herself face down on the bed once more the robe tight about her, her slim body shaken with her grief within it. Larry, bewildered, looked at the girl and then slowly, a step at a time, backed to the door, opened it, and went out.

# CHAPTER 17

### ... But a Wolf Howls

DUCK BUNN'S CAB WAS AT THE CURB WHEN LARRY emerged from the Oxford Hotel. Duck, standing beside the hack, tried to explain his absence from the cab rank but Larry, shaken, was in no mood for talk. "I want to go some place where I can ask you some questions, Duck," he said. "How about your place?"

"Good with me," Duck agreed. "You et, Larry?"

Larry did not answer and Duck, assuming a negative response, frowned ferociously. "Got to eat," he announced. "All right, git in."

221

Larry climbed into the hack and Duck drove off.

Twice on the way to the western edge of town he stopped and went into stores, making purchases. When they did reach his adobe Duck got down and broke into Larry's silence. "Look after the team," he commanded. "You don't need to take off the harness. Just unhook an' water an feed 'em."

Larry was glad for something to do. At the little barn behind the adobe, he pumped a though full of water for the horses, threw down hay from a little stack and found a battered tin pail in which to measure oats from a meager store. Duck Bunn lived on the edge of poverty but his horses did not lack.

Returning to the house after the team was cared for, Larry found Duck frying steak.

"Duck," Larry announced, "I need some information."

Squinting his eyes to avoid the smoke of hot grease, Duck made answer. "You can have it if I got it," he assured, turn, ing the steak. "Set the table. This meat's a'most done."

Larry found utensils in a cupboard nailed to the wall. While he placed them he spoke. "Here's the layout, Duck: "DeWitt Bolton's in jail for murder and I've got to get him out. I got him in, I reckon."

Duck, dishing the meat, paused with his fork in midair.

"You got him in?" he said incredulously. "How come?"

"I just feel that I did," Larry answered.

Larry freed his mind to old Duck Bunn. He knew that talking to Duck was like throwing it down a well, it would never turn up to bother him again. And so he told of writing the will, of Don's actions, and of how Don

222

wanted to stay with Lester. Constance Bolton came into the tale. Annette Bondreaux entered it. By the time Larry had finished, they were through eating and Duck had stuffed a pipe while Larry rolled a cigarette.

"Yeah," said Duck Bunn, lighting his pipe, "I reckon yo're some responsible, Larry. Findin' that will kind of brung things to a head, it looks like."

Larry nodded glumly. "They made the frame-up on DeWitt when the will came to light," he said.

Duck squinted solemnly at the smoke. "Luella Seemans likes a dollar," he announced. "she's closer'n a burr in a sheep's hide. I reckon she's behind it."

Again Larry nodded.

"An' that Bolton girl," said Duck. "You think you're in love with her." He did not ask a question, simply stated his belief.

Larry flushed. "She's Don's girl." he said. "I . . . well, I like her . . ."

"You think yo're in love with her," Duck refuted Larry's statement placidly. "Better forget it."

"Why?" Larry was alert and perhaps a little angry.

"She ain't our kind," said Duck. "She's been raised gentle. She ain't never saw the rough string, Larry. Better forget her."

"What do you know about it?" Larry snapped.

"I was in love onct." Duck puffed placidly. "Preacher's daughter back in Ioway. I wasn't her kind nor she mine. We found it out in time. I know plenty about women, I do."

Larry sniffed, and Duck, his calm ruffled, took the pipe out of his mouth. "Yo're nothin' but a kid," he said scornfully. "Women's a life study, boy. You don't learn 'em in a minute. Wait 'til yo're as old as me."

"All right, grandpa," Larry said. "Then tell me what I

did wrong this afternoon when I went to see Annette."

"You let her know that you was stuck on the other gal." Duck put his finger unerringly upon the weak place. "That's what you done wrong. Still I wouldn't be surprised if she come through for you. There's a gal," Duck's tone was admiring, "that a feller wouldn't have to look back to see was she along. She'll do, Annette will."

"Well," said Larry, "I'm no judge of women. Let it go at that. Now what about this Fernald and this man Morton?"

"Morton runs the Crystal Palace for Abe Seemans," stated Duck. "Fernald lives over to yore hotel an' caps the games. He drags in any strangers that look like they had the dinero. Seemans owns 'em both."

"I thought that, but where can I get hold of them?"

"You can't buy 'em off," warned Duck. "They'll have to go through for Seemans. He'd kill 'em if they didn't an' if he didn't get 'em, Whiteman would. They know it."

"I wasn't figuring to buy 'em off," said Larry. "I want to talk to them."

"Together?"

"If I can."

"Then you can find 'em in the Crystal Palace restaurant along sometime after midnight," Duck stated positively. "I've seen 'em there every night I looked in."

"Then I'll look for them tonight," Larry stated. "Maybe I could get them to come out here and talk."

"Not unless you had 'em at the end of a gun," said Duck.

"Well," Larry drawled, "I've got a gun. You'd drive me out, wouldn't you, Duck?"

"Sure. But gettin' 'em."

"I made a fool of myself last night," Larry stated. "Now it looks like I could maybe use that. Here's what we'll do, Duck. Listen." He bent forward across the table, and Duck Bunn, pipe forgotten, listened closely.

Duck and Larry talked over a plan based on audacity and reckless disregard for their own and others' safety.

While Duck and Larry talked another disregarded her own safety and took her life in her two hands. Annette Bondreaux, after Larry's departure, remained on the bed, face down, sobbing. When finally she gained control of herself her first movement was toward her mirror. Powder and rouge erased the ravages the tears had wrought, and then rapidly the girl began to dress. She had some time before she was due at the theater, time that she generally spent in leisure. Now having decided upon a course of action, she hastened. Her toilet completed, Annette left her room, locked the door and leaving the key at the desk down stairs, went out to the street. She waited there until a hack came rattling by, and hailed the driver with a lifted arm.

When he swung in to the curb the girl asked to be taken to Judge Lester's. Riding up the hill to Lester's, with the sun gone and only its aftermath remaining over the Cantandos, Annette stared at the worn upholstery of the opposite seat. So preoccupied was she with her thoughts, that the driver was forced to inform her that she had reached her destination.

Directing the driver to wait, Annette knocked at Lester's door and asked the servant who answered the summons for Miss Bolton. Invited to enter, Annette stood in the hall, her hands nervously touching her hair or rearranging her dress until Constance appeared.

"I am Annette Bondreaux," the girl announced when Constance came to meet her. "I . . . I wanted to see you.

225

Is there some place that we can talk?"

Constance's face showed her surprise, and then collecting herself, the girl smiled wanly at her visitor. "We can go into the music room," she said. "I didn't expect you, Miss Bondreaux . . ."

"I didn't expect to come," Annette interrupted. "I thought . . . well," calmly, "I just wanted to see you."

Constance led the way into the music room just off the hall and gestured toward a chair. "Won't you sit down?" she invited. "Is it about DeWitt that you have come?"

Annette refused the seat but answered the question. "In a way it is about DeWitt. I . . . Miss Bolton, did you ask Larry Blue to come to see me?"

The surprise on Constance's face was answer enough. Annette went on rapidly. "Have you talked to Larry Blue?"

"Yes." Constance was frank. "I talked with him. I asked him to help us if he could."

"And what did he say?"

"He promised to help. I don't know why I tell you this. I don't know by what right you come here. After all, my brother . . . my brother would be here with us now if it were not for you. You infatuated him. You . . ."

"Can't we leave that out?" Annette's voice was weary. "What I've done doesn't matter. Will you answer one more question?"

"There is no reason why I should "Constance was haughty. "After all . . ."

"One more question: What is Larry Blue to you? Do you . . . ?"

"Mr. Blue is a friend!" Constance drew herself rigidly erect. "He has been very kind. His brother, of course, is

226

DeWitt's counsel. Naturally, Larry would . . ."

That one word was enough. "Larry!" Annette lowered her eyes. "I think I understand," she said softly. "I've come to help you, Miss Bolton. Can I speak to Don Blue or to Judge Lester?"

"Why . . . why, yes!" Constance was eager. "They will be here in a moment. I didn't understand, Miss Bondreaux. I didn't know that you had come to help. Sit down. As soon as Judge Lester comes . . ."

"I can't wait for him." With an effort Annette controlled her emotions. "Tell him this: Tell him that Wayne Justice said that he was going to get your brother. I'll swear to that on a witness stand. I'll swear to it!" Annette's voice had risen until it was almost a scream. Constance Bolton, moving toward the distraught girl, caught at Annette's shoulder.

"I don't understand," she began "I don't know . . ."

"Judge Lester will understand." Annette pushed aside the restraining hand. "Tell him what I said. I must go now. I . . . I must go."

She brushed by Constance, hardly seeing her, reached the door and caught at the jamb. Then, more steadily, she passed through the opening and when Constance reached the hall, Annette was at the outer door. She let herself out, Constance running after her, went to the cab and got in. The cab rolled away just as Constance Bolton reached the doorway of Lester's home. Constance looked after the cab, watched it as it turned out on the driveway and started down the hill, then closing the door the girl reentered the house. Constance Bolton's mind was in a turmoil, but the seething within it was as nothing to the tumult that raged in Annette's brain.

Annette had scarcely entered her hotel before George

Whiteman stepped from the curbing and approached the driver.

"Miss Bondreaux, wasn't it?" asked Whiteman of the driver.

"Yeah." The cabman nodded, pocketing the money that Annette had given him. "Want to go someplace, Mr. Whiteman?"

Whiteman shook his head. "Where did you take her?" he asked.

"Up to Lester's. Waited for her an' brought her back. She's sure a swell actress, ain't she? I seen her the other night an' . . ."

The driver broke off abruptly. Whiteman had stepped back to the curb and was favoring the front of the Oxford with a long, slow stare. Presently he turned and walked slowly down the street. He went a few steps, turned, and retraced them. Pushing open the door he went into the lobby.

Annette had just taken her key from the clerk and reached the foot of the stairs, when Whiteman's call stopped her.

"Annette!"

The girl turned. "Yes?" she said, and then seeing who had called to her, she paled. Whiteman, smiling, came to her side. "You have had a distressing day, my dear," he said gently. "Are you too tired to have supper with me tonight? Just a quiet supper at the Crystal Palace. We'll go to the restaurant."

Annette hesitated. She was tempted to refuse. Then she smiled at Whiteman and nodded. "I'll like to, George," she said disarmingly. "Just we two."

"And no one else," assured Whiteman.

At thirty minutes after midnight Duck Bunn's hack

228

pulled up before the Crystal Palace and discharged a passenger. The man who alighted seemed much the worse for liquor, for he staggered as he waved a bill toward the driver. Duck, leaning down to take the bill, heard a surprisingly sober voice give final directions.

"Don't forget, Duck. When I come out, alone or not, you pick me up."

Duck grunted his understanding and then, loudly so that the loafers on the walk could hear: "Wait a minute, mister, and I'll give you yore change." But the object of his call had already made his somewhat unsteady way into the barroom.

The Crystal Palace received Larry Blue gladly. The bartenders and the waiter that met him at the door of the restaurant had not forgotten the previous evening. Larry had laid a good foundation when he had gone on his spree.

"Yes, sir," said the somewhat soiled waiter. "There's a party of ladies back this way. They're alone, sir. Would you . . . ?"

"No women," Larry stated thickly. "Wine. Maybe women later."

Yes, sir," said the waiter.

He seated Larry at a table the cloth of which was none too clean, and stood by, waiting for the forthcoming order. "What you had last night?" suggested the waiter, smiling faintly.

"That's it," Larry agreed. "What I had las' night."

When the man was gone Larry stared owlishly about the room. There were two or three giggling women whose faces seemed familiar. They smiled and nodded invitingly. Evidently last night's acquaintances, although he could not remember one of them. Across the room at another table were two men and two

229

women, the men well dressed and with masklike faces, the women evidently showgirls. Further along the wall Annette Bondreaux sat with one of the men who had called that morning at Don's office. Larry knew that it was Whiteman although he had not met the man. Duck's description and warning had identified the lawyer. The two were talking, Annette bent forward over the table toward her escort. Beside Larry's elbow a cork popped. The waiter had returned and was opening champagne.

Champagne was common enough in Franklin. Booming Franklin was no stranger to any form of wealth or dissipation. The railroad, the mines to the west, the business that flowed back and forth across the border, all brought their tribute to Franklin and the town assimilated it all. Still the popping of that cork caused eyes to turn. Larry saw Annette raise her head and look at him. Without taking his eyes from the girl he groped for the glass that he knew must be on the table before him. Finding it he lifted it high and rising to his feet stood weaving. There was no mistaking his motion. Larry lifted his glass toward the girl and then drank. Annette flushed and George Whiteman, leaning toward her, spoke swiftly.

"Who is that?"

"I used to know him," Annette answered, the color still flaming in her cheeks. "That is Larry Blue."

"Ah, yes." Whiteman's voice was cool. "Mr. Blue. I have heard of him. He was quite a character last night. A brother to young Blue who is Lester's partner?"

Annette nodded. Larry had seated himself again and now was looking around the room.

"By the way, my dear," Whiteman's voice drawled on, "if I were you I would stay away from the Blues,

230

this one and that other. I would stay away from Lester's. No more little trips."

Annette almost gasped. What did Whiteman know? "Sympathy is all well and good," he continued, "but don't let it lead you astray. You'll testify against young Bolton, you know." His voice hardened suddenly. "You'll testify or I'll break your pretty neck, my dear. You will excuse me?"

George Whiteman got up without waiting for an answer and crossing leisurely to the table where sat the party of four, bent down and spoke. "It looks like your man is about right, Morton," he said. "The one you spoke of today. You might as well get what there is to be had."

The man he addressed looked up, his face stony, and nodded. Whiteman returned to his table. Larry sipped again from his glass. He wanted attention, wanted it particularly from that party of four. Duck Bunn had been direct and explicit in his description of Morton and Fernald. They were sitting over there. Presently Morton rose, smiled at his companions, and strolled over to Larry's table. Bending down he spoke. "All alone?"

"All by m'self," agreed Larry. "I'm lonesome."

"My name is Morton." The bending man thrust out his hand. "Glad to meet you, Mr. Blue. Would you care to join us? Just a little party and I hate to see a stranger in town not enjoy himself."

Larry weaved in his chair, straightened his mouth and then smiled broadly. "If I can join party I'll buy wine," he stated. "Can't buy wine, can't come."

Morton laughed. "You can buy all the wine you please," he announced. "Come on, Mr. Blue."

As Larry came up out of his chair Morton beckoned to the hovering waiter and tucked his hand under

231

Larry's arm. At Mortan's table introductions were in order. Larry heard names: Lola Montgomery, Carmen LaVerne, Carl Fernald. That last name pleased him. Both the men he wanted were together. He gave the waiter five dollars for bringing a bottle and ordered more wine.

The party waxed loud. Lola had a shrill giggle. Carmen tried to be genteel, becoming more and more polite and ladylike with each drink. Larry could hold a good deal of wine, particularly on a coffee foundation. By one o'clock things were well organized. Morton and Fernald were not drinking a great deal. It was evident that they had plans for Larry. They talked about roulette and the big winnings that Fernald had made. Larry wavered in his chair. Once he looked at Annette and saw her eyes on him. It was hard to read what was in the girl's dark eyes. Larry thought that it might be disgust.

Fernald and Morton brought the talk back to gambling. Larry was willing. He was lucky, he said, and taking the vagaries of drunkenness as a springboard, suddenly decided that he desired action for his money. Lola and Carmen demurred but were silenced by glances from Fernald.

"Got to have a game," Larry stated. "Goin' to take thish li'l or town apart an' shee what makes it tick. Goin' play."

He staggered up as he spoke and Fernald came to his feet. "There's a game upstairs," said Fernald. "Best game in town. We'll go up and trim it. Come on,"

But now, apparently struck by a new idea, Larry shook his head. "Can't leave the ladies," he objected. "Got to look after the ladies. I always take care of 'em." He leered wickedly at Lola who giggled.

Fernald scowled at Lola and she subsided. Morton

had also risen. "The girls can come along," he said. "They can. . ."

"Nope." Larry was very positive. "Goin' to take the ladies home. Goin' to shee 'em home. . . 'It was from Aunt Dinah's quiltin' party I wash sheein' Nellie home . . .' "This last an attempt at song.

Every eye in the restaurant was fixed on Larry Blue and his party. Fernald saw that and so did Morton. The attention was distasteful. They wanted to get out and get this piece of work done. "We'll take them home," Fernald assured. "Come on, we'll take them home." He seized Larry's dangling arm. The waiter was hovering anxiously near by. The tip of Larry's roll of bills showed from his vest pocket but he made no move toward it, but only stood wavering, held by Fernald. Morton paid the check, took the expostulating Lola and the protesting Carmen firmly in tow, and the five made their way out of the Crystal Palace. Duck Bunn's hack stood at the curb.

Duck saw the party come out. He came down from his seat and opened the door, standing beside it. As was the natural thing to do, with an inebriate and two women who were the worse for liquor on his hands, Morton made for the cab. He loaded his group in, putting Larry on the seat with his back to the driver, helping the girls to enter, and he and Fernald wedging themselves in place.

"Oxford Hotel, driver," directed Morton.

Duck climbed back to his seat and the cab rolled away.

At the Oxford Hotel Morton took the girls to the door.

Fernald stayed with the cab. Larry playing his part, had apparently passed out on the way to the hotel, sat

233

lolling on the front seat, his head hanging. Morton came back and got in.

Duck asked, "Where to, boss?"

"Go back to the Palace," directed Morton. The cab started with a jerk and only Fernald's quick movement kept Larry from falling.

"He's passed out," announced Fernald. "What's the use of going back to the Palace? He won't be able to play. Why not just take it and let him go? We can say that we left him at the Oxford and when he wakes up in an alley he won't know the difference."

"We'll sober him up," snapped Morton. "Whiteman said . . . Hey, where are you going?" This last a yell to Duck Bunn.

Larry sat erect in the front seat. There was something his hand that gleamed wickedly in the light that came from a corner lamp.

"Sit still!" snapped Larry. "We'll go out to your place, Duck."

"I was headin' there," answered Duck from the seat "Here, Larry, I'll put this lamp behind you."

The interior of the cab filled with light. Duck had pulled one of the lamps from its bracket beside the seat and now held it so that the light streamed down into the interior the hack through the partially opened top. The short gun in Larry's hand, held low in his lap, was the most prominent feature of his ensemble. Larry's voice was a smoothly pleasant drawl.

"Stay still," warned Larry. "Move and I'll shoot, and the driver and I will both swear that you tried to roll. me and I killed you when you did it. Drive along , Duck."

Duck drove along. Morton and Fernald sat stock still on back seat, their eyes fixed on that ugly blue weapon Larry's hand, as a bird's eyes might be fixed on the flicker of a snake's tongue.

The cab stopped before Duck Bunn's adobe. There bad moment there. Larry had reckoned on it, but he had not counted on Duck. Duck was on the job, Duck said, "Let 'em get out, Larry. I'll hold 'em."

That meant that Duck had a gun. Larry got as far back in the seat as possible and reached up his right hand for the lamp. He held it while Morton and Fernald, under Duck's orders, left the cab. When Larry got out he saw that he was right. Duck did have a gun. In the dim light it looked like a shotgun but Larry could not be sure. Duck unlocked the door of the adobe.

"Go in," directed Larry briefly. Morton and Fernald, their hands held shoulder high, filed toward the door, Larry following them with the lamp.

Inside the adobe he held the lamp high while Duck struck a match and lit the lamp on the table, then without instruction Duck moved on Fernald and Morton. Larry saw the two exchange glances and spoke once more.

"Don't try it! Stay out of line, Duck."

"Think you got to tell me that?" grunted Duck scornfully.

He walked behind Morton and Fernald, took a gun from Fernald and a revolver and a derringer from Morton, patted them carefully under the arms and on their pockets and around their waist bands, and stood back, nodding to Larry.

Larry held out the cab lamp. "Better put this back," he said.

Duck took the lamp, went out, and came back in.

Fernald wet his lips with the tip of his tongue. "This isn't going to get you anything," he said. "We haven't any money."

235

"I don't want money," Larry answered cheerfully, putting the short gun back under his arm. "You planned to roll me, didn't you?"

Fernald growled, "What if we did?" and stopped at a look from Morton.

Larry gestured toward a bench by the table. "Sit down," he ordered.

Both men sat down. Morton, the cooler of the two, spoke again. "This will cost you," he said. "You can't stay in Franklin and pull a thing like this. I thought there was something fishy about your being drunk."

"That's a lie," answered Larry cheeerfully. "You wouldn't have fallen for it if you thought anything was fishy."

Fernald fixed Duck with a baleful eye. "I know you driver," he snarled. 'This will cost you. You'll go to the pen . . .'"

"No he won't." Larry interrupted. "Not on your testimony."

Larry's voice was casual but there was a sinister significance in the words that made Fernald and Morton look at each other. Fernald wet his lips again. He was nervous, but Larry was looking at Morton. Morton was a heavy, stolid sort of man and yet Larry's eyes told him that Morton would crack under pressure.

"Whch one of you two killed Justice?" snapped Larry. "You?" his arm shot out, a finger pointing to Morton.

Morton flinched under the impact of the words and the pointing finger. He leaned away from it. "No," he began, "I . . ."

"Shut up!" snapped Fernald.

"Then it was you!" Larry turned his attack to the man. "You think that Justice didn't have any friends?"

236

"Young Bolton killed Justice," snapped Fernald. "He's in jail for it. Turner and I saw him do it, didn't we, Turner?" He looked at Turner Morton for corroboration.

"We saw him," agreed Morton. "You . . ."

"If you're a friend of Justice and think we had anything to do with his killing, I might pass this up," offered Fernald smoothly. "I know how a man feels about his friends. You . . ."

"You never had a friend," Larry interrupted. "Young Bolton didn't kill Justice. One of you did it. Bolton was drunk as you thought I was tonight. Which one was it? Speak up!"

Neither man spoke. Larry nodded to Duck Bunn "All right," he said. "Take this one outside." He nodded toward Morton.

It was a shotgun that Duck had, a very queer shotgun. Someone had cut off the barrel until there was about a foot left, and then carved a pistol grip out of the butt. The weapon looked like a club with a hole as big as a tunnel in the end.

Duck had his shotgun cocked. "Come on!" he growled.

Morton got up. Larry produced his own gun, under his coat and then reaching down with his left hand brought a knife from a sheath at his hip, the blade shining wickedly in the lamplight. As Morton moved toward the door, Larry essayed as evil a grin as possible. The effort must have been a success for Morton flinched and Fernald recoiled on the bench.

"Close the door, Duck" directed Larry, "and stay close."

Sure," grunted Duck. The door closed.

Larry looked at Fernald. "I don't want to be hard

237

about this," he said cheerfully. "I know that you were working under orders. Which one of you killed Justice? Cough up and the other one will get loose. Did your partner do it?"

Fernald maintained a sullen silence. Larry waited patiently. Fernald shifted nervously on the bench.

"Well," said Larry, "if you will have it that way . . ."

He moved catlike in on Fernald. Fernald rose to meet him coming up to fight. Larry had expected that. He lashed out with the gun, a carefully calculated blow. Fernald had not been expecting a blow. Fernald was expecting a shot. The gun struck home on Fernald's soft hat. Fernald went down, eyes glazing, and Larry watching the man fall, screamed, hoping as he yelled that he had put sufficient terror in his voice.

Fernald sprawled out on the floor. Larry watched him to see if another blow was necessary. Apparently it wasn't. Stepping to the door Larry opened it and spoke to Duck. "Bring him in."

Duck's growled, "Git inside," answered the command.

When Morton entered, Larry was bent over Fernald, wiping his knife blade on Fernald's dark trousers.

"He wouldnt talk." Larry said casually. "How about this one, Duck? He softened up any?"

Duck did not answer. He had closed the door behind him and he and Morton were both looking at Fernald with wide, horror-stricken eyes.

"Well?" demanded Larry. "Who killed Justice, you or your partner?"

Morton gulped. "We didn't . . ." he stammered. "My God, let me out of here. We didn't kill Justice. Whiteman shot him. He was waiting in my office at the Crystal Palace and when the girl went out he stepped in and let Justice have it. We didn't . . .!'"

Larry put his knife back in its sheath, holstered the Smith & Wesson and smiled pleasantly. "Sit down, Morton," he ordered. "Duck throw some water on this gent on the floor. He'll come around in a minute. I didn't hit him very hard. What do you reckon we'd better do with these two? We can't have them running loose."

Duck said, "Well. . ." speculatively, and looked hard-eyed at Morton and Fernald. He had drenched Fernald with water from his bucket and Fernald was stirring, trying to sit up.

"If we could get them out of town," Larry suggested.

"Tie 'em an' throw 'em in a boxcar," suggested Duck. "There's a freight that pulls out early every mornin', headin' east."

Larry nodded. "We'll do that, but we won't tie them," he said. "They might starve to death before anybody found 'em."

"Then what?" demanded Duck.

"Got any liquor?"

Duck produced a jug from beneath his bed, and shook it. "Pretty near full," he stated. "That's about half a gallon of tequila."

"Enough," declared Larry, grimly. He turned to Morton and to Fernald who was now sitting up and holding his head. "You've got a choice," he announced. "You can get good and drunk, or else I'll slap you over the head with my gun. One thing sure, youre leaving Franklin and not coming back."

"Why not?" Morton rasped. He had regained some confidence, "If you think for a minute that you're goin' to get away with this . . ."

"I've got away with it," snapped Larry. "And you're

not coming back because in about an hour some cop down town is going to pick me up out of an alley with my clothes dirty and a cut on my head. I'll be broke, and all will swear that you took me into that alley. They'll know you rolled me. Do you think that Seemans or Whiteman will stand for that? Try to come back. Your boss would kill you, and you know it."

He paused triumphantly. Morton glowered. Fernald shook his head weakly. "And now start drinking that liquor," commanded Larry Blue.

# CHAPTER 18

### BEHIND CLOSED DOORS

THE SWITCHMEN WHO WORKED AT NIGHTS IN THE Franklin yards had need to be alert. Beside the ever present danger of losing a thumb or a finger or so to the link and pin couplers, there was always the added chance that someone would borrow from a loaded car. The switchmen carried brake clubs as part of their professional equipment and on occasion they used those clubs for other purposes than twisting down brake wheels.

It was Mike Rafferty, a fine upstanding young son of Erin, who had driven many a spike as the road progressed westward, that spotted the door of the boxcar. The door was opened a trifle and had no right to be. Mike called in his partner, one Clarence O'Brion, and lanterns in hand and brake clubs cocked for action, they investigated the phenomena. No one answered their raucous orders to "Come out of there, youse bums!" and so they slid open the door and climbed in. It was

240

Clarence who discovered two bodies at the far end of the partially laden car, but it was Mike, always quick that way, who by way of precaution tapped twice with his brake club at the heads he saw.

"There!" said Mr. Rafferty, "let that be a lesson to ye."

The slower moving Clarence bent down and sniffed. "Drunk," he announced. "A beautiful pair of drunks. What would you give, Mike, to be as drunk as that?"

Mike's olfactory organs were in as good working trim as his partner's. He added their evidence to Clarence's statement and made answer. "It's a grand way to get," said Mike. "We'll drag 'em out of here, Clarence."

Accordingly, their feet bumping over the bottom boards, the two limp bodies were pulled from the car and none too gently disposed close to an empty siding. Mike and Calrence went on about their work, having donr their good deed for the day.

Their unfinished task was taken up by Dan Tully, a thick-set gentleman who gloried in the title of Special Officer. Mr. Tully, a railroad bull in any language, coming upon recumbent shapes in his rounds of the yards, kicked at inert feet, beat a tattoo upon a shoe sole with his stick and then did as the switchmen had done: bent down and sniffed.

"This" chided Mr. Tully, straightening, "is a hell of a place to sleep off a drunk. Supposin' one of ye was to roll an' the yard engine would come along an cut off the head of you? Then what? Would the railroad be liable?" With that, he bent down, possessed himself of two coat collars and hauled away.

The load was heavy. Mr. Tully was willing but quick witted. He bethought himself of the fact that the City of Franklin maintained a police force and a Black Maria

241

for such contingencies. Mr. Tully walked away whistling, and returning presently, spoke to his companion.

"There they are, Sherm. Two sleepin' beauties if I ever seen one."

Sherman Clay, one of the Railroad Avenue squad, bent down and, like his predecessors, sniffed. "Drunk as two boiled owls," drawled Mr. Clay in his soft Texas voice. "He'p me haul 'em out in front, Tully, an Ah'll send for the wagon."

So by devious ways, Turner Morton and Carl Fernald began their journey, a journey which eventually terminated in the bullpen of the Franklin jail. There, with two natives; a woman who shrilled: "Wait 'til I tell Abe Seemans about this. Just you wait!"; a teamster who snored on the only bench; and a little, disheveled man who sniffed incessantly through a running nose, Mr. Morton and Mr.Fernald slept.

They were not alone in their slumber. In an adobe at the west edge of Franklin Larry Blue smiled pleasantly beneath his dark mustache, as though his dreams were pleasant.

Duck Bunn snored the snore of the just and whistle of the outward bound freight blew a blast that shook the house, Duck turned over and gave up the unequal competition.

The preliminary hearing of DeWitt Bolton was set for ten o'clock in the morning. It was not held. Judge Goshan, who consented to sit as committing magistrate, was in his court. Don Blue and Judge Lester were present, as was pale-faced Constance Bolton. George Whiteman appeared, and Abe Seemans hovered in the background. Annette Bondreaux, wan of face and showing the strain, had come with Whiteman but she was not called upon. The State's two premier witnesses, the men upon whom the fate of DeWitt Bolton hung, were not there. Whiteman fumed, Seemans rumbled, albeit he kept a bland and pleasant mask; Annette looked her relief, and Judge Goshan was disgusted.

The judge had thought this a routine matter, a favor to his friend, Seemans, and he had risen early. Now that early rising was wasted. The good judge frowned and fumed and was almost tempted to sign the writ of habeas corpus that Don Blue presented to him when the hearing was postponed. There being no other magistrate available to sign the writ, DeWitt Bolton, his handsome face showing his worry and a heavy growth of beard, was taken back to his cell. Judge Goshan retired to his chamber where he had a bottle of six-year-old Ripple whisky, and George Whiteman and his honor, the Mayor, adjourned to Seemans' office. Annette went back to her hotel, and Constance, accompanied by Don, visited her brother. Through all these proceedings Larry Blue slept peacefully. Larry knew that DeWitt's hearing was scheduled, he knew that DeWitt was, in the course of events, to be bound over to a Grand Jury. He was not worried. You cannot indict a man when the witnesses against him are riding a boxcar toward the East. Larry got his sleep out.

He was clean-shaven and alert, and a devil sported in his eyes when at two o'clock he strolled into Lester's anteroom. He had done his part, Larry felt, and now it was up to Don and his partner. Larry had disposed of the witnesses against DeWitt, and he knew who had shot Justice. What more could Don. and Lester ask? Surely, with that help they should be able to get somewhere.

Both Lester and Don were in. Through Don's open door Larry could see Constance Bolton sitting beside Dods desk. They were talking and Larry did not intrude. Lester came out from his room to greet the visitor. The judge looked much better than on the preceding day. He shook hands cordially and invited Larry to enter. Larry accepted.

"How are you coming along?" Larry asked when he had taken a seat. "How did the hearing come out?"

"It was postponed," Lester answered. "Two of the witnesses were not present. Whiteman asked for a continuance and Goshan granted it. DeWitt is still in jail."

"Teach him to pick his playmates after this," commented Larry callously. "What is your next move, Judge?"

"To get a magistrate that will sign a writ of habeas corpus," answered Lester. "They cannot hold DeWitt indefinitely. We can get him out of jail on a writ and prepare for the hearing when it comes up again."

"If those two witnesses don't show up, what are DeWitt's chances?" asked Larry. He knew the answer to his question before he asked it.

Don's voice came from the door behind his brother. "Then they haven't a case," he stated. "If those men are gone, they have fled through a sense of guilt. The evidence against DeWitt is purely circumstantial if they do not testify, and we can beat it. Miss Bondreaux came to the house last night and told Constance that Justice had threatened DeWitt's life and that she would so testify. They haven't a case without those two men."

Don entered Lester's office, having finished his statement, closely following Constance, who smiled at Larry. Don too was cordial, at least he was not frowning

244

at his brother.

Larry arose, as did Judge Lester, when the girl entered the room. "Annette came out last night?" he asked puzzled. "I thought . . . Well, never mind."

Don was in high good spirits. Things were coming his way and he knew it. "Whiteman was surprised when I told him what the girl had said," he stated. "Quite surprised. It is possible that he will drop the whole thing, let the case go by default. He knows he is beaten."

Larry's eyes narrowed. "You told Whiteman what Annette said?" he asked incredulously.

Don flushed. Lester was frowning. Apparently this was the first he had heard of Don's indiscretion. "I wanted to make him see how useless all this was," explained Don. "He and Seemans were here yesterday, offering to trade their influence if we would relinquish the claim against Archer Bolton's estate. Of course we would not do that." He smiled fondly at Constance.

Larry studied his brother, looking at him with a long, slow survey that covered Don from his shoes to the top of his head. He said nothing, simply looked. Don, after his glance at Constance, turned to Larry again. "Did you come to see me?" he asked. "If you have something that you want to talk about I'm sure that Constance and the Judge will excuse us."

"I came up to tell you good-by." Larry's voice was strained and a little hoarse. "I was going back to Denver tonight. I thought that DeWitt would be loose and that you would be able to take care of anything else that came up."

"I'll be sorry to have you go." Just the words and not the voice said that Don was sorry. "As soon as we clear up this matter I'll try to run up to Denver for a day or two and visit you. I . . ."

"You poor damned fool!" said Larry slowly. "I'm not going now."

"What do you mean?" snapped Don, instantly angry. "You may be my brother but that gives you no right to insult me! After the display you made of yourself I'm . . ."

Larry Blue said two words: "Shut up!" His voice was as savage as his face as he spoke, and under the impact of facial expression and voice, Don Blue checked his words, leaving his sentence unspoken. Larry eyed his brother again; a slow, insulting survey.

"And you told Whiteman that Annette would testify for you?" he drawled. "The kid goes to bat for you, puts her life in your hands, and you throw it away. You poor damned fool!"

"You should not have given Whiteman that information, Don," Lester spoke abruptly. "It was dangerous. Whiteman is utterly unprincipled. He . . ."

Larry interrupted. He had walked across to the wall and, now, turning, he faced the others in the room. Constance Bolton he disregarded entirely. Judge Lester he did not see. He looked only at his brother and to him he spoke.

"And I was going home," Larry drawled. "I thought I'd fixed things so you could handle them. I meddled in this when I shouldn't have. I wanted you to win your case, so I wrote that damned will. Sure I wrote it!" He laughed harshly. "Last night, after I'd seen what I'd started, I was going to fix things. I went to see Annette. I talked to her and she wouldn't do a thing. She changed her mind and turned out to help you. You threw her to the wolves. Last night me and a friend of mine got those witnesses drunk and loaded 'em in a boxcar headed

246

East. With them out of the way Whiteman didn't have a case. Sure I meddled. I got you into this and I got you out. You poor fool! I thought I'd raised a man, I did. And you turned out to be a wet-eared kid."

Constance Bolton's eyes were on Larry as he read his slow indictment of Don, as he recapitulated the things he had done since his advent in Franklin. Dark eyes they were wide with a question at first, and then as Larry drawled on, filled with another look. Her hand dropped from Don's arm when Larry finished.

Don stammered. His face was dark with blood and his eyes were blazing with anger. "You have no right to talk like that!" he began. "I won't listen. I . . ."

But Larry, his talking done, was moving toward the door, paying no heed to his brother or to Lester who had risen from his chair. It was Constance who stopped Larry. Constance who, moving swiftly, caught his arm and held him. "Where are you going?" she demanded. "Don't go, Larry. Don't leave me here."

"I'm going to find Annette, if she's alive," said Larry. "I'll try to find her and see if she's all right. Then I reckon . . ." He said no more. His blue eyes were light with the flame behind them and there was about him a thing that caused the girl to shrink away even though she retained her hold on his arm.

From Larry's set face Constance turned to Don. She looked at him, searchingly, measuringly, and then again turned to the man whose arm she held. "Take me with you!" Constance almost whispered.

"No," Larry's answer was short and stern. "I can't You wouln't want to see."

He pulled his arm gently from the girl's grip and without looking at Don Blue or the anxious Lester, walked out of the office. As he passed the door he heard

Lester voice a question.

"Why did you talk to Whiteman, Don? Why did you tell him?"

Down stairs the faithful Duck was waiting. Duck saw at once that something was amiss and scrambled down from the seat of his hack. "What is it, Larry?" demanded Duck. "What's wrong?"

"You take me to the Oxford Hotel," said Larry. "And take me there quick, Duck!"

In Lester's office Don Blue had not answered the older man's question. He stood, head hanging, eyes on the floor. Constance Bolton it was who made the answer. "Does it matter?" she demanded. "It's done. And now we must do something. What can we do, Uncle Judge!"

Judge Lester, taking his eyes from Don, answered the girl's words. "We can telegraph to Austin once more," he said wearily. "That is all we can do. Telegraph and ask for the Rangers."

Abraham Seemans' office was in the city hall. Part of the city hall was the jail and the rest housed the municipal departments. Being Mayor, Seemans had taken two rooms in the long adobe structure. Now Seemans sat behind his desk in the outer room. The inner door was locked and the key lay before Franklin's Mayor. Annette Bondreaux was behind that locked door, Annette whom Whiteman had tolled to this place. Looking at the key Abe Seemans considered the disposition of Annette. There was only one thing to do with the girl, he thought. Shut her mouth, shut it permanently. He would have trouble convincing George Whiteman that that was the thing to do.

The outer door of the office opened unceremoniously

and Whiteman stamped in, tossing his hat on the floor in a corner. "I found 'em," he snapped. "Found 'em, and you'd never guess where!"

Seemans got up and came over to the smaller man. "Where, George?" he demanded. "Had they pulled out?"

"In jail!" Whiteman swore viciously. "I dropped into the police court and there they were. Gallegos was the most surprised Mexican I've ever seen. He didn't know what to do. I soon told him."

"But . . . in jail? What were Morton and Fernald doing there? How did they get into that sort of a scrape? I don't understand it. I don't . . ."

"I took them to the hotel to sober up," snapped Whiteman. "They were drunk. Still drunk after an all day's sleep. They talked a little. Very little!"

"What did they have to say?" demanded Seemans. "What happened?"

"That damned Blue happened!" answered Whiteman. "Larry Blue. That young whelp's brother. He happened to them."

"But I don't understand," Seemans said again. "I don't . . ."

"I'll tell you as much as I know," said Whiteman. "I got a little out of those two. They were at the Crystal Palace last night, in the restaurant. I was there with Annette. This Blue came in, drunk to all appearances. He had been on a bender the night before. Got thrown out of the Empire for raising a disturbance, and made the rounds of every place in town, buying wine and generally playing the fool. I thought that if he had all that money to spend, I'd see that we got some of it. I sicked Morton onto him. How did I know that he was shamming?"

"Then he wasn't drunk?"

"Not by a damned sight! He went with Morton and Fernald and a couple of women in a hack. They took the women home. Then they started back to the Palace to get him into a game. On the way he pulled a gun. The hack driver helpled him. He took Morton and Fernald out to a place on the edge of town and worked thcm over."

"Both of them?' Seemans expressed his incredulity in his tone.

"Both of 'em," stated Whiteman grimly. "I think he got what he wanted, too. Turner didn't say, but I think Blue knows who killed Justice. When he had pumped those two he made them drink half a gallon of tequila. They woke up in jail. I haven't found out yet just how they got there. I talked to Turner after I took him to the hotel and then I came here."

"Who put them in jail?" demanded Seemans. "Every man on the force knows Turner Morton. I'd like to know what fresh cop it was that threw them in. By God, I'll have his job!"

"A young fellow on the Railroad Avenue squad named Sherman Clay," Whiteman answered. "Your hand-picked Chief of Police, Vance, hired him and a couple of others a week or so ago. Clay didn't know who Morton was, of course."

"Vance has got no business taking on men without asking me about it," snapped Seemans. "I'll tell him so. He . . ."

"Let your little politics go!" ordered Whiteman. "They can wait. We've got some other things to attend to."

"What?"

"That man Blue. He knows too much."

250

Seemans nodded. "He does," he agreed, his face serious. "We've got to attend to him, George."

Whiteman's face was suddenly old and tired. His voice was almost weary when he spoke. "You mean I've got to attend to him, Abe," he said. "Me, George Whiteman." He broke off and stared musingly at the other man.

"Funny," Whiteman seemed almost to be making casual comment, "isn't it, Abe? I started out because a drunk got tough with my mother. I killed him because of that. She wasn't worth killing a man for, but I didn't know it. The drunk had some friends. They took it up and I had to down two of them and run because the country got too hot for me. I lit out here and it seemed like trouble followed me. First it was one thing and then another. Andrews hired me to get him the Tanks and I killed Haslip. Tom Blue got hung for that. Then old Cardwine had to put his nose into it and I had to get him too. Now here's this fellow Blue, sticking his nose into things."

"You getting soft, George?" questioned Seemans anxiously. "Are you . . . ?"

"Soft, hell!" Whiteman snapped the words petulantly. "What do you think? I'm going through with this, ain't I? It's just that the whole thing is a damned nuisance! Why can't these people leave good enough alone? Why do they always have to stick their bills into my business? I'm getting tired of it, Abe."

Abe Seemans stared at the smaller man. He had never heard Whiteman talk so, had never heard him express his sentiments one way or another. Apparently George Whiteman, whose business was death, was getting weary of that business. "How many men have you killed, George?" he asked curiously.

Whiteman considered. "Do you count Mexicans and Indians?" he asked.

Seemans nodded.

"I don't know then," Whiteman's tone was still petulant. "What difference does it make, anyhow? Well settle this Larry Blue's business tonight."

"And then . . . ?" said Seemans.

"Then we'll go ahead like we planned," Whiteman continued. "Morton and Fernald will testify against Bolton and we'll go through."

"What about the girl?" Seemans nodded his head toward the locked door.

"I'll attend to her," snarled Whiteman viciously. "Give me a little time with her and she'll be glad to do whatever I tell her to."

Behind that locked door Annette shuddered. She had been in that closed room for two hours. She had tested every window, tried the door, and had given up. The windows were barred and the door was thick and locked. She knew why she was there, knew that somehow George Whiteman had learned of her visit to Lester's home, and her offer there. Whiteman had told her when, snarling, he had thrown her into the room and locked the door. Now she crouched beside that portal, her ear to the keyhole, listening, listening to learn if she could, what was to happen. She knew now, knew what was in store for her, and worse, the thing that was in store for Larry Blue. Whiteman had said that he would take care of Larry Blue. That could mean only one thing.

"You going to talk to her now, George?" asked Seemans.

"Not yet," Whiteman rasped. "Give her time to think things over. I'm going back to the hotel to see if those

252

two are sobered up a little. I want to find out just what Morton told Blue. You coming?"

"I think I'll stay here a while," answered Seemans. "I want to see Vance. He ought to be here pretty soon."

"Let the girl alone," warned Whiteman. "I'll handle her." He picked up his hat, pulled it on and nodding to Seemans went on out. Seemans, fat hands folded, placed his thumbs together and stared at the wall. Things were going wrong, very wrong. Still they couldn't help but turn out all right. George would kill this nuisance, Larry Blue, and they could go ahead as planned. But after that what? George Whiteman was getting out of line. He was not fitting into Abe Seemans' plans at all. Seemans nodded. He would have to do something about Whiteman, when this was done. The question was just how?

Abe Seemans considered that question for a long time. He unlocked his hands and with an effort that brought a grunt, got his feet up on the desk. Whiteman was a problem. He was still useful but it would not be long before he outlived his usefulness. There must be some way. . . Abe Seemans sought for it.

Dusk crept into the office. Whiteman did not return and Seemans glanced uneasily at his watch. Steps sounded in the corridor and Seemans brightened. George was coming back. Perhaps he had attended to the matter in hand. Perhaps. . . .

The door opened. Frank Vance, the Chief of Franklin's Police, thrust in his head and, seeing Seemans, came on into the room. Vance was agitated, his face showing his disturbance.

"What is it, Frank?" asked Seemans without changing position at his desk.

"I got this at the depot," said Vance, placing a square

253

of yellow paper before his boss. "I was there when this telegram came in and I got it from the operator."

Seemans picked up the paper. His eyes crinkled against the fading light as he read the message.

TO JOHN LESTER, FRANKLIN,—

ANSWERING YOUR TELEGRAM ADVISE YOU RANGER FORCE IN FRANKLIN CONTACT SHERMAN CLAY WITH INFORMATION GOOD LUCK.

The signature was that of the Attorney General of the state.

"I thought you'd better see that," said Vance. "I hired that man Clay. We needed a couple of men and he had recommendations and . . ."

"It doesn't matter, Frank," Seemans interrupted calmy.

"It's all right"

"Then you think..?"

"You let me handle it," comforted Seemans. "You go on, Frank. I'll look after things."'

Vance hesitated. The placid calm of Seemans overcame his fears. He smiled. "I'll go along then," he said. "You sure can handle things, Abe."

Left alone in his office Abe Seemans read the message through once more. Then crumpling it, he threw it in the waste basket, lowered his feet from their elevation, and got up. He did not look at the closed and locked door of the inner office, but donning his hat went on out into the dark corridor. Leaving the municipal building he rounded the corner of the jail. There he spoke to the native who came to meet him.

"Get the rig, Juanito. I'm going home."

Annette Bondreaux heard the fat man's departure,

254

listened at the door, crouching against it. No sound from the office. Straightening, the girl looked about the room. She was alone, she believed. Upon the wall hung a heavy barreled Sharps rifle, a tasteful decoration, with the Indian bows and quiver of arrows beneath it. Moving swiftly the girl pulled a chair beneath the gun, climbed up and took down the dusty weapon. She had to get out, had to get out and warn Larry Blue!

Jim Cardwine would have approved the use to which Annette put his old gun then. Would have approved it and sanctioned it, fond as he had been of "Ol' Sal." Empty and useless as a weapon, still the heavy Sharps made a battering ram. Annette beat against the panels of the door, struck wildly and awkwardly. But wood cannot stand against steel. A panel cracked, splintered and a gap widened. Now the battering ram became a pry. Now the center strip groaned under the applied pressure. Hands aching, Annette pushed and strained, and with a final crackling the wood gave way.

# CHAPTER 19

### MADNESS

ANNETTE TORE HER DRESS GETTING THROUGH THE door. That was of no moment. What was important was to find Larry and get him out of George Whiteman's way. Annette had no idea that Larry Blue, the grown-up boy that she had worshiped, that she still worshiped, might be or was able to meet and cope with Whiteman on his own account. Annette knew George Whiteman, knew the things the pale-eyed, buck toothed man had done; and she was frightened, not for herself

255

particularly, but for Larry. Dress torn, hair disheveled, pale face streaked with dust from the old Sharps, and eyes wide with fright, she left Franklin's city hall and almost ran the two blocks to the Plaza Hotel. The clerk disdainfully answered her panted inquiries. Mr. Blue was not in. He had not been in. The clerk did not know when he would come in. Indeed, while Mr. Blue was registered at the Plaza, he had not been using the hotel of late.

Annette left the hotel. There was one other possible place where Larry might be: Lester's house. Annette remembered Constance Bolton, she remembered that Larry had been with Constance, and too, she knew that Larry's brother lived at the Lester home. She must get there at once. She had no money and Judge Lester had built upon a hill a long way out from the Plaza. Taking a cab at the stand at the corner she told the driver her destination, and settled herself nervously in the seat. Larry must be at Lester's, and if she could keep him there, keep him out of danger, she have accomplished her task.

And where was Larry Blue? At the moment he was talking to Duck Bunn down on a corner of Railroad Avenue.

"She wasn't at the hotel," Larry recapitulated. "They said she'd gone out with Whiteman. She wasn't at the Palace anyplace else that we've been, the theater or anywhere. It's no use looking for her, Duck. We've got to find Whiteman."

Duck nodded soberly. Duck was worried, not about Annette Bondreaux, but about Larry. He did not want Larry going up against Whiteman but he could not stop that. Larry was determined. Duck was a follower, not a leader, and Larry was his boss.

"I don't know where we'd find him neither," Duck contributed. "Seemans has went home, they said at the city hall. Whiteman might be out with him."

Larry shook his head impatiently. "I'm going to the Palace, Duck," he announced. "I'll stay there. That's where Whiteman and Seemans hang out. If one of them shows up I'll talk to him. You work around. You know the ropes. Ask questions and find out what you can. If you locate Whiteman or Seemans you come and get me."

Duck was dubious. "I don't like you projectin' around alone," he announced. "Seems like I ought to be with you. Whiteman's bad, Larry."

"I know it," Larry answered impatiently. "That's why I'm looking for him. Go along, Duck. I'll walk over."

"Um," said Duck but took the order. Larry swung off along the walk and Duck, clucking to his team, moved toward the depot. Some cronies of his held down the cab stand by the depot. Maybe he could pick up a little information. He glanced back as he drove, watching Larry's sturdy figure as it swung along the walk.

The hack stand by the depot held but a single cab. Duck drove up, stopped his team and alighting fell into conversation with the other driver. He did not push things, but by degrees brought the conversation around to the proper subject. The other driver had not seen George Whiteman or Abe Seemans, not all day. He had not heard a word concerning them. Duck said that there were no trains due and that he had just as well go back uptown. The other driver thought the same. He told Duck "so long" and getting up to his seat, drove away before Duck, unwieldy as he was, could mount his cab. Duck was just gathering up his lines preparatory to driving away, when a tall, blond-haired man issued from the station door and hailed him. Duck could barely make out the tall man's features in the failing light.

"Wait a minute," called the tall man. "I need you."

Duck waited. The tall man came to the side of the hack and peered up. "Know where Judge Lester lives?"

Duck said that he knew.

"I'll want to go there pretty soon," drawled the man beside the cab. "You can take me. Got a couple of places to stop first."

"Listen, mister," Duck spoke earnestly, "I got work to do, I have. I got to scout around an' find a man. I got a friend in trouble an' I ain't got time to fool with you."

The tall man laughed, opened his coat and Duck following the motion saw a familiar badge. "Oh!" exclaimed Duck. "Uh . . ."

"Yeah," drawled the tall man, "Ranger service. Git a goin'. Take me down to Barker's alley an' we'll stop there. I got to pick up a couple of fellows."

"Honest, Ranger," Duck tried again. "I got a friend in trouble. I got to find a man an' . . .'"

"We'll find him," Sherman Clay grinned humorously. "I'll help. Right now the State of Texas needs yore hack. You do like I say."

There is no use arguing with a Ranger. Duck knew it. Everybody knew it. The Rangers have a persuasive way of getting what they want. Duck sighed. "Git in," he said. "You want Barker's alley?"

"Right," agreed Clay, and climbed into the hack. There was a telegram in Clay's pocket, a telegram that had been delivered.

Annette Bondreaux could not pay her driver when he stopped his cab in front of Lester's house. She told him to wait, and the driver, suspicious as he was because of her disheveled appearance, got down from his seat and

258

attempted to argue the matter. The girl brushed him aside and running to the door, beat a swift tattoo against its oak. She was there, wildly refuting the driver's accusation that she meant to stand him up for her fare, when the door opened. The sound of the altercation carried past the servant who had opened the door, and reached Lester's ears. The old man came to the door and when he appeared the driver ceased his argument.

"What is this?" demanded Lester, testily, not recognizing Annette in the dusk. "What is happening here? I can't have a disturbance . . ."

Annette caught at his arm. "Larry," she exclaimed. "Whiteman means to kill him. I heard him say so."

Lester knew the girl now. He pulled her into the house and turned to the hackman. "Here," he said shortly, thrusting out a handful of change. "Take this!" The money dropped to the ground and the door closed in the startled driver's face as he reached for the fare.

Inside the hall there was light. Constance Bolton appeared at the end of the hall and Don Blue came from a side door. Both man and woman paused, astonished at what they saw.

Annette was pouring out her story to the Judge. Excitedly, urging haste now that she had discovered that Larry was not in this house, she told what she knew and what she heard. Lester pieced complete sentences from the broken words she uttered, and having learned the purpose of her visit, made rapid decision.

"We must find Larry," he said. "I'll have the carriage brought around at once. Don, you will go with me. Constance . . ."

But Constance had disappeared. Before the Judge finished ordering his carriage, she had returned, a bonnet tied on her head and firm determination written

259

in every line of her body.

"I'm going with you," she announced.

"You can't," Lester answered. "You must stay here and look after this poor girl. Don and I . . ."

"I'm going to Larry," Annette cried. "I've got to find him!"

"We'll find him, my dear," Lester soothed. "We'll find him. Felipe! Where in the devil . . . !"

When he left the City Hall, Abe Seemans sent his light rig along at a spanking pace. Juanito, beside him on the seat, held on with both hands. Seemans kept the trotter at his work. He drew rein in the driveway beside his house. Giving Juanito the lines, he also gave orders.

"Drive around back and turn," he said. "I'm going back down town pretty soon and I'll want the horse."

"Si," agreed Juanito, and the buggy wheels crunched upon the gravel.

Abe Seemans entered his home cautiously. Luella, he thought, might be waiting for him. He hoped not. If she were waiting he would have to change his plans and Abe Seemans, a course once decided, hated to change it. His cautious footsteps brought no call, no welcome, and satisfied that his wife was out, Seemans slipped up the stairs. There in his room (for he did not share a room with his wife), he worked swiftly. Abe Seemans filled the telescope bag beneath his bed, with shirts and socks and other appurtenances. He was leaving Franklin, leaving for good. That message Vance had given him was enough for Abe Seemans. Let others stay and fight and hold the sack. He, Abe Seemans, was all through. When the Rangers came Abe Seemans left. It was time to go when the Rangers came time and past time. But he would not go empty-handed. There was that safe

260

downstairs, the safe behind the picture, and to which he had the combination, painfully memorized. Strapping the telescope, Seemans lifted it and on tiptoe made for the door. In the hall a board squeaked complainingly beneath his weight. He paused and then reassured by silence, went on down the dark hall.

At the end of the hall Luella stirred upon her bed. She had had a splitting headache in the afternoon. She had had many headaches recently and could not throw them off. The doctor thought that it was migraine. Perhaps it was. Moving made her headache worse but she had heard a noise in the hall. Luella sat up.

It could not be that her husband had come in He always called to her when he arrived. Luella hated to be surprised and Abe Seemans had learned that fact from her sharp tongue. No, it could not be Abe, for he had said that he would be late, busy over that matter of the river land which was so unjust and so tiring She had imagined the sound. She had heard nothing. She was . . . The sound came again, the squeaking of a board, carefully stepped upon. It was in the lower hall. Downstairs, close to the parlor, close to the safe that was in the wall.

Luella Seemans shuddered. She was frightened, more than frightened, almost frantic. There was someone down there, someone who moved stealthily, someone who had no business in this dark house. It was dark. She had lain upon the bed longer than she realized and now, alone in the dark, there was someone prowling beneath her. Luella Seemans' thin shoulders shuddered convulsively.

But she could not sit there in the dark, could not sit passive while she was robbed. There was money in the safe, valuables on the lower floor. The silver was there,

261

the silver of which she was so proud; and there was a bond upon the table where she had carelessly left it, and money in a purse. She couldn't just sit there.

And she could not go down. There was a man downstairs, a man who had a gun or a knife . . . if she went down . . .

But the money. The silver! Luella forced herself to rise from the bed. Noiselessly she crossed the room to the bureau. Clark Andrews' old long-barreled gun was in a drawer. Loaded, it lay there amid little piles of silk and finely stitched cotton and lacy garments. An ugly, worn, long-snouted weapon. The touch of the cool wood of the butt reassured Luella. She took the gun from the drawer and cocked it.

And now she would go down. Now she would go down and meet that prowler. Now she would . . . The board in the hall floor protested under her foot, and downstairs all was silent, quiet with a grave-like stillness. Luella went on, reaching out and feeling for the banister.

The parlor, the parlor where she and Whiteman and Seemans had sat and talked so deliberately, was just off off the lower hall. From the parlor door the bottom of the stairs was visible. From the bottom of the flight she could look into the parlor; could stop, just as she went up, and see the picture on the wall and imagine the little safe, closed and tight and secure, behind it. The bottom of the stairs . . . There was a light in the parlor, a dim glow that died and then, momentarily, came again.

Light in the parlor and Luella Seemans at the bottom of the stairs gun raised, mouth open to speak or to scream, eyes wide. The light flickered, showed the picture gone and the door of the safe gaping open, its black maw despoiled. Beneath the light, a match held

262

high, was a bulky figure. In the instant that her finger closed convulsively upon the trigger, Luella Seemans recognized the man. The roaring shot drowned out her scream. The light died, swiftly, dropping in half a glowing line and vanishing. In the parlor a body thudded down and then, long and heavy, a man groaned. That was all.

Luella dropped the gun, dropped it to the thick piling of the carpet. Her hands, reaching out, clutched the heavy walnut of the banister and then through the darkness of that house a laugh rang out, mad, terrible, shrill. A laugh that would go on and on and on through the years that were to come.

# CHAPTER 20

## WOLF TURNED LOOSE

LARRY BLUE WAITED IN THE CRYSTAL PALACE BAR. Out on the street the lamplighter passed, leaving a dim glow upon the street corners. In the Crystal Palace the lights were bright. A second bartender had come on shift since Larry's advent and now he conversed in low tones with his fellow, their eyes occasionally shifting to the man who stood lounging nonchalantly, right elbow on the bar, right foot on the rail. Back in the restaurant waiters moved about and the odor of food drifted into the barroom to mingle with the smell of beer, the sourer odor of wine and the sharp tang of the whisky. Men came into the Crystal Palace, paused for a drink, spoke to the barmen, and went on to the restaurant or out to the street again. Impassively Larry surveyed each face. He was waiting. Long ago he had learned to wait. It was

263

worthwhile knowledge, that. Waiting and patience, and things came to a man.

The dinner hour in the restaurant was over. There were a few loiterers in the barroom. It was not yet time for the Crystal Palace to do its real business. That would come later. Now was the lull, the time just after mealtime and just before the evening business. One of the barmen, coming along behind his walnut counter, spoke to the waiting man.

"Lookin' for someone, friend?"

"For George Whiteman," Larry answered. There was no necessity of making a secret of his business.

"He ain't been in," said the bartender needlessly. "Usually comes in for supper an' a drink, but he ain't been in tonight."

"He'll come," said Larry, easily.

The bartender went back to his partner and again they fell into conversation. Larry shifted his foot on the rail.

The doors of the Crystal Palace bar were half shutters, green painted and swinging both ways. Legs appeared beneath the shutters and they opened a trifle and stopped, as though the men outside hesitated to enter. Then the shutters swung wide and three men entered. Two of those men, once they were in the room, recoiled at the sight of Larry Blue. The other, buck-toothed, pale-eyed, came steadily to the bar and spoke to the attendant. "Pony of whisky, Bill."

The barman served the little glass and bottle, putting them on the bar top. He nodded his head toward Larry Blue. "Man lookin' for you, Whiteman," he said.

George Whiteman poured his drink with a steady hand, tossed it down, and turning, surveyed the motionless Larry. "You want to see me?" he asked casually.

They were not five feet apart. Behind Whiteman, standing back from the bar, Turner Morton and Carl Fernald watched Larry Blue. Morton had his hand under the tails of his coat, the fingers resting on the butt of a gun in his pocket. Carl Fernald, eyes bloodshot, was holding himself erect with an effort. Fernald had a bandage on his head.

"Where's Annette Bondreaux, Whiteman?" Larry asked impassively.

"You looking for Annette?" Whiteman pulled a pipe from his pocket and tapped it against the edge of the bar. "I don't know where you'd find her. You tried the theater?"

"Where is Annette Bondreaux?" demanded Larry once more. He had not changed his position, had not moved. He stood, right elbow upon the bar, right foot lifted to the rail, lounging there.

"I thought that you were looking for me," said Whiteman. He laughed appreciatively when the words were out, the long, yellow teeth showing between his lips. Larry, watching the man, knew that Whiteman, whatever his other faults, was not afraid. Whiteman had sized the play and was backing his hand. The time had not yet come for shooting and Whiteman knew it.

"That's the man, George," announced Morton, hoarsely. "That's the man."

"Of course," Whiteman tossed the words over his shoulder. "No, Mr. Blue, I haven't seen Annette."

He brought a pouch from his pocket, a beaded buckskin bag, worn and dirty with use. Long, big knuckled fingers opened the pouch and stuffed tobacco into the pipe. Whiteman let the pouch lie upon the bar when he had filled the pipe.

"So you want Annette, do you?" he drawled. "That's

too bad, Mr. Blue. I fancy her myself."

Larry looked at the tobacco pouch upon the bar. He knew that pouch, his fingers had traced every beaded line, touched every angle and turn of the design upon it. That was Jim Cardwine's medicine sack, that pouch lying there upon the dark walnut. Instinctively Larry glanced down at Whiteman's feet. They were small, neatly booted, and as the man stood, the toes turned in. Boots like that would make a small, neat pigeon toed track in sand.

"So," said Larry Blue, "so you were there."

The words seemed to startle Whiteman. They were out of line, they should not have been spoken. They did not belong in the dialogue. "I was where?" the buck-toothed man demanded, recovering his poise. "I've been in good many places."

"I know you have," Larry answered.

The green half shutters banged open. Men and women pushed into the Crystal Palace barroom. Behind the bar the attendants stood, frozen by what they knew was coming, and at the far end of the bar a bleary-eyed man, recovering his senses, shuffled away bearing his glass in his hands. Constance Bolton and Judge Lester, Don Blue and Annette Bondreaux, were in the room. Larry saw them, saw them and did not heed. His eyes had now that vacant stare, that all seeing look that encompasses each detail and does not consider those that have no meaning.

"Larry," exclaimed Constance. "Larry."

Annette was here and safe. A weight lifted from Larry's chest. She was safe! He had not known before how much that meant. And Constance Bolton. What was she doing here? And Lester and Don. Why had they come? They had no business here, they had no place in this thing that was slowly tightening here in the Crystal Palace.

"A good many places," Whiteman drawled. "You've been around yourself. Last night, for instance."

"And before that." Larry made no movement. His face was as expressionless as granite, his eyes slits in the hardness. "I was at a camp up the river one time, Whiteman. The camp where you got that pouch."

Whiteman did not look toward the pouch. He dared not move his eyes from the impassive man before him.

"I was Jim Cardwine's pardner, Whiteman," drawled Larry Blue, a judge pronouncing sentence, a judge in a black robe and black cap. "I killed the other two, but I lost your tracks. I'm sorry."

Annette had pushed herself forward until she stood beside Don Blue, just behind Turner Morton. To Judge Lester's right was Constance Bolton, face working, eyes wide with terror. Judge Lester was gray, face and hair and eyes blending into a mask of monotone.

"And so," said Larry Blue, "I'll finish the job I began."

George Whiteman had killed men, sometimes in fight, sometimes from a growth of tornillo, or behind a rock. His way, and it was a successful way, was to egg the other fellow on, to make the other fellow angry, to make the other fellow reach first and clumsily for his weapon. That was the pattern, that was the shape of his success. But this man who had calmly stated his intentions was not angry, was not flurried made no movement. In the street a vehicle stopped. Men's voices came, rough and growling.

"And you mean to kill me?" said George Whiteman. "I'll have something to say about . . ."

He moved then, hand flashing down from where it

toyed with his watch chain, reaching for the gun in its holster just at his waistband. The hand met wood and steel and lifted the weapon, and from that five-foot distance Larry Blue, who had matched movement with movement, shot once and again and again, the altered Smith & Wesson flaming in his hand.

Constance Bolton screamed, flinging herself at Don Blue, her arms going about his neck, her head buried against his chest. Don held her close, sheltering her from the thing that was happening. Annette Bondreaux also screamed, but it was no cry of fright. Of anger, rather. She too flung herself upon a man, her hands claws that struck at Turner Morton's hair and face, that grappled with his arm as he tried to bring his gun from his pocket. Carl Fernald had moved back thrusting himself against Judge Lester, trying to get clear. And George Whiteman, an expression of surprise upon his face, let the gun he had drawn drop to the floor of the barroom, and stood swaying. For a moment he stood so and then, swiftly, like an old suit falling to the closet floor, crumpled and went down into a heap.

There were others in the room: A big blond man who held a gun, and a small man that chewed vigorously, and another, unshaven, stocky fellow. Duck Bunn was at the door, face white behind his whiskers, eyes wide. The stocky, unshaven man, moving swiftly, reached Annette Bondreaux and the struggling Morton. The stocky man twisted a hand into Morton's coat collar and spoke mildly.

"Let him go, ma'am. You scratched him enough."

The blond advanced on Larry Blue, an odd smile on his face. "I reckon," he said, his voice a soft Southern drawl, "I'll take that gun. You don't need it. Ranger business, mister." Larry dropped the gun into the broad,

268

extended palm. He was watching Constance Bolton, watching her shaking shoulders, watching the mingled expressions that played on Don's face as he held the girl close.

"He pulled first," Duck's voice was high and excited. "Whiteman pulled first."

The small tobacco-chewer spoke contemptuously. "Of course," he agreed. "But first wasn't soon enough."

"I reckon," said blond Sherman Clay regretfully, "I'll have to arrest you, Mr. Blue. I kind of hate to do it too."

Larry paid no attention to Sherman Clay. His shoulders slumped, the mask on his face was broken, his lips twisting as he stepped toward a woman. "Annette," said Larry Blue. "Annette!"

Rangers are efficient people. A little, dried-up tobacco-chewing Ranger Tim McCoy can foregather with such men as Carl Fernald and Turner Morton and pry information from them, make them give out their knowledge as Aaron's staff made the rock give water. A blunt, bewhiskered Ranger like Jerry Tobin can close a place such as the Crystal Palace tight as a drum; hie a trembling justice of the Peace from his home and bring together a coroner's jury. A tall, blond, drawling Ranger like Sherman Clay can direct affairs, can cope with a mad woman, a woman who laughs crazily and babbles incoherencies; can be courteous and not too hard on a man like Larry Blue. Three Rangers can sit on a town like Franklin and keep on the lid.

Rangers in town! Let's leave, gamblers, let's pull out touts and procurers. Let's close up, clean the till and get away. Let's get out! It takes time. Sure it takes time. Everything takes time. Takes time to talk to Judge Goshan until his belly quivers and his fat jowls shake

269

with the fear that's in him. Takes time to put a chief of police into his own jail. Takes time to listen to the dirt after the first shovelful is thrown. But what's time? Two, three days, maybe. Maybe two, three weeks. There's a citizens' committee with their complaints (the big men and the little men, the honest ones and those that have something to hide) to deal with. Sure it takes time, but what's time? Rangers in town, mister! Don Blue appointed special prosecutor. Judge Goshan whipped into line. A special session of the grand jury and, helping along, behind it all, the fact that the big guns behind the crookedness are dead. Seemans' wife killed him. She's crazy. George Whiteman tried against that fellow Larry Blue. Didn't have a chance, they say. Smelter company coming into Franklin. Lots of jobs and they want a clean town. Railroad company helping out. Lester and Blue, attorneys for the railroad. Editorial in the newspaper. News articles on the front page. Franklin's cleaned up. Good town to live in. Good town for the wife and kids. Going to have a new school; going to have a special election. Mighty good town, mister. And if it does get tough again there's always the Rangers.

Larry Blue sat in a hack. There was a girl beside him on the rear seat and on the seat facing Larry was Duck Bunn, Denver bound. Duck had his grip on his knees and was holding it tightly. He had traveled by stage, by wagon, on horseback, and afoot, but never before by train. A little afraid of his first railroad journey, Duck. Behind the hack Judge Lester's matched bay trotters pulled his barouche. Don Blue sat on the back seat of the barouche, a girl beside him, too, and facing Don and the girl were Judge Lester and a chastened DeWitt Bolton. Ten minutes to train time and the hack and the

270

barouche rolled right along.

Larry Blue looked at Franklin, rolling past outside the window. He was not seeing Franklin. Larry was thinking about Denver, thinking about Royal Truman who waited impatiently for him there, thinking about the house that he would build on Federal Street, thinking about . . .

A soft hand touched Larry's, locking around it. Larry looked down at the girl beside him and smiled. Back in the barouche Don Blue smiled at another girl.

"Sorry, Larry?" asked Annette Blue.

Larry's hand closed on the soft fingers of the girl. It was answer enough. Sorry! Larry thought of the other girl back in the barouche, sitting beside Don; thought of Constance Bolton. A wonderful woman, Constance; a woman who would make a man a wife. But not for Larry Blue. Not for him. This girl, this dark-eyed, blond woman who sat so quietly: Annette, that was the kind of girl for Larry Blue. Slowly Larry voiced his thoughts.

"You and me, Annette," said Larry Blue, "we've seen it all, haven't we, kid? We've seen the rough edges, haven't we?"

In his grasp the girl's hand tightened.

"And we'll see some more," said Larry. "Maybe rough, again. It won't make a difference, will it?"

"No, Larry."

A smile broke across Larry's face. "Not with you it won't," he said. "Not with you, Annette."

We hope that you enjoyed reading this
Sagebrush Large Print Western.
If you would like to read more Sagebrush titles,
ask your librarian or contact the Publishers:

## United States and Canada

Thomas T. Beeler, *Publisher*
Post Office Box 659
Hampton Falls, New Hampshire 03844-0659
(800) 251-8726

## United Kingdom, Eire, and
## the Republic of South Africa

Isis Publishing Ltd
7 Centremead
Osney Mead
Oxford OX2 0ES England
(01865) 250333

## Australia and New Zealand

Australian Large Print Audio & Video P/L
17 Mohr Street
Tullamarine, Victoria, 3043, Australia
1 800 335 364